Uncle Drew
and the Bat Dodger

Thomas Cochran

PELICAN PUBLISHING COMPANY
GRETNA 2016

The word "Pelican" and the depiction of a pelican are
trademarks of Pelican Publishing Company, Inc., and are
registered in the U.S. Patent and Trademark Office.

ISBN 9781455622092
E-book ISBN 9781455622108

Printed in the United States of America

Published by Pelican Publishing Company, Inc.
1000 Burmaster Street, Gretna, Louisiana 70053

For Kate

Chapter 1

He closed his eyes and braced himself for the sound he knew was coming. It was a sharp, tinkling noise, abrupt as a gunshot. In the silence that followed he thought he might as well just go on over to Merritt Mortuary and make arrangements for himself. He could already see the headline in the *Oil Camp News:*

LOCAL YOUTH BREAKS NEIGHBOR'S WINDOW, IS EXECUTED

The story would say that he had been tossing up and hitting a baseball from one side of his front yard to the other when for some reason he forgot that he wasn't in Yankee Stadium and took a full cut. The good news was that he made solid contact. The bad news was that the resulting line drive went directly into (and through) a side window of the house next door.

He would rather have broken just about any window in Oil Camp other than one in the house next door. It wasn't that the old man who lived there, Mr. Weems, had ever done anything mean or un-neighborly since he moved in, because he hadn't. He'd just never done anything particularly kind or neighborly either. He arrived in the middle of February and had lived over there being old and mysterious and therefore unnerving ever since. If you thought of him at all, you thought of him as somebody who kept his distance and left no doubt that he would prefer you to follow suit. Breaking one of his windows was certainly no way to make his acquaintance.

He was dead, all right. He was the late Teddy Caldwell, nine, of Oil Camp.

Unless he denied what he'd done. That would be easy enough for some people, but Teddy had denied something once and vowed never to again. This happened one day the year before, when he was in third grade. Rain fell particularly hard that day, and those members of Teddy's class who had brought their lunches were allowed to stay in Mrs. Stoker's room instead of walking from the First Building to the cafeteria, which was in the high school, which was on the other side of the Middle Building. The elementary principal, Mr. Sherman, agreed to look in on them periodically. This was a Friday, the one day of the week Teddy's mother packed him a lunch. He had a ham sandwich and a pear. He ate the sandwich, but the pear was ripe to the point of having gone mushy. It was like applesauce in a pear-skin wrapper. The room's wastebasket stood in a corner by the door, fifteen or twenty feet away from where he was sitting. He decided to take a shot.

"If I make this I get all As for the rest of my life," he thought.

The door opened just as he was bringing his arm forward. He couldn't stop the motion, so the pear was on its way when Mr. Sherman stepped into the room. It caught him at the knee. Being soft, it opened upon impact, leaving a stain on the principal's trousers. He looked down, then up. Teddy bowed his head as if that might help him disappear. It did not.

Mr. Sherman picked up what he could of the pear and held it between a thumb and index finger.

"Please step forward, whoever is responsible," he said.

There were five students in the room, including Teddy. Nobody moved.

"Fine," Mr. Sherman said. "Here's what we'll do, then. I'm going to ask each of you if you threw this, and you are going to answer me truthfully. Do we understand each other?"

Nobody spoke. The girls nodded their heads, the boys theirs.

"Was it you, Donna?" Mr. Sherman asked.

"Nosir," Donna Sanders said.

"Lonnie?"

"Nosir," Lonnie Williams said.

"Cindy?"

"Nosir," Cindy Franklin said.

"Molly?"

"Nosir," Molly Barnett said.

"Teddy?"

"Nosir," Teddy Caldwell said.

Mr. Sherman sighed.

"I don't think this or any other pear is capable of defying gravity, of flying through the air on its own," he said. "Children, please. Am I mistaken?"

Nobody spoke. The girls shook their heads, the boys theirs.

"That being the case, the fact of the matter is that one of you had to have thrown it," he said. "I hate the word I'm about to use because it's an ugly word that designates an ugly thing, but the truth here is that one of you is a liar. Are you a liar, Donna?"

"Nosir."

"Lonnie?"

"Nosir."

"Cindy?"

"Nosir,"

"Molly?"

"Nosir."

"Teddy?"

"Nosir."

Mr. Sherman sighed again. He dropped the pear into the wastebasket and took a handkerchief from his coat pocket. He wiped his hands. He studied the stain on his trousers. He considered his options. All of the oxygen seemed to have gone out of the room. It was so quiet that the usually silent ticking of the clock above the chalkboard became audible.

Teddy took this opportunity to consider his own options. There weren't many. He could tell the truth or he could continue lying. Having done it twice within the space of a minute and a half had taught him that in addition to the obvious problem of its simply being wrong, lying was complicated. One lie demanded another. First you lied, then you had to lie about lying. Where would it end? Telling the truth might get you in trouble, but you were bound to be in trouble already if you had lied in the first place. Besides, unlike lying, telling the truth was a onetime deal. You didn't have to keep track of what you'd said or not said. You just had one thing to say. You could repeat it if you had to, but that's as complicated as things would get.

Teddy raised his hand.

"Yes, Teddy," Mr. Sherman said.

"Can I change my answers?" Teddy asked.

"'May I,'" Mr. Sherman said. "You're asking permission, not wondering if you are capable of something."

"May I change my answers?"

"You may."

"My first one should have been 'yessir,' and so should have my second one."

"Very good, Teddy," Mr. Sherman said. "Come with me."

Everybody knows that being sent to the principal's office means that you have committed a serious infraction. Being summoned there by the principal himself, in person, obviously puts you into a higher category of misbehavior. Following Mr. Sherman down the long hallway, Teddy wondered if his age would save him from going to Angola Prison. Outside, rain pelted the building. Thunder rumbled.

In the office, Mr. Sherman told Teddy to have a seat in the huge chair in front of his main desk. The principal then stood with his hands resting on the high-backed leather chair behind the desk. He was deep in thought. At first Teddy sat perfectly still. Then he began to fidget. To relieve the tension that was building up inside of him, he started to look around. He had delivered his share of notes to Mr. Sherman's secretary, but this was his first trip into the principal's actual office. The walls were decorated with framed certificates and shelves of books. The main desk was covered with stacks of folders and loose papers. An auxiliary desk held a computer. Among the certificates were newspaper clippings and photographs of Mr. Sherman's family. In some they were on a snowy mountain. Others showed them beside blue water. It was hard for Teddy to imagine that the Mr. Sherman in the pictures, who wore sunglasses and a red ski jacket and, even more amazingly, sunglasses and purple bathing trunks, was the same Mr. Sherman who now stood across from him wearing no glasses at all and a plain gray suit. It was, in fact, hard for Teddy to imagine Mr. Sherman anywhere other than at school doing anything other than being the principal, same as it was hard for him to imagine any school adult out of that context.

"Why did you put off telling me the truth, Teddy?" Mr. Sherman asked at last.

"I was afraid," Teddy said.

"Of what were you afraid?"

"Of you."

Mr. Sherman covered his smile by making a pyramid of his hands and bringing them to his mouth. He folded his fingers into church-and-steeple position, tapping his lips with the steeple.

"And why were you afraid of me?" he asked.

He began to walk slowly back and forth like a lawyer in a courtroom. This made Teddy feel even more vulnerable and on edge. He needed to be sure that everything he said from now on was not only the truth but also the whole truth and nothing but the truth.

"Because you're the principal of the school and I'd just threw my pear at you," he answered.

"Thrown," Mr. Sherman said. "The verb is irregular. Throw, threw, thrown. It's a complex mistake, actually, making an irregular verb regular. Nevertheless, let us not confuse mangling the language with complexity of mind. It is precisely the opposite. Now. You hadn't just thrown the pear at me. You had just thrown it at the wastebasket. I merely happened into its path at the worst possible moment for both of us. The fruit hit my knee, and when I wanted to know who was responsible for having thrown it you made the assumption that I was angry. Am I correct so far?"

Teddy answered the question with an uncertain nod. His mind was still on what Mr. Sherman had said about where he had aimed the pear. Telling the truth, it seemed, was not itself without certain complications.

"Yes, well, assumptions are tricky things," Mr. Sherman said. "They might be right and they might be wrong. Which do you think yours is in this case?"

"I think it might be right," Teddy said.

"It is indeed," Mr. Sherman replied. "But do understand why. I wasn't angry because the pear hit me. I would have been angry if the pear had not hit me. I was angry because somebody had thrown a pear. We do not throw pears or anything else in the classroom, Teddy. I won't tolerate it, and I'm certain that Mrs. Stoker feels similarly."

"She definitely does," Teddy said.

"The more serious problem, of course, is that you failed

to own up to what you had done," Mr. Sherman continued. "There's another irregular verb for you, by the way. Do, did, done. At least you did not own up to it initially. I must say that the decision you made to reverse that course impressed me. It's a good sign. Do you know that I sail, Teddy?"

"Like boats?" Teddy asked.

"Not 'like' boats," Mr. Sherman said. "I sail actual boats. As in, I know how to use the wind to my advantage."

"How do you do it when the wind blows in the wrong direction?" Teddy asked.

"The wind never blows in the wrong direction," Mr. Sherman said. "There are ways to use it in your favor no matter which direction it comes from. My point is that when you are sailing you sometimes find yourself either headed for or already in troubled water. Your task then is to tack, which means to take a course, a route, away from that trouble. This is what you did today. You could have sailed headlong into some very heavy weather, but you tacked out of it. Because of that, I'm going to give you something of a break. I'll consider the matter over and done with if you will promise me two things. Does that sound fair?"

"It depends on what you want me to promise," Teddy said.

The principal did not cover his smile this time. He let Teddy see it, and that made Teddy almost comfortable enough to return the gesture. He tried but managed only to slightly raise one of his eyebrows.

"You're a thinker," Mr. Sherman said. "I like that. First, you must promise not to throw things in the classroom. If you have something to discard, walk to the wastebasket and drop it in. If you have something to throw, wait until you are outdoors. Yes?"

"I promise," Teddy said.

"Fine," Mr. Sherman replied. "Second—and this will be

slightly more difficult—I want you to tell your parents that they will be receiving a dry-cleaning bill from me sometime during the next few days and why that is."

He lifted his knee so that Teddy could see the stain on his trousers.

"I'll tell them," Teddy said.

"Good boy," Mr. Sherman declared. "You're dismissed."

"Thank you, Mr. Sherman," Teddy said. "I'm sorry I denied what I done."

"Did," Mr. Sherman corrected. "Simple past. No need to drag the participle into it."

"Yessir," Teddy said.

He made good on the second of his promises at the supper table that night. His parents listened to the story but did not immediately respond.

"Are y'all mad?" Teddy asked.

"Not too," his father said. "Sounds like you and Mr. Sherman worked things out pretty thoroughly. Back in my day, though, hoo me. If you got in trouble at school you were in even worse trouble when you got home. We got licks."

"Licks?" Teddy asked.

"Spanked," his mother said. "But we don't believe in spanking in this house."

"Do we not?" his father asked.

"We most certainly do not," his mother said.

"I'm kidding," his father replied. "Of course we don't. But you're still in trouble, Teddy. We'll pay the cleaning bill for Mr. Sherman's pants, and you'll pay us back."

"How?" Teddy asked.

"Oh, I can think of a few more chores around here we could use a hand with," his father said.

The one chore Teddy had been responsible for up until then was setting out the trash every Wednesday evening and retrieving the can the next afternoon. His new ones were clearing the table and loading the dishwasher after each meal, sweeping and vacuuming the house after school on Mondays and Thursdays, and folding and putting away his clothes each time they came out of the dryer. After a month of this, his parents told him that he could consider his debts for getting in trouble at school and for the dry-cleaning bill squared but added that he'd been such a big help that they would like for him to take on two of the tasks permanently.

"Which one would you rather hand back over to us?" his mother asked. "Not that we'd mind if you kept doing all three."

"I think I'll let y'all fold my clothes," he said. "That's the most frustrating thing in the world."

"Tell me about it," his father said. "And if you think clothes won't cooperate, wait till you have to deal with a fitted sheet. Nobody can fold one of those."

His mother cleared her throat.

"Except your mother, that is," his father said.

"Why, thank you, Mr. Caldwell," his mother replied.

"You're more than welcome, Mrs. Caldwell," his father said.

Teddy's parents regularly addressed each other that way, as Mr. and Mrs. Caldwell instead of Chris and Becky or, as some of his friends' folks did, Mama and Daddy. It was an unusual habit, but it always made him feel good somehow, which was quite unlike the way he was feeling at the moment, looking at the broken window. He wondered if there was any chance at all that Mr. Weems would just send a bill for its replacement. As if to answer that question, the old man himself suddenly appeared. He stood like a ghost behind the broken glass, scowling. He leaned forward and held up the ball for Teddy to see.

"This yours, boy?" he asked.

His voice was deep and strong, like a movie announcer's.

Teddy debated his response. It was a short debate. He'd learned his lesson about what to say in such a situation. Besides, he was standing there all alone, holding a baseball bat. He couldn't have been a more obvious culprit.

"Y-yessir," he said.

The old man's scowl deepened. He put his lips together and blew a puff of air dismissively. Then he was gone.

Chapter 2

Teddy was not supposed to call his parents at work unless it was an emergency. He'd never had to do it before, but he'd never been allowed to stay home alone before either. This was his first summer of that. It was, in fact, his first day of it. His parents hadn't been gone two hours and here he was with a definite emergency on his hands. They'd probably send him back to Mrs. Gaither's the next day. Mrs. Gaither was a retired schoolteacher who kept kids for working parents during the summer. Teddy liked her, but he thought he'd outgrown having to go to her house two summers ago, last summer at the latest, and talked his parents into giving him a try on his own this year.

"I won't even be here till but eleven when the pool opens anyway," he said. "Mr. Belcher'll be over there, plus all the lifeguards. It's not like I won't have people watching out for me."

"Good point," his father said. "Jack Belcher's been running City Pool for a hundred years. He practically raised me and my bunch during the hot months."

"I guess y'all turned out all right," his mother said.

Teddy waited for Mr. Weems to come out and kill him, but the old man did neither. Inside his own house, he sat at the kitchen table and stared at the phone, wondering which of his parents to call. He was equally comfortable with both of them under normal circumstances, but these circumstances were hardly normal, so he decided that he would be better off getting his mother's advice first. His father was probably on the road somewhere anyway. He worked for an oilfield supply company and was always either at or on the way to a drilling site. His mother kept the books over at the lumber company. She also answered the phone. Teddy punched in the numbers.

"Builders Lumber," his mother said after two rings.

"It's me, Mom. Teddy."

"Where are you?" his mother asked.

The note of panic in her voice was unmistakable.

"I'm home," he said. "And the house is not on fire or anything like that. Everything's okay, except I think I might be dead."

"What in the world is that supposed to mean?" his mother asked. "What happened? Do I need to be there?"

"Not really. I'm thinking now I might should've waited till dinner to even call."

"Well, you called and I answered and I'm thinking now I'm very definitely ready to hear how come you called."

The note of panic had left her voice. A note of anger had replaced it.

"I hit a ball through a window next door," Teddy said.

"Which one?"

"The kitchen one, I think."

"Not which window, Teddy. Which house?"

"The one you wouldn't pick to hit a ball through if you had a choice. I'm sorry, Mom. I just swang the bat too hard and the next thing I knew that old man was standing there looking at me through the busted glass."

"What were you doing hitting a baseball out there in the first place?"

"I just was. I don't know. I wasn't hitting it hard. Not mostly. I got all of that one, though."

There was a long pause.

"What do I do?" Teddy asked.

"The obvious thing would be go over there and apologize and tell him we'll pay to have it fixed," his mother said.

"But I'm scared of him," Teddy protested.

His mother laughed at that.

"It's not funny," Teddy said.

"Sorry," his mother replied. "I know it. Mr. Weems is kind of intimidating. Your daddy and I walked over there to say hey a couple of times when he first moved in after the Anglins left, but he hasn't been real friendly."

"I wish the Anglins were still there."

"I won't say I don't either, honey. But they're not."

Teddy thought for a moment.

"Maybe you could call him for me," he said.

"I don't think so," his mother replied. "It might not be a bad idea for you to, though. Let me see if he's in the book, which I don't see how he could be in this one since it's last year's but I'll check."

Teddy looked over at the old man's house. The broken window gave it a creepy, haunted appearance.

"Nope, he's not listed," his mother said. "So. I'm not sure what to tell you, sweetie. I don't blame you for not wanting to go over there by yourself, but looks like you're just going to have to."

"How mad you think he'll be?" Teddy wondered.

"Just tell him we'll get his window fixed," his mother said. "That's all you can do, no matter how mad he is."

"Y'all won't send me back to Mrs. Gaither's, will you?"

"No, but this doesn't exactly ease my nerves about you staying home by yourself. And I know you'll hardly even be there with the pool and everything. But still."

Just as she said it, Teddy felt his nerves come to life. The knocking was like an assault.

"Somebody's at the door," he said. "What if it's him?"

"It's probably the mailman with a package," his mother said. "He won't leave one without knocking, and I bet he has those boots I ordered online the other day. They're going to be one of your daddy's Christmas presents this year. Ostrich."

Teddy shook his head. Who other than his mother would ever think of Christmas in barely June?

"But what if it's him?" he asked. "That old man."

The knocking became more insistent.

"I don't think you have to worry about that," his mother said. "Mr. Weems has never knocked on our door."

"He never had a reason to," Teddy said. "We never broke his window."

"It's not him, Teddy. But if it is, just tell him you're sorry, your mother knows what happened, and she said we'll be in touch about fixing his window. Now go answer the door. My other line's ringing. I'll see you at supper. And please maybe try to play baseball somewhere else, like at the baseball field, from now on. I love you."

"Okay, Mom. Love you too. Bye."

Teddy was certain that it was Mr. Weems knocking on the door. But his mother had been right. It was the mailman, Mr. Bilberry, and he was holding a box, which he handed to Teddy.

"How you today, buddy?" he asked. "Guess you're glad school's out."

Teddy thought about saying, "Not necessarily," but that would require an explanation. He *was* glad school was out. He just wasn't glad about the way his vacation had started. Still, there was no need to go into all of that.

"It's always good when school's out," he said. "How you?"

"Can't complain," Mr. Bilberry said. "Getting ready to be a hot one, but when is it ever not around here after about March? Oh, by the way, I have something for you."

He took an envelope from his back pocket and laid it on the package Teddy was holding. It hadn't been addressed.

"Who's it from?" Teddy asked.

"Andrew," Mr. Bilberry said. "He asked me to bring it over. I'm not supposed to deliver anything that's not addressed or stamped, but I won't say anything if you won't."

"Andrew who?" Teddy asked.

He couldn't think of anybody he knew named Andrew.

"Andrew Weems next door," Mr. Bilberry said. "Interesting fellow, your neighbor. You be good, now."

Distracted by the envelope and by the idea that Mr. Weems had a first name, something he'd never considered, Teddy didn't respond. Mr. Bilberry left to continue his route. Teddy stood in the doorway for some time. He wished that he'd asked what kind of mood Mr. Weems was in.

Teddy set the package on the couch and walked to the kitchen. He looked at the envelope, glancing at the house next door with its broken window. He wondered what the mailman had meant by calling Mr. Weems an interesting fellow. "Interesting" could mean a lot of things, including "strange" or "weird." But it could also be used in the sense of something or somebody that made you want to know more. What did Teddy know about Mr. Weems? Not much. He always wore overalls and a real hat. He sometimes drove a pickup truck, slowly. He cut his grass with a mower that he had to push to make the blades turn because it had no engine. He never waved. He never smiled. Teddy tried to think of something else. He couldn't come up with anything. He shrugged. Mr. Weems was just an old man. He kept to himself and didn't invite you to try to change that. How much was there *to* know about him?

Teddy picked up the envelope, which in addition to being unaddressed and unstamped was unsealed. He held it up to the window. It contained an index card. What was written there could be anything—a death threat, say, or a ransom note demanding an outrageous sum of money for the safe return of the baseball. It might just be an estimate of the cost for repairing the window. That would be the best thing. His parents could send a check, and Teddy could pay them back by assuming a few new chores. It would be like the pear incident with Mr. Sherman, minus the interview and the promises.

He thought about trying to forget the envelope and what

was inside until later. It was only 9:45, but he could kill the hour before going to the pool by reading. He was in the middle of one of his father's old Hardy Boys books. In the part he read just before going to sleep the night before, Frank and Joe had been captured trying to rescue their father from drug smugglers. Teddy was interested in seeing how they got out of the bind they were in, but he decided to save that for later because he wouldn't be able to concentrate on a book. His mind was elsewhere. Now that he thought of it, here was something else to know about Mr. Weems. What had he sent over in the envelope? If Teddy didn't go ahead and find that out now, he would think about nothing else for the rest of the day.

"Might as well get this over with," he said.

He folded back the flap and removed the index card. He read the note:

I like baseball. You?

Your neighbor,

A Weems

Teddy could have thought for a solid week and that message would never have crossed his mind. Relieved, he read it again. He studied the letters. They were half-printed, half-cursive, and all shaky. Only a few of them fit between the lines. Some of the tops rose above; some of the bottoms dipped below. And the *A* that stood for Andrew was connected to the *W* that started Weems. Teddy had never seen a name signed in such a way.

"That's cool," he thought.

He took a ballpoint pen from the plastic Oil Camp Roughnecks cup on the counter. Using the envelope, he tried signing his name as Mr. Weems had signed his. He made his usual cursive *T* and continued the tail up and over into a *C*. Then he made a printed *T* with the cross slanted up to form the top of the *C*. He liked that. It looked good and it was quick. Down, cross, curve. *TCaldwell. TCaldwell. TCaldwell. Sincerely, TCaldwell. Yours truly, TCaldwell. Best wishes, TCaldwell. Your neighbor, TCaldwell.*

"Whoa," he said.

He had an idea. He needed to act on it right then or he would talk himself out of it. He searched the kitchen drawers for an index card. There weren't any, so he settled for one of the scraps of paper his parents used for grocery lists. It wasn't the exact size he wanted, but it would do. He trimmed it into the proper shape with scissors. That done, he wrote a reply to Mr. Weems:

I do. Sorry I broke your window.
                              Your neighbor,
                              TCaldwell

A little while later, he leaned his bicycle against the huge pin oak in front of the house next door and walked as nonchalantly as he could to the porch steps. He tried to tread lightly on the porch, but the boards creaked. He froze and listened, not sure if he was hearing approaching footsteps or his own heartbeat. Knowing that he needed to get in gear no matter what, he slid the half-rolled envelope that contained his note behind the handle of the screen door, knocked twice, returned to his bicycle, jumped on it, and pedaled away. He wanted to look back but didn't.

City Pool was just a little over a mile and a half from his house and the route to it was mostly flat, though there were a few places where the pavement rose so that he had to stand and pump. They made for tough going on the way over but promised an easy (and exciting) return trip. The mailman's prediction had been correct. The mildness of the morning was already giving way. It was going to be a hot afternoon. Teddy felt himself begin to sweat. By the time he got to the pool, streams were sliding down his back and sides. He stood his bicycle in the rack out front. A couple of muscular high-school boys wearing sleeveless *OCHS FOOTBALL* T-shirts were playing ping-pong on the gallery. A couple of junior-high girls were pretending not to watch them. One of the boys tilted his head back to acknowledge Teddy, who waved at him with an index finger.

Inside, Mr. Belcher was lifting a block of ice into the snow-cone machine.

"Ran into your daddy other morning," he said. "Told me you'd graduated to coming here on your own this summer. I remember him and that bunch of nuts he grew up with. Lord, they had themselves a time out there. Looks like a good day to open."

"Looks like," Teddy said.

Mr. Belcher patted the ice with a gloved hand.

"Come get you one of these gentlemen after while," he said. "They on the house today and you can't beat that price."

He turned on the machine. The loud, shuddering noise it made crushing the ice was as much a part of City Pool as the smell of chlorine.

Teddy knew that the water was going to be cold, but he was not fully prepared for the shock it gave him when he cannonballed in. It was an indescribably wonderful sensation, available only once each day. He let himself sink until his feet touched the cement bottom, then he sprang toward the surface with a smile that stretched his entire face. Summer was officially under way. He was by no means in the clear regarding the central event of an unusually eventful morning, but he felt confident that writing a reply to Mr. Weems' note and leaving it on his door had been a pretty good idea.

They'd each made a move. Off and on throughout the long, hot afternoon, Teddy wondered what the old man's next one might be.

Chapter 3

Mr. Weems was sitting on his front porch when Teddy pedaled by on his way home from the pool. The old man didn't smile, but he did lift a hand. That was a first. Teddy almost had a wreck waving back. Something told him not to stop, though, so he coasted up his driveway and parked. The driveway was on the other side of his house. He decided to go in through the front door instead of the back, thinking that he might say something to Mr. Weems or at least give the old man a chance to. But Mr. Weems was no longer on his porch. Teddy looked at the window he had broken. What he saw surprised him.

At the supper table, he told his parents about his day. They let him talk without interrupting.

"And then I saw the window fixed," he said. "That's three things he did you wouldn't expect."

"That and the note and what?" his father asked.

"When he waved at me," Teddy said. "Like nothing happened."

"Interesting," his father said.

There was that word again. Teddy was beginning to think of it as the very way to describe Mr. Weems.

"But something did happen," his mother said. "And we need to pay for it, whether it's already fixed or not. They don't give glass away. It's expensive."

"Plus, unless he did it himself, which I doubt, he had to pay somebody to do it for him," his father said.

"I think we ought to wait and see," Teddy suggested.

"Like I said, he never waved at me before until a while ago."

"Or anybody else that I know of," his mother added.

"Say again what you put in your note," his father prompted.

"I told him I like baseball too and sorry for breaking his window," Teddy answered.

"I guess that would have to count," his father said.

"It's not the same as saying it in person," his mother stated.

"Maybe I'll get a chance to sometime."

"I'd hate him to think we know about this and let you slide," his father said.

"I bet he's not even thinking about y'all. It's between me and him, not y'all and him. Wouldn't he come over here and yell if it was?"

His parents looked at each other. Both of them raised their eyebrows, as if they had no reason not to agree with him.

"What would y'all's parents do if you were in my shoes?" Teddy asked.

Of the four, only his mother's mother was still living. Two-Moms had an apartment in a retirement village in Shreveport.

"My daddy'd've whipped my butt and marched me over there and asked Mr. Weems if he wanted to do the same," his father said.

"Oh, he would not have," his mother protested.

"We've had this conversation before," his father said. "We spanked at my house. Whipped. For quite a while."

"Well, we didn't at mine," his mother said. "And we don't here."

"I'm not talking about here," his father said. "I'm just answering the question. That's what would have happened. What would your folks have done?"

"One thing they would not have done is worry about me

breaking somebody's window with a baseball," his mother said. "Or anything else. I never got in trouble until I started running around with you."

"What kind of trouble did y'all get into?" Teddy asked.

His mother shook her head. His father smiled.

"Your mother never got in trouble."

"Except at home for being the girlfriend of somebody who quite often did," his mother said.

"Like how?" Teddy asked.

"Nothing serious," his father said. "Some of it might could've been, but—well, for example, there was the night just before the end of our sophomore year. Me and Kevin Branch set some tires on fire in the alley behind the drugstore and rolled them past the police station. Remember that, Mrs. Caldwell?"

"I surely do, Mr. Caldwell," his mother said.

"Sounds pretty serious," Teddy pointed out.

"It was more like plain idiotic is what it was," his mother said.

"Oh, we just thought we'd have a little fun with old Willis Williams. He was a town cop, and he was one of those good-natured fellows who just invite you to pick on them. You could do that sort of thing in a place like Oil Camp back in those days. It ain't exactly New Orleans around here now, but we got away with a few things you might not ought to try anymore. Everybody knowing everybody is the biggest difference. Sometimes they'd blow the whistle on you; sometimes they'd take care of you theirself; sometimes they'd let you slide. It all depended on their mood and how interesting they thought what you'd done was. There was a give and take that made it fun for both sides, at least up to a point. Nowdays, there's no give and take. It's a lawsuit because there's more strangers, and strangers don't generally appreciate people telling them how to raise their kids, thus the lawsuits or at least the threat of them. And, lord, I'd hate to think Mr. Weems might be thinking we've thrown the rod away in favor of flowers and Frisbees over here. Not that you need the rod, as we have discussed.

"Anyway," his father continued, "that night we saw old Willis sitting out there in front of the cop shop—on duty supposedly—and Branch came up with the fine idea of putting him to work, so we went and got five tires from out behind Shackleford's Texaco and took them into the alley, where we coated them good with gasoline, lit them one at a time, and sent them rolling past Willis, who didn't even stand up till the third one went by. We were about to beat each other to death laughing. He'd start this way then he'd go a few steps the other trying to decide whether what he was seeing was real or a dream and then, once he figured out which, between whether to go put them out or investigate who was pulling the prank. This was about two o'clock in the morning, so it wasn't anybody but us and him even still awake. Finally he went inside and came out with a fire extinguisher and headed down to where the tires had stopped and fell over. Once we knew he was good and occupied we got back in Branch's pickup and eased down there like we were just happening by.

"'Need a hand there, Willis?' Branch said, and Willis said, 'Y'all see anybody could've did this?' and Branch, who could keep a straight face better than anybody I ever knew—I mean, I was about to pull some muscles over there trying not to make too much noise laughing—Branch said, 'We just took our dates home and's headed that way ourself.' Which was actually true for me, except that I'd dropped your mother off two hours before and ran into Branch on my way to the house. So Willis just keeps on spraying those tires for a minute, then he says, 'I don't know how dumb you boys think I am, but if you think I'm dumb enough to fall for this hook and line y'all're the dumb ones. Reckon what your daddies'd say was I to call them in the middle of the night and wake them up just to tell them their boys was up to no good?' Branch says he figures his daddy and probably mine wouldn't be able to see what us trying to lend the law a hand putting out a fire has to do with being up to no good, and Willis says, 'I know y'all done this but I can't prove it, so what we're going to do is we're going to have y'all get out that pickup truck and load this mess up and haul it out to the dump and then go straight home. After that if I see either one of you so much as make a turn without your blinker or hear about you arriving to class late or crossing the street outside the crosswalk, your daddies are going to hear from me and we are going to see some young butts blistered. And oh by the way, I'll expect the both of you to address me as Officer Williams from now on. Are we eye to eye on this?' Well, Branch looks at me like, 'What?' I'm still tickled but not quite as much. As I'm opening the door to get out I hear that idiot say, 'I didn't know we had crosswalks in Oil Camp, Officer Williams,' and Willis say back to him, 'Shut up, Kevin, and help me get these tires in that truck.'"

"So y'all didn't really get in trouble?" Teddy asked.

"Not until a few minutes later," his mother said.

"What do you mean?" Teddy asked.

"Mr. Caldwell?" his mother prompted.

"Now this was truly idiotic," his father said. "But I didn't have nothing to do with it. For some reason Branch got the bright idea of peeling out leaving. Then he laid rubber in second. I looked back and saw Willis headed for his cruiser. I guess he'd had enough. Sure enough, he blue-lighted us about a mile out the highway. Wrote Branch a ticket that said he was going thirty-five on Main Street and ran a red light. Wasn't much we could say, never mind that the stoplights just blinked yellow after midnight. Branch's daddy whipped him for the ticket and mine me for not getting in until three in the morning."

"And when he heard about it the next afternoon mine told me he didn't want to hear the name Chris Caldwell cross my lips ever again under any circumstances," Teddy's mother said. "He said our little romance was over and done with and made me call your daddy to tell him right then while he stood there and made sure I said it. After we hung up I cried and cried, and my mama said the world wasn't really coming to an end even though I probably thought it was. I'll never forget it. She said, 'You'll see. Before you know it you won't even remember his name to say.' And she might've been right if he'd been somebody else."

"I sure am glad he wasn't," Teddy said. "I wouldn't be here if he had been."

His mother stood and gave him a hug.

"I'm glad he wasn't too, sweetie," she said. "I can't imagine me without either one of y'all."

She kissed the top of his head and gave his shoulders a squeeze before sitting back down.

"How'd you change their mind?" Teddy asked.

"Mama and Daddy's? Well, first I didn't say his name in front of them for a while. For a *long* while. Almost two years. Second, we kept things secret. At least we thought we did. They knew all along, of course, which we found out later. At the time, all along, we thought we had them completely fooled. Finally, homecoming our senior year, when the football boys chose who was going to walk for them, we knew something was going to have to give because our pictures were going to be in the paper, so it was either wait for that to come out or go ahead and tell them. When I did they said they'd been wondering how we were going to try to get homecoming past them and named every movie we'd seen in Magnolia and Shreveport for the past two years, every gift we'd exchanged, every party we'd been to. I sat there with my mouth hanging open. I was just amazed. I told them I really thought we'd been a secret, and Mama said, 'There are no secrets in a town this size, young lady. Never forget it if you're ever tempted to do anything you don't want anybody to know because somebody will, every detail of it, and they will consider it their obligation to report what they know.'"

"They just let y'all, then," Teddy said. "What about yours, Daddy?"

"Wasn't a problem with mine to start with," his father said. "Your mother was a fine upstanding girl, ha, and they thought I was playing well up out of my league, which of course I was and still am. But once the cat got officially released from the bag over at the Bower residence it was obvious to both of us that we were the ones been fooled. Hard not to run into folks in a town this size and like you just heard, back then everybody knew everybody, and when folks run into each other they can't stand not to talk. Your mother's folks knew all along because mine and everybody else did too. I think they all thought it was funny."

"It was funny," his mother said. "I mean, we really thought we were getting away with something. Can you imagine? I will say this about the other thing we're talking about, though. Not that there aren't better methods than whipping to deal with bad behavior, but the only reason your daddy ever got one was because he deserved to."

"It was generally worth it," his father said. "And that one after the tire shenanigans was one of the last. My mama had a talk with my daddy and they decided that whenever I got into any mischief they'd handle it constructively, sort of like we did with you and Mr. Sherman and the dry-cleaning bill. They put me to work. I painted, I washed windows, I weeded flowerbeds, I raked pine straw, I cut and hauled wood, I did whatever needed doing. It was stuff somebody would normally've helped me with, but when I was in trouble I'd have to do it on my own, and always on Saturday."

"Sounds like you were in trouble a lot," Teddy said.

"I missed a few Saturdays," his father admitted.

"I'd rather not," Teddy said.

"That's because you've got good sense," his mother remarked. "I just hope you don't lose it somewhere along the way like your daddy did."

"I never had any to lose until later," his father said. "I'll admit that. But you got to admit I kept pretty good track of it ever since."

"With a little help from somebody who everybody thought had no sense at all getting involved with you," his mother said.

His father smiled and shook his head.

"So then," he said. "We're waiting and seeing?"

"I believe we might should," his mother said. "For the time being."

"Fine with me," his father said. "What's in that box I saw?"

"What box?" his mother asked.

"The one in yonder on the couch," his father said.

"I don't know what you're talking about," his mother replied.

His father stood and left the room.

"I should've told you to put that in my closet," his mother said.

"I forgot all about it."

"So did I," his mother said.

His father returned carrying the box.

"Oh, you mean that box," his mother said. "Never saw it."

"Let's have a look, then," his father said.

He took a folding knife from his pocket and acted as though he was going to open the box, but his mother swiped it away from him.

"I believe this is addressed to me, Mr. Caldwell," she said.

"Don't you want to see what's in it, Mrs. Caldwell?" his father asked.

"I know what's in it," his mother said.

"Something you ordered?" his father asked.

"Could be," his mother said.

"Where from?" his father asked.

"Somewhere," his mother said.

"Somewhere like maybe the North Pole?" his father asked.

"I think I've answered enough questions about this box, Mr. Caldwell," his mother said.

"Only your mother could think about Christmas and summer not even officially started," his father commented.

"I know it," Teddy said. "How can you think of Christmas when it's just getting hot outside?"

"Never y'all mind," his mother said. "We'll see who has a problem with it come December twenty-fifth."

"Point to Mrs. Caldwell," his father said.

"Game, set, and match to Mrs. Caldwell," his mother corrected. "As usual."

Chapter 4

Teddy was only mildly surprised when the mailman brought him another note from Mr. Weems the next day. Again, the envelope was not addressed or sealed, but this one had a stamp with a red *X* drawn across it in the upper right-hand corner.

"I told him we best not make a habit of this," Mr. Bilberry said. "He said, 'Why in the world not?' And I said, 'Because it's illegal.' Then he said, 'Robbery.' And I said, 'Come again?' But he didn't say anything. Know what he did do?"

"What?" Teddy asked.

"He said, 'You just wait right where you are,' and left me standing there. When he came back he said, 'Give me that.' Then he snatched this envelope right out of my hand and made a show of licking that stamp and putting it on. 'There you go,' he said. 'Used to be the mail'd get hijacked, and now it's the dadblamed Post Office itself doing the banditry. Think forty-four cents'll cover the price of you carrying this next door for me?' And I said, 'I'd taken it without the stamp, Andrew. You know that. All I was saying is I don't want to make a habit of it. Just putting a stamp on there doesn't make it any more legal anyway. The stamp's not canceled.' He sort of snorted at me and took a marker out of the bib of his overalls to draw that *X* with. 'There,' he said. 'How's that? Legal as a new penny, is how,' and shut the door in my face. Been anybody else, I'd put an *Undeliverable Mail* sticker on here and left it in his box. Andrew, though, what can you say? I just laughed, and here you go. What's this all about anyway? I been carrying the mail for twenty-some years and never had anything like this come up."

"I think it's about baseball," Teddy said.

"Baseball?" Mr. Bilberry repeated.

"It's a long story," Teddy said. "You know Mr. Weems? You said he was an interesting fellow yesterday. I used to not think much about him except that he scared me, but now I'm starting to see what you mean."

"Hard to miss," Mr. Bilberry said. "All that foolishness with the stamp a minute ago? That's interesting. That old car of his? Same thing. Oh, and sometimes he cooks. The smell over there when he does is like God Himself stirring the pot. Tastes about that good too. He gives me something to take with me every now and again. Stew, beans and rice, that sort of thing. One time he gave me a whole pie. Coconut. My wife said it put hers to shame. I argued her side, but that was just to keep the peace."

He lifted his hat and scratched his head.

"What old car?" Teddy asked. "I've never seen anything but his truck."

"Oh, he has quite a collector's item of a car parked back in his shed," Mr. Bilberry said. "It's open over there sometimes and you can see the back end. I believe it's a Hudson, which you probably never even heard of. A once great name now long defunct. Baseball, huh?"

"Baseball," Teddy said.

"Interesting. See what I mean?"

"Like I said, I'm starting to," Teddy answered.

That day's note was in the form of a question:

Who is your favorite player?

Your neighbor,
A Weems

Teddy cut another of the grocery-list scraps into the proper shape and wrote his response:

Derek Jeter. Who is yours?
Your neighbor,
TCaldwell

He wasn't in quite as big a hurry approaching Mr. Weems' porch the second time. He figured that they had established a routine and that the old man wouldn't change it. He even looked back as he pedaled away this time. But the door was still closed and his note was still there.

The exchange continued for the next several days. The mailman would deliver a note to Teddy from Mr. Weems, and Teddy would deliver his response himself on his way to City Pool. He didn't tell his parents about the notes because he thought of them the way he thought of the broken window. They were between him and Mr. Weems.

When he brought the third one, Mr. Bilberry said that he was out of the trying-to-explain-U.S. Mail-regulations-to-Mr. Weems business. The envelope was once again neither sealed nor addressed, but on it was another red-*X*'d stamp.

"I said to him, 'Forget it,'" Mr. Bilberry explained. "Said, 'No need to do this anymore. Save your stamps. It's not a problem.' And it ain't. I can just tell myself I'm doing it as a friend. I did ask him why he didn't bring these over himself, though."

"What'd he say?" Teddy asked.

"He said, 'Wouldn't be the same,'" Mr. Bilberry replied.

"Thanks for doing it."

"My pleasure," Mr. Bilberry said.

Figured you'd say somebody like Jeter. You're too young to know better.
Your neighbor,
AWeems

You didn't answer my question.
                                    Your neighbor,
                                    TCaldwell

Bopeep Shines. Best pitcher who ever lived.
                                    Your neighbor,
                                    A Weems

Never heard of him.
                                    Your neighbor,
                                    TCaldwell

Now you have. Look him up.
                                    Your neighbor,
                                    A Weems

Another summer rule Teddy's parents had laid out for him was that he was not to get on the computer when he was home alone. This had been no inconvenience to him until he received Mr. Weems' last note. He wanted to know something about Bopeep Shines before he responded, but when he tried to break the computer rule, he discovered that he couldn't. His parents had changed the password the three of them shared during the school year. He didn't know which made him feel worse, the fact that his parents didn't trust him or the fact that he'd found it out by not being trustworthy.

Other than a red dictionary, the only reference books in the house had to do with plants and animals. Teddy had a small library of his own, including several volumes about baseball, but they were biographies of players everybody knew. He'd read all of them more than once, and he was pretty sure that he would have remembered if he'd come across a name like Bopeep Shines. He went to his room and thumbed through each of the books, hoping that he'd just forgotten. But he hadn't. Mr. Weems' favorite player wasn't there. Teddy wondered how that could be, especially if he was the greatest pitcher who ever lived.

"You'd think somebody would at least mention him," he reasoned.

For the first time all week, Teddy did not leave a note on Mr. Weems' door. He had nothing to say except that he was looking, and that didn't seem worth saying. Mr. Weems would surely figure it out for himself. Teddy also took a different route to City Pool so that he could stop by the library. He didn't think his parents' summer computer rule would be in effect there.

The Oil Camp branch of the parish library was on Main Street between McKeithan's Drug Store and Pyle's Auto Parts and Supply, the stores that fronted the alley his father and his father's friend had rolled the burning tires out of. There were only two computers there for patrons to use, half an hour at a time, and three people were signed in ahead of Teddy, not including the lady and the high-school girl who were already at the workstation. He was going to have to wait longer than he wanted to, so he didn't sign in. Instead, he asked the librarian, Mrs. Delhomme, if she minded looking up somebody for him when she got the chance.

"Why, I'd be happy to, Teddy," Mrs. Delhomme said. "Who is it you're interested in today?"

"A baseball player named Bopeep Shines," Teddy said.

"Oh, my. That's certainly an interesting name. For whom did he play?"

Teddy remembered the confusing lesson about "who" and "whom" in English period earlier that year.

"I'm not sure whom it was," he said.

The word was awkward to say. No wonder almost nobody ever used it.

"Who," Mrs. Delhomme said.

She wrote something on a pad.

"Bopeep Shines," Teddy said.

"Yes. I meant 'who' as in who it was, referring to his team. You said you weren't sure whom it was."

"I'm not," Teddy replied.

"'Whom' is fading away, I'm afraid," she said.

"I can see why."

"Laziness is why," she said. "Pure laziness. At any rate, I guess I've spelled 'Bopeep' correctly, but I suppose it could be hyphenated or that the first *p* could be capitalized. I'll do a search for your ballplayer this afternoon. Looks like you're headed for the swimming pool."

"Yes, ma'am," Teddy said. "I'll be back by on my way home."

"I hope you're spending some time reading this summer."

"I am. I'm on the Reading Program list for a book a week. I have a Hardy Boys going right now. It was my dad's. He has a bunch of them from when he was a kid. I might just read them this summer."

"That may well be my very favorite part of reading— choosing a new book after I've finished one."

"Sometimes it's hard to decide, especially after something really good."

"Oh, I know exactly what you mean," Mrs. Delhomme said.

"The Hardys are pretty good. Kind of old-timey, but I like that. Anyway, thanks for the help. I'll see you after while."

"I hope to have some information about your ballplayer," Mrs. Delhomme said.

Chapter 5

Teddy's parents were home when Mr. Bilberry arrived with Saturday's mail and the latest message from Mr. Weems. He also had something else to deliver. It was covered with tinfoil, and the envelope containing that day's note was taped on top.

"I didn't look, but you can smell it's coconut," Mr. Bilberry said. "Mine's chocolate. Got it out there in my truck. Y'all ever talked yet, or he just send you these notes? Not that it's none of my business."

"Just notes so far," Teddy said. "I leave one on his door every afternoon after you bring his."

"Still baseball?" Mr. Bilberry asked.

"Still pretty much baseball," Teddy said. "You ever heard of a pitcher named Bopeep Shines?"

"Bopeep Shines?" Mr. Bilberry asked. "Can't say I have. Course, I don't follow the baseball too much. My sport is football. Roughnecks on Friday, Tigers on Saturday, and Saints on Sunday. You a baseball man?"

"I like all sports," Teddy said. "Baseball right now because it's summer."

"Good way to look at it. Got a favorite team?"

"Yankees. And Derek Jeter's my favorite player. Mr. Weems said that didn't surprise him. I mean wrote that it didn't."

"Don't surprise me neither. Little as I follow the baseball, I know that Jeter. Team-wise I'd have to go with the Cardinals myself. The Yankees're like the baseball version of the Cowboys to me, and being a Saints fan I'm anti-Cowboys. I have to listen to New Orleans on the radio because the Shreveport station always shows the dad-blasted Cowboys."

"Me too. I hope the Cowboys lose every week, just like my daddy does."

"He's raising you right. Well, y'all enjoy that pie. Bopeep Shines, huh? That's a new one on me."

"Mrs. Delhomme at the library tried to look him up for me yesterday, but she said she got so busy with other people that she didn't have time to do a real search. She's going to look some more for me on Monday. We tried to here last night, but something's the matter with our computer. He's Mr. Weems' favorite player is why I'm wondering about him."

He and the mailman locked eyes. Teddy knew that they were thinking the same thing.

Interesting.

The pie tasted like a cloud might if you could taste it, like one of those great white mysteries that ease across the sky on perfect summer days.

"This is unbelievable," his father said.

"It's impossible," his mother agreed.

"I didn't even used to like coconut," Teddy said.

"You have to thank him for us," his mother told him.

"Oh, I will," Teddy said.

"How do you thank somebody for something taste like this?" his father asked.

"Mr. Bilberry said Mr. Weems cooks real food like stew and stuff too," Teddy remarked. "He gave him a chocolate pie today."

"Well, he ought to open him up a restaurant," his father said.

The note was on the table beside Teddy's placemat:

Missed hearing from you yesterday. Hope you like pie.
Make sure your folks get a bite.

Your neighbor,
A Weems

"What does he mean he missed hearing from you?" his father asked.

"Want to see his other notes?"

"I thought there was just the one before this," his father said.

"There's more. We've been sending them back and forth."

"Well, why didn't you say something?" his father asked.

"I didn't see any reason to," Teddy answered.

"I'd say that's strange," his father commented.

"Sending notes?" Teddy asked.

"I was thinking you not saying anything was. But, yeah, writing notes to your next-door neighbor seems kind of strange too."

"I think it's more interesting than strange," his mother said.

The word was everywhere.

"How do you do it?" his father asked.

"Just like the first time," Teddy said. "Mr. Bilberry brings me one from Mr. Weems with the rest of the mail, then I write something back and leave it on his door on my way to the pool."

"What do y'all talk about?" his father asked.

"Baseball," Teddy said. "I'll show you."

As he headed to his room, he pictured his parents looking at each other with "I don't know either" faces. He took the notes out of his drawer and put them in order.

"Okay," his father said. "He writes this and you write what?"

Teddy said what he'd written.

"That's funny about Jeter," his father noted. "What did you say to that?"

"I said he didn't answer my question," Teddy replied. "Look what he wrote back."

"Bopeep Shines," his father said. "That's a hell of an answer. Sorry. You know who that is?"

"I don't," his mother said. "Do you?"

"I don't either," Teddy said.

"I've heard of him. He's kind of a legend. He played ball in the old Negro Leagues during the depression."

"The Negro Leagues?" Teddy asked.

"Back then they wouldn't let black players in the Big Leagues, so they had their own league," his father said. "I don't know that much about it. Everything was separate, not just baseball. It was ridiculous. 'Negro' is where 'nig—'"

"Don't say it," his mother warned.

"I was just . . . ," his father protested.

But his mother held up a hand.

"Okay, okay," his father said. "You're right."

"It's not like I don't know the word," Teddy said. "I remember a long time ago you talking to me about it."

"Around here you can't help know it," his mother said. "You should hear some of those guys down at Builders. They come in and get to talking and it's *n* this and *n* that like we're still in 19-whatever. It makes me sick."

"You'd need earplugs in the oilfield," his father said.

"What did you mean by 'everything was separate'?" Teddy asked.

"I meant everything was divided by a line you didn't cross," his father said. "Like even around here now in at least one way I can think of. I'm still waiting for the first black family to try to buy a house outside one of the Quarters."

"Nobody'd sell them one," his mother said.

"But back then it was literally one side 'Colored' and the other 'White,'" his father went on. "Down to water fountains."

"And baseball," Teddy said. "So you mean Derek Jeter and A-Rod and them couldn't have played for the Yankees?"

"Not for anybody," his father said. "It was a big deal when they finally let the first black player in. Jackie Robinson. I don't remember what year, but it wasn't long after World War II."

"He must've been pretty good," Teddy said.

"Lots of them were pretty good. But Robinson was extra pretty good, and they picked him to let in. There's no telling how many were just as good, though, and probably even better. Definitely there were some a lot better than some of the white players."

"I don't get it," Teddy said. "Wouldn't you want the best players on your team no matter what?"

"You'd think," his mother said.

"People talk about the good old days. My granddaddy used to say, 'You want a taste of the good old days? Wait till the middle of July and turn off your air-conditioner.' In other words, the good old days really weren't. Not that everything's perfect now, but imagine the Yankees without Jeter or the Cardinals without Pujols before he went to the Angels. You could go on and on. And that's just baseball."

"The Negro Leagues would have whole teams of All-Stars today," Teddy said.

"Well, everybody's not an All-Star. Black or white. But there's no doubt that some of the best players who ever lived never got a chance to prove themselves."

"Like Bopeep Shines," Teddy said.

"Probably," his father agreed. "Really, though. I don't know anything about him except that he was supposed to've been a great pitcher who just sort of came and went. Disappeared. You wonder how come he's the old man's favorite. A guy his age, I'd said he'd pick somebody from the old days for sure, but not somebody as obscure as Bopeep Shines."

"Are you going swimming today?" his mother asked.

"I am," Teddy said. "I'll leave Mr. Weems a note on my way."

"Be sure to thank him for this pie," his mother said. "Profusely."

"Tell him we definitely got that bite," his father said.

Interestingly, Mr. Weems had not made an appearance since he waved to Teddy on Monday. Nor had he mentioned the broken window in any of his notes, not even to acknowledge the apology Teddy had written. Up until the arrival of the wonderful coconut pie, their relationship was based strictly on the brief written exchanges about baseball, specifically Bopeep Shines—whoever Bopeep Shines was. Now that Teddy knew something about him, Mr. Weems' favorite player somehow seemed even more mysterious.

Teddy's note that day read:

Thanks for the pie. It was too good to say. My folks think the same.

> *Your neighbor,*
> *TCaldwell*

P.S. I found out something about Bopeep Shines.

No mail was delivered on Sunday. Teddy half-expected Mr. Weems to find a way to send him a message, but he didn't. The sky was overcast and threatening, so he took a break from the pool and spent the afternoon finishing the Hardy Boys. He liked it enough to try another one and read a couple of chapters to get started. The story had the same comfortable rhythm and some of the same characters as the first, including Frank and Joe's buddy Chet Morton, who drove a yellow car called the Queen. The boys referred to it as a *jalopy*. Teddy found the word funny and wonderful.

After supper that night, he asked his mother to see if she could log him on to the computer. He wanted to try Bopeep Shines again. She couldn't do it. The machine was still acting up.

Chapter 6

Teddy wondered how long he and Mr. Weems would exchange notes before they met face to face. Although they lived not a hundred yards apart, they might as well have been in different towns, or even different countries. The old man was certainly from a different world. Teddy knew only the littlest bit about the past from history period and from stories Two-Moms told him when they visited her in Shreveport. His father had said that the good old days really weren't, which may have been true, but Teddy was beginning to find himself fascinated by the idea that the past was actual, that the world had been full of real people living real lives long before he arrived. This made him look at everything differently, from the streets to the houses and buildings to even the trees of Oil Camp.

He tried to picture the town in his parents' day when, as they'd told him, Main Street was just at the beginning of going downhill toward the way it was now, mostly closed and boarded up. In Two-Moms' day that same street was thriving, bustling, busy.

"Many's the time I drove around for seemed like a half of an hour trying to find a place to park," Two-Moms would say. "Why, we had everything in Oil Camp. Three groceries, if you can believe it, and, law, I don't know what-all. A movie theater. Two shoe stores. You didn't have to go anywhere else to shop for clothes or food or anything else. Oh, you might go to Shreveport for a special occasion once in a while, but most of us spent the better part of our time

49

right here where we lived. It was the same everywhere, I suppose. And then the world got big. Now, look at me. Here I am *living* in Shreveport, and if I didn't, I'd have to come over here like your folks do for any but the most basic things."

He thought back to before that, when Oil Camp wasn't even Oil Camp. It was Sherman's Store, a settlement of cotton farmers and the one business. Then came the big strike and with it jobs. People found their way to northwest Louisiana from all over and set up camp where they could, mostly following the lay of the railroad tracks until they had a town. Sherman's Store became Old Store, and the camps became Oil Camp. Main Street was just a strip of dirt that turned to mud in the rain, lined by the first buildings. Teddy crossed the tracks every day on his way to the pool. His house was on Gantt Street, three blocks east of the highway.

Now he sat in the living room waiting for the mailman. He was looking at the pin oak in front of Mr. Weems' house. Its bottom limbs were gone, so it was very old, maybe older than the town itself, a leftover from the big woods, when these houses and this street didn't exist, when Oil Camp didn't exist, when not even Sherman's Store existed, back when everything he knew was nothing but the pure world.

His thoughts were interrupted by the mailman's knock.

"Got you another one," Mr. Bilberry said. "How'd you like that pie?"

"That pie was just fine," Teddy said.

"Wait'll he gives you a chocolate one. I thought the coconut was good. This one, there wasn't even any point to my wife saying it put hers to shame. That was plain as day. He's cooking real today. You'll smell it when you go over there. It's, well, just good Lord. Maybe he'll offer us a taste tomorrow."

"Bopeep Shines played in the Negro Leagues," Teddy said.

"I be dog."

"You know them?" Teddy asked.

"Just only that it was all niggers," Mr. Bilberry said.

Teddy stared at him.

"What?" Mr. Bilberry asked.

Teddy shrugged.

"Nothing," he said.

"Wait a minute. I see. I don't guess you kids say that anymore."

"Some do," Teddy replied. "My mom hates it."

"It's an old habit," Mr. Bilberry said. "I can't help it sometimes. I'm sorry. It's a serious thing."

"Okay," Teddy said. "Well, I guess I'll see you tomorrow."

"I hope you won't hold saying that against me. It's just a word."

Teddy nodded as he closed the door. He was disappointed in Mr. Bilberry, and he wanted him to know that. But he wasn't sure why hearing the word that morning bothered him so much, exactly. It wasn't as though he didn't regularly hear it. Maybe it was the conversation he'd had with his parents the day before and being reminded of how much it upset his mother. Maybe it was the surprise of hearing Mr. Bilberry use it in front of him so casually. But it *was* just a word, after all. To somebody from a foreign country it would just be a sound. Teddy had even used it himself before he knew better. He remembered the day he became aware of it as something his mother considered taboo. They were in the car. He was five. They passed some children walking along the side of the road, and he asked his mother where she thought they might be going, using the word as his reference.

"Don't say that, Teddy."

"Say what?"

"The word you just called them."

"Why not? Two-Pop says it."

"Well, Two-Pop is wrong."

"How?"

"Because it's an ugly thing to say. It's like a cuss word. People use it to be mean. That's the only reason."

"Two-Pop ain't mean. He's your daddy."

"Isn't. No, he's not mean. But he should know better than to say it in front of you."

"I wasn't being mean."

"I know it, sweetie, but let's just take the word out of your vocabulary right now because it is mean. It's complicated."

Thinking about that reminded him of Two-Pop, who died the next year. Teddy hadn't known his father's parents at all, and the little bit of memory he had of Two-Pop was beginning to fade. He wondered how much of what he knew about being with him was real memory or just stories his parents and Two-Moms told. Like the one about the time at the lake when Two-Pop got a strike from a good-size bass then tried to give the rod to Teddy so they could reel it in together but Teddy, who was three, wouldn't take the rod and the fish almost pulled it out of Two-Pop's hands and he had to juggle it back under control, but by the time he had it steady again the fish was gone because the hook wasn't set.

"Funniest thing I ever saw," his father would say. "And the best part was Two-Pop trying to act like he wasn't mad. He was fuming. I'm talking about ready to bust, because that was a really good fish. And poor Teddy standing there scared half to death so Two-Pop has to take a knee and hug him and tell him it's all right. Boy, he hated losing that fish."

Teddy had a picture of the incident in his mind, but it was like something he'd read or seen in a movie, not something he'd actually done.

The word that had just sent his mind all over the place was something he hadn't thought about much either way in quite a while. Some people said it. Some people didn't. Probably more didn't. Now that he was back to thinking about it, he realized that he wasn't even sure of its specific definition, so he looked it up in the dictionary and read that it meant "Negro," which meant black, which was undoubtedly what his father was going to say when his mother stopped him the day before. But there was more. Teddy didn't completely understand all of it, but the message was clear that his mother was right to think about it the way she did. Ironically, Mr. Bilberry was also right. It was a serious thing.

That day's note from Mr. Weems read:

> *Glad you all liked the pie. Look in my mailbox.*
> *Your neighbor,*
> *A Weems*

Teddy tried to think of a reply, but there was nothing to say to that except another thank-you for the pie. Saying he'd look in the box seemed unnecessary, too, because that would be something he'd already done by the time Mr. Weems got the note. Teddy realized that his brain had not had much of a vacation so far that summer. He was thinking at least as much and maybe more than he did in school, as a matter of fact. The difference was that everything that was on his mind now was interesting, even the tenses of verbs. He pictured Mr. Sherman saying the parts of "think": think, thought, thought. Was that regular or irregular? Maybe it was regular irregular, or perhaps irregular regular.

"Enough!" Teddy said.

Mr. Weems' mailbox was a converted birdhouse nailed to the wall beside his front door. The hole was still in it, but the roof had been fixed on hinges so that it would open and close. The wood was weathered, unfinished. Teddy studied it, aware of a cooking aroma so rich that it made him want to close his eyes. It was a dizzyingly good smell, some kind of gamey meat simmering in a broth along with what must have been a whole garden. He breathed it in, unable to place any single thing.

He lifted the roof of the birdhouse-mailbox and reached inside, but he wasn't tall enough to get his hand all the way down into it. He stood on his tiptoes and tried to see through the hole. It was just over his head. He jumped, but whatever was there was either off to one side or shadowed. He jumped again and then a third time, without success.

He looked around. There was nothing on the porch he could use to stand on. Mr. Weems' rocker would be unsteady. He heard a sound inside the house. This time it was definitely footsteps and not his own heartbeat. His heart hadn't pounded like that since his first trip to the porch. He knew he was welcome there now, but he wasn't sure he was welcome enough to bring Mr. Weems to the door. Teddy turned and moved toward the steps. He was on them when he heard the lock turn. He stopped. He heard the door open, then the screen.

"What's all the commotion?"

At close range the voice was even more commanding than it had been the other time Teddy had heard it. He turned and saw the old man standing there holding the screen open with his forearm. He had on his usual overalls with a collared short-sleeve shirt and rough-side-out cowboy boots. His forearms were tanned from a lifetime of outdoor work and thick with muscle, not the pale sticks Teddy expected an old man to have. His hair was white and cropped close to his head, his face seamed with wrinkles. His eyes were blue and they were as clear as a cat's.

"It's me," Teddy said. "Your neighbor."

"What's that *T* you sign stand for?" Mr. Weems asked.

"Teddy," Teddy said. "And you're Mr. Weems. Your *A* is for Andrew. The mailman told me."

"Let's be a little less formal than all that," Mr. Weems said. "Call me Drew. That mailbox a little high for you?"

"I can't reach inside of it," Teddy said.

Still holding it open, now with a hand whose skin looked like the hide of his boots, the old man stepped around the door. He lifted something from the box with his other hand.

"You said this was yours other day. Had a lump in your throat at the time."

He lobbed the ball. Teddy caught it with both hands.

"I'm real sorry about your window, Mr. Weems," Teddy said. "My folks said tell you we'll pay you for it."

"Nothing to pay for," Mr. Weems declared. "Window's fixed. Call me Drew."

"But don't you have to pay somebody, Mr. Drew? For the glass, I mean?"

He couldn't quite bring himself to drop the "Mr." entirely.

"Not if you know where to look. And, no, I don't have to get no handyman to do no job for me. Window's fixed. Anything you owed you paid with your note. That told me a lot about you. About your folks too. Apology accepted."

"What're you cooking?"

"A bite to eat. Smells good, don't it. You hungry?"

"Nosir, I'm not. And, yessir, it smells about as good as anything I ever smelled. What is it?"

"No need for all the 'yessir' and 'nosir' business, son. Just talk to me normal. Deer gumbo."

"I ate a lot of deer meat but never in gumbo."

"Good land, boy. Where you been for—how old are you anyway?"

"Nine. Be ten in August."

"Ten come August. Well, well."

Teddy had eaten two peanut-butter sandwiches before he left the house. He truly wasn't hungry, but he was tempted to say that maybe he was after all just so he could find out what deer gumbo was like. He didn't think the old man was the kind of person who cared for people changing their mind, though, so he didn't.

"Tell you what," Mr. Weems said. "You stop by on your way home from wherever it is you go ever' day. I'll have you a taste set out by the door here. See what you think."

"I'd appreciate that, Mr. Drew," Teddy said. "I go swimming."

"Can you not hear, child?" Mr. Weems asked. "I'm Drew. Or Uncle Drew if you want. I always liked that. Where you swim at?"

"City Pool."

"I much preferred something a little less manmade when I was your age."

"Closest place to go like that's five miles out the highway. Mitchener's Pond."

"Oh, I know Mitchener's Pond."

"How you know it?"

"Lord, boy, I grew up out that way. Walked to it from our place a thousand times as a youngster. Fished the water, hunted the property, knew ever' pine needle out there."

"You're from Oil Camp?"

"That would be a fact. Been gone a while, though. Come back to spend my final days in familiar surroundings."

"Where you been?"

"Here and there."

Teddy expected him to say something more specific, but that was it.

"What did you do?" Teddy asked.

"This and that. Man lives long's I have and he gets around. Unless he stays in one place, if you know what I mean."

"Are we going to quit writing notes now we talked?"

"Depends."

"On what?"

"Depends on if you want to. Save time you just come over here, seems to me. Set on the porch with me or step inside. Take what we established just now, as a for instance. That'd be quite a few notes, quite a few days. I might not have enough days left to do it that way."

"What are we doing?"

The old man smiled. His teeth were startlingly white.

"Why, I reckon we're seeing what there is to see about each other," he said.

"When can I come over?" Teddy asked.

"I'm here except when I'm not," Uncle Drew said. "Come over any time you take the notion."

Teddy didn't think there was much to see about himself, but he suspected that he was going to be taking a regular notion to visit Uncle Drew during the coming days because there was obviously a great deal to see about the old man.

He worked up a good appetite at the pool that afternoon. On his way home, he detoured over to Main Street and stopped by the library to see if Mrs. Delhomme had found out anything about Bopeep Shines.

"I came across several references to him, Teddy," she said. "But they all say essentially the same thing. I printed this one for you. It's representative of what is available."

He thanked her for her help, folded the sheet of paper she gave him, and stuck it into the waistband of his swimming trunks.

"Aren't you going to read it?" Mrs. Delhomme asked.

"Not right this minute," Teddy said. "I need to get going. Thanks again."

He had that taste of deer gumbo on his mind. Pedaling across the railroad tracks, he thought he might knock on Uncle Drew's door and show him the printout. They could look at whatever it said together.

But Uncle Drew's truck was gone. Teddy leaned his bicycle against the pin oak and walked to the porch. On the rail was a small bowl covered with tinfoil. The handle of a utensil protruded from the tinfoil. He removed it and picked up the bowl. Unless his nose was playing tricks on him, the gumbo smelled even better now than it had earlier. The bowl was still warm. Uncle Drew must have just left. Teddy stirred the thick soup into the rice and spooned up a bite. The flavor astonished him. Everything that was in it tasted exactly like itself—the okra, the garlic, the onion, the bell pepper, the venison—but all of it instantly came together to make something brand new and so gloriously right that he didn't want to swallow it, ever. The only reason he did was so that he could take another bite. He repeated this process until nothing was left. Then he licked the bowl. Until he opened them, he didn't realize that his eyes had been closed the entire time.

Chapter 7

The printout Mrs. Delhomme had given Teddy contained the following entry, taken from an Internet source:

CANTRELL "BOPEEP" SHINES (1910?-?) Negro League pitcher about whom most information is anecdotal and therefore unreliable. After a single spectacular season with the New Orleans Po' Boys of the Negro Southern Association, Shines vanished from history and entered baseball mythology. Stories about his depression-era exploits persist among old-timers. According to legend, Shines is said to have traveled from town to town accompanied by a white valet several years his junior (name unknown) with whom he rounded up hitters to face him at up to one dollar per pitch, a significant sum at the time. Although baseball historians consider his one-man barnstormer legacy purely apocryphal, Shines' official 1935 record with the Po' Boys is testament to a singular mound prowess. Blessed with uncanny control and speed, the lanky southpaw posted a record of 17-0, including 1 perfect game and, amazingly, 3 no-hitters. Shines was the winning pitcher of record in the 1935 NSA All-Star Game, played in Shreveport on July 1. Working three innings, he faced 12 batters, striking out 10 and allowing 0 hits. Said to have earned his nickname from his habit of calling opposing batters "a bunch of sheeps [sic] I'll herd straight back to the dugout," Shines abruptly left the Po' Boys and organized baseball a few weeks prior to the end of the '35 campaign. No newspaper *accounts, photographs or newsreel footage exist to verify his subsequent whereabouts, but the legend endures—much like that of the Loch Ness Monster. Born in New Orleans, ca. 1910, Bopeep Shines provides an intriguing footnote to Negro League history.*

Uncle Drew read the entry in silence and handed the sheet of paper back to Teddy. They were sitting on the old man's porch the morning after their first conversation. Uncle Drew had brought out a lawn chair for Teddy and was himself sitting in his rocker. Beside the rocker was a Piggly Wiggly sack. The top of the sack had been folded over twice.

"What's 'anecdotal' mean?" Teddy asked.

"Means based on a story," Uncle Drew said.

"What about 'apocryphal'?"

"Same thing, except the story's not likely true."

Teddy thought about that.

"You mean a story like something made up?" he asked.

"Yep," Uncle Drew said.

"Is what they say about Bopeep Shines made up?"

"Nope."

Neither of them said anything else for a few moments. Teddy watched a robin hopping around pecking for worms out by the pin oak. When Uncle Drew finally spoke he sounded at first as though he were talking to himself, not to Teddy.

"What I never understood about these so-called historians is why they can't just believe what somebody tells them," he said. "They think they know everything already anyway, so when somebody says something that don't fit what they got in their head they dismiss it right off the bat. They want an account, something wrote down somewhere. These days they'd want a picture, preferably moving. But maybe there ain't no record. Or, let's say in this particular case, more accurately, that maybe they ain't nobody *found* a record yet. What difference does it make?"

Teddy realized that he'd been asked a question.

"Don't automatically mean it ain't true," he said.

He heard the voices of his mother and Mr. Sherman in his head correcting him, but he paid them no attention. He liked the way the old man talked and thought he might as well take a break from rules and regulations too.

"Sure's hell don't," Uncle Drew said. "It'd be like me telling you Cedric Vicknair taught me how to make that gumbo you tasted yesterday and that pie you tasted Saturday, which he did, and you running off trying to find a record of Cedric being a cook but can't do it. Now. You done tasted the pie from my oven, and you done tasted the gumbo from my stove. And I'm telling you Cedric taught both them dishes to me. You going to come back over here and claim him to be apocryphal?"

"Nosir, I ain't," Teddy said. "I'd believe you."

"I guess you wouldn't make much of a historian then," Uncle Drew said.

He looked over at Teddy, who didn't immediately get the joke. Then he did and smiled.

"Guess not," he said.

Uncle Drew rocked a minute.

"Anything in that library story bring out your antennas?" he asked.

"Mainly how good Bopeep was that one season," Teddy said.

"I mean other than the obvious," Uncle Drew prompted. "A small detail."

Teddy looked at the printout. He scanned it, searching in vain for something that should stand out but hadn't when he'd read it before.

"Not really," he said.

"Let's say for some reason you took a notion to prove

that what they say about Bopeep Shines after he left the Po' Boys ain't made up. Something tells you it's fact and you have just got to get to the bottom of it."

"Like a report for school," Teddy said. "Okay."

"Where'd you start?" Uncle Drew asked.

He rocked while Teddy considered this.

"I'd probably look around for somebody to tell me a story and swear to it," Teddy said.

"Who'd be the person you'd most wish to come forward and do that for you?" Uncle Drew asked. "I mean, if you could scare up any one person of all the old-timers who have a memory of Bopeep Shines, which one you think could most likely help you get him—what does it say there? Hold me that over here."

He indicated the printout and leaned toward Teddy, who moved the sheet of paper so that Uncle Drew could see the words.

"That's it," Uncle Drew said. "Help you take Bopeep out of mythology and put him back in history, where you believe he rightly belongs."

He was still leaned toward Teddy, his forearms on his thighs.

"Look there," he said.

He stabbed the printout with an index finger. Teddy read where he pointed.

"The valet," Teddy said, pronouncing it as it was spelled. "I meant to ask you that too. What's a valet?"

"You say it 'valay,'" Uncle Drew explained. "It's foreign. It means a servant, somebody who waits on you."

"I don't guess a lot of black people ever had white servants," Teddy said.

"It'd be highly unusual," Uncle Drew agreed. "But a valet ain't always just a servant like a slave. He could be a companion, a traveling partner. Think Bopeep's could help you with your project?"

"He could tell more stories than anybody, I bet," Teddy said. "But they'd still just be stories."

"What if he had a record to back it all up?" Uncle Drew asked. "What if he had a list of every pitch Bopeep Shines ever threw after he left the Po' Boys?"

"Then we'd be in business," Teddy said.

Uncle Drew resumed rocking. He seemed to be looking past the yard and the tree, past the street, past anything he could actually see. Teddy took the opportunity to study him up close. He noticed how beaten up his hands were. They were huge and had brown spots on them. His nails were thick and yellowed but neatly trimmed. A spot similar to the ones on his hands, though larger, was visible at his temple, visible because his hat was tilted back on his head. Deep lines creased the skin of his face like furrows in a field.

One of the things Teddy had always heard about old people was that they smelled bad. His experience told him that this was not necessarily true. At least it wasn't true of the two old folks he knew. Two-Moms smelled soft, like soap and powder. Uncle Drew smelled clean, like right before rain. He looked clean too. He looked like his truck, old but immaculately kept. The truck was parked in his driveway, the paint and chrome gleaming in the sunshine. Teddy hadn't been inside Uncle Drew's house yet, but he imagined that everything in there had a place and that the smell was good, like food cooked or cooking.

"You like to read, Teddy?" Uncle Drew asked.

"I do," Teddy said.

"So do I. Don't have much schooling but I always enjoyed a good book. What're you reading right now?"

"A mystery story. Hardy Boys."

"Frank and Joe. Good companions for a boy."

"I think I'd like them in real life."

"Undoubtedly," Uncle Drew said. "Reason I bring up

reading is I got something I think might interest you. It's books, just not what you'd call 'real' books."

"How can books be not real?"

"I mean not printed. These're handwrote. And it ain't sentences in them mostly, just lists. Like I said, it's a record."

"Who did the writing?"

Uncle Drew had continued to look straight ahead while they talked. Now he turned his head toward Teddy. He reached down beside his rocker and picked up the sack. He held it in his lap.

"I did," he said.

It took a second for Teddy to sort through the conversation they'd been having and for the full meaning of the last answer to become clear. His mouth dropped open. Goosebumps crawled across his shoulders and down his arms. Uncle Drew had been leading him toward this moment the whole time, all the way back to the note he'd written after Teddy broke his window. He wanted to say something, but all he could do was sit there with his mouth hanging open and stare at the old man, who didn't say anything either. He just rocked and nodded.

Chapter 8

Teddy sat cross-legged on his bed. Before him were three cardboard accounting ledgers he had taken from the Piggly Wiggly sack, which lay on its side on the floor. Written in faded ink on the front of each ledger were these words:

Bopeep Shines
"The Bat Dodger"
Bets/Balances
Kept by AWeems
"Uncle Drew"

The ledgers were arranged in a fan, like three outsize playing cards. They were all dated in their top right corners by year: 1935, 1936, 1937. Teddy looked at the years, which he had seen only as numbers printed in books, never actual dates written by a real person who was living in them.

Uncle Drew had handed him the sack and told him to take it home before he opened it.

"You'll have to use your noggin for a minute, but I expect you'll find it fairly self-explanatory," he said.

"You were his valet?" Teddy asked.

"I was," Uncle Drew said. "Now you know whose name they don't have on the Internet."

"How'd it happen?" Teddy asked.

"We'll get to that another time," Uncle Drew said.

"Meanwhile, you just go take a look and see what's in the sack. I need to rest."

"Why me?"

Uncle Drew looked at Teddy seriously.

"Because you like baseball," he said.

Teddy pulled the 1935 ledger toward himself and carefully opened it somewhere near the middle. He studied that page and turned to others, comparing. They were uniform in their setup, the information always recorded in the same hand. At the top was the name of a town followed by a date. A column of consecutive numbers ran down the left-hand side. Often the column filled the entire page, ending with *27,* and continued on to the next and sometimes even the next after that. Occasionally it ended after just three or four entries. Beside the numbers were amounts, written inside parentheses. Most were followed by three slash marks, */ / /,* though the occasional *0* appeared. After that was another amount, not in parentheses, and a plus sign. Teddy turned to a page with five entries, and it looked like this:

Gulfport, Miss.   October 17
1. (25c)   / / /   .75+
2. (25c)   / 0 /   .50+
3. (10c)   / / /   .30+
4. (50c)   / / /   1.50+
5. (10c)   0 / /   .20+

He spent some time with each ledger, noting the names of the towns and figuring out how the system worked. Apparently the parenthetical amounts were bets, the slashes strikes, and the *0*s hits. The final amounts must have been what Bopeep had won during the encounter—or lost. There were a few places where the right-hand columns contained minus signs. The last entry in the 1935 ledger caught his eye because it was different. It was in a three-page list headed Valdosta, Ga., and dated December 15.

63. (all/auto) /   *auto*

Something had been written beneath the entry and partially rubbed out. A few of the letters were still visible enough to read with a little imagination. Teddy tried briefly to decipher it but couldn't. He didn't think it mattered anyway. What did matter was that if he was right about how the system worked, the entry indicated that Bopeep had won a car with a single pitch. He wondered if *all* meant just the all of that particular day or the all period, everything. He looked back over the previous sixty-two entries and saw only four 0s. The rest were /s. Bopeep had already thrown 186 pitches, 182 of which were strikes. That seemed impossible, but there it was, in ink. All of the bets were for at least a dollar, but there were quite a few for five and several for ten. Teddy added them up and discovered that Bopeep was over five hundred dollars to the good when the sixty-third batter stepped up to face him. Whoever it was must have been mighty confident he could get a hit because even back then a car was bound to have been worth much more than that. And Bopeep must have been equally confident in his ability to throw one more strike, because that was definitely a lot of money, no matter when, to put on the line. It might have been even more. It might have been everything he had.

Teddy put the ledgers back into the Piggly Wiggly sack and slid it under his bed. He lay with his hands behind his head, trying to decide whether he should tell his parents about the ledgers or just keep the knowledge to himself for the time being. They would surely be interested in them, but he didn't really have much in the way of a story to explain it all yet, so he thought he'd wait until he did. He stuck to that plan even when his father brought up the subject of Bopeep Shines at the supper table.

"Ran into an old codger down in Jonesboro this afternoon," his father said. "We got to talking about this and that—he was a black man—and I thought I'd run Bopeep Shines by him, see if he knew who I was talking about."

"Did he?" Teddy asked.

He took a bite of fried chicken and began to chew.

"He did," his father said. "Said he even saw him pitch one time. Funny thing, though. It wasn't in a game."

Teddy stopped chewing.

"What do you mean?" he asked.

"Don't talk with your mouth full, Teddy," his mother said.

"I mean they weren't playing two sides and nine innings and all that," his father answered. "Reach me a biscuit if you wouldn't mind there, hon. These are some kind of good."

"They're from a tin," his mother said. "Two-Moms'd have a fit she knew I was feeding y'all store-bought biscuits."

"I don't care if they're from an oil can," his father said. "And neither would she if you didn't tell her. Anyway, this old man said they were having a fish fry one afternoon way out in the country somewhere over in Mississippi. He's from Mississippi, he said, and this was when he was a kid. Said it was a big to-do. Everybody was out there, dancing and carrying on and everything, and all of a sudden here comes a Hudson followed by a cloud of dust up the dirt road leading out to the place."

He stopped to take a sip of ice tea. Teddy finally swallowed his bite of chicken.

"A Hudson?" he asked.

"It's a kind of car they used to make," his father said. "A company, like Ford or Chevrolet. Not many around these days."

"I know," Teddy said. "Mr. Bilberry told me there's an old car in Mr. Weems' shed. He said the door's open sometimes and he's seen the back end and thinks it's a Hudson."

"Small world," his father marveled. "Maybe he'll show it to you sometime so you'll know what one looks like. I wouldn't mind seeing it myself. So anyway, here comes one up the road and driving it is a white kid not much older than the old man telling me this was at the time, which did get some of their attention. What got the rest of it was that also in the car was a black man. Car pulls up and stops. The driver gets out, goes around, and opens the door for the passenger. He's a tall, skinny, black-as-night fellow dressed to the nines. Tie, hat, everything. The old man said there was a band playing for the dancers, so of course the music stops and everybody gathers around to see who this is and it's guess who."

"Bopeep Shines," Teddy answered.

He spoke the name reverently.

"In the flesh," his father said. "How they worked things, that day anyway, was the kid who drove the car said his man would give anybody who wanted to bat against him three pitches, his two-bits—what they called a quarter back then—his two bits against theirs per pitch and they could choose their own umpire to judge his placement. Anything the ump considered out of the strike zone didn't count, no questions asked. The kid himself would catch. Well, naturally, there were a few old boys out there who might've had themselves a taste or two from the jug, and when they looked at this rail in a suit standing there they thought, 'Shoot, this easy money.' But it wasn't. By the time he was done, the old man said, he'd been through just about everybody who could lift a bat, some two and three times, and the bets were up to an even dollar a shot. He said Bopeep didn't even loosen his tie or roll up his sleeves. Said he just took off his jacket and mowed them down one after another. Said, 'Law, that boy he had hissef a ar-um. Ball go ever' whichaway.' Said, 'He kick up that long leg, haul back almost to the ground behind him, and then come I'm talking about *at* you with it. Thing'd dance up, down, this side, that side, who know where? And him talking the whole time.' Said he, the old man now, said he like to busted a gut, him and his friends, they got to laughing so hard at their daddies and brothers and uncles turning plumb around trying to get some wood on the ball and Bopeep saying, 'Ain't no kinda way now, sheeps. Y'all *got* to know better'n think I ain't herdin' today.' And the kid was writing all of it down in a notebook, every pitch. He kept it off to one side, and after he threw the ball back he'd put a mark in it."

"Did he say what year this was?" Teddy asked.

"Don't believe he did," his father answered. "Sometime during the depression, I guess. Thirty-something."

"I wonder if any of the batters got mad at him," his mother said. "For all the talking, I mean, not to mention that he was taking their money. I bet some of their wives and girlfriends did if the men didn't."

"I thought about that too," his father said. "I asked the old man, but he just shook his head and said, 'Shoot, ain't no way to be mad, man entertain you like that. My daddy say later, say, "You know, I look at it like we got to see something special today." That's what he called it. "Something special." Now, my mama, she wasn't exactly in full agreement. He done lost six dollars, see. Two turns at the plate. But she did say she got a kick out of seeing the menfolks up there acting the fool like they under attack from a bee every ball he threw.'"

The whole time his father was talking, Teddy was going back and forth between picturing the scene and picturing the ledgers that were in the sack under his bed.

"Are you done, Teddy?" his mother asked. "You're not eating."

"I'm just wondering," he said.

"Imagine what those ledgers would be worth to a baseball collector," his father remarked. "Who knows where they are, though? Probably long gone by now. Kid probably is too. If not, he's well on his way to it. But people do collect baseball stuff. Like that one card of Honus Wagner supposed to be worth I don't know how many thousand dollars."

"But that's famous," Teddy said. "Nobody's hardly heard of Bopeep Shines. They say the stories like that old man's today are all just made-up legends."

"No reason not to believe it," his father replied. "Why would he make something like that up?"

"It'd be cool to prove it's true," Teddy said.

"Sure would," his father agreed. "Maybe Mr. Weems knows something about it. He ever tell you why Shines his favorite player?"

"He just says he was," Teddy replied.

"That's a good answer," his mother commented. "You don't have to have a reason for so-and-so to be your favorite whatever. Sometimes they just are."

"I wonder if he ever saw him play or just heard about him," his father said.

Teddy smiled without moving his lips. It was an inside smile.

"I think he probably saw him," he said.

Chapter 9

For the next few days, Teddy skipped going to the pool in favor of spending his time either listening to Uncle Drew talk or thinking about what he'd said. They'd start out on the porch, Uncle Drew always adding another episode or two to the story of his adventures with Bopeep Shines, then they'd move inside to have a bite of dinner, after which they returned to the porch to let their stomachs settle. Uncle Drew would end the visit by saying that he had to go rest. Teddy could have gone to the pool then, but even though some of his friends started calling to ask where he was and why he wasn't coming swimming anymore, he would always just walk back over to his house and either thumb through the ledgers looking at the entries that went with Uncle Drew's stories or lie on his bed daydreaming. He told his friends he had an earache or he had to go visit his grandmother in Shreveport. The truth was that, for the time being, he wasn't interested in his friends or City Pool or much of anything at all that had to do with the world he lived in. He was interested in Uncle Drew and the world the old man took him to as they talked.

On the morning of the first day of this new schedule the mailman, Mr. Bilberry, stopped for a minute.

"Glad to see you two fellows finally got together," he said.

"Young Teddy here wants to know about the old days, and I'm telling him."

"Ever get the Bopeep Shines mystery solved, Teddy?" Mr. Bilberry asked.

"I know a little bit," Teddy said.

"Well, I'll say again I'm sorry about the other morning."

"It's okay," Teddy replied.

"My wife said tell you, Andrew, that that chocolate pie of yours'd win the gold medal. Unless it was up against the coconut, in which case there'd have to be a tie."

"You tell her I said I'll send y'all a couple of slices of huckleberry over tomorrow'll drop them others into second," Uncle Drew replied.

"Have mercy. Y'all take care, now."

Uncle Drew nodded. Teddy did the same. They watched Mr. Bilberry resume his route.

"What's he sorry for?"

"I asked him if he ever heard about the Negro Leagues and he said he only knew it was all just the *n*-words played in it," Teddy answered.

"Well, he ought to be sorry," Uncle Drew declared. "I ain't saying I ain't used it myself in my day, and I'll have to, telling you some of this. But I want you to understand that I have heard it said the wrong way too many times to take it lightly, I don't care who says it, and that includes black folks themselves. You'd figure they'd just as soon want to erase it from the language, but some of them use it fairly regularly, which is a wonder. If they think they're taking it away from them who means harm by it they're dead wrong. Keeping it alive is all that does. You say anything to him about it? Must have, him to apologize."

"I did," Teddy said. "Why're people mean, Uncle Drew? Not that Mr. Bilberry's mean on purpose I don't think."

"I'd second that," Uncle Drew said. "As to your question, if I could answer that I'd be on the TV explaining it for a fee. People're mean because they're people. Some don't even know when they're being mean. Most do, though. I guess they're trying to verify that they exist somehow, treating the other fellow like he's second class. One thing

I learned real quick running with Bopeep is there's a deep meanness sometimes comes out in folks. Not him, though. Lord, Bopeep Shines was as peaceful a human being as is possible to be. The man didn't have a mean bone in his skeleton."

He paused as if he were remembering something that wasn't pleasant. Then he shook his head and turned to Teddy.

"The road'll take some twists on you," he said. "Now. Where were we before the postman dropped by?"

"You were saying how it used to be."

"Yessir, well, how it used to be just in my lifetime's undoubtedly as distant to you as the Ottoman Empire or Sparta," Uncle Drew said. "Which is understandable. History has a way of piling up on a fellow. Hard to keep up with it. But let's us see about establishing a frame of reference here. When you're talking about history you need you a perspective. And one thing I can tell you for sure is that while the passing years do take just about everything else away from you, they will give you perspective. It ain't much of a trade, but time don't negotiate. It just passes."

Teddy noticed that Uncle Drew was once again looking beyond what was in front of them toward something he couldn't actually see. But maybe he was seeing something over there. Maybe it was as clear to him as the pin oak.

First thing you got to understand [Uncle Drew said] is the obvious point that everything was different. It was also exactly the same. People don't change. Our species is just as infuriating and inexplicable now as it was the day Eve had to have a bite of that apple and Adam couldn't stand not to too. Two humans in Paradise and all they have to do's follow one rule. So what do they do? They break the rule at the first available opportunity and get theirself kicked out the pool. Nothing's changed on that front. Details might have, what we've surrounded ourself with. But us? We're the same as we ever was.

Primarily, to get oriented to how it used to be, the detail you need to know is that the United States of America was at the time all this happened a country divided by race. And I ain't talking about the kind of division we have now, this leftover, behind-the-back, smile-on-your-face kind of prejudice. Most folks do a fair job of hiding that part of themselves anymore. Look what they done in the voting booth electing your president, for instance. I'm sure as we're sitting here that a good many of them didn't think a thing in the world about the black and the white of it, but I'm just as sure there was that many more thought about nothing else and either had to hold their nose to pull his lever or pulled the other one against him as much or more as they pulled it for his opponent. But he was on the ballot for everybody to do with what they would, and him just being there—never mind him actually becoming president of the United States—is a stride forward that was once unimaginable, because this country was not too very long ago defined by flat-out racism and absolute segregation.

Now you take your school and the teams y'all have. They're mixed, black and white kids getting along happy as pigs in a puddle for the most part. Didn't happen in the old days. *Couldn't* happen in the old days, due to the law of the land and the attitude folks held. If you wasn't white, you had very few privileges. You came and you went through the back door. You lived in a certain part of town, which is still the case here in Oil Camp today and'll give you a little bit of an idea. You drank from a fountain had a *Colored* sign above it and you did not so much as glance at the one below the *White* sign. Same water through the same pipe, same need for it. But, mister, I don't care if you dying of thirst, you had better sip yours over there and stay out of ours. Else, you fixing to have more problems than a parched throat. We'll put a strap across your back and sleep no less well for the memory of your suffering. Might even sleep better.

Hard as it undoubtedly is for you to imagine such foolishness, it was a fact of life, no questions asked. Nothing was mixed and I mean no exceptions. Not schools, not churches, not places of business, not baseball. But black folks did go to school, they did go to church, they did buy and sell, and they did play baseball. They was human after all and them're things humans do. Black humans just had to do them separate because that's how the hammer hit the nail.

Segregation. Because of it, as you now know, professional baseball was closed to the black man. Don't matter how talented, don't matter how smart, all that, they were not welcome. And they had plenty of talent. Had talent to burn, talent to spare, talent to throw away. Not the problem. Problem was skin tone. You ain't born with a certain pigment, Major League Baseball ain't interested in your services. Never mind you can throw a ball nobody can see or hit one from here to Mitchener's Pond. Do not apply. It wasn't fair, to say the least. But then again, nothing else was fair for black folks at the time. They was used to making something out of nothing, though, and the solution in this case was plain as day. They said, "You won't let us play ball in your league? Fine. We'll make our own league."

Actually they made several, the original right around the time I was born, maybe a year or two before. Whatever the case, the original Negro National League was a successful venture, which is just the type of a venture that tends to get copied. Well, lo and behold, guess what starts popping up like dandelions. Professional black baseball outfits. Included among them was the one your library article mentioned, the Negro Southern Association, which had among its teams the New Orleans Po' Boys, which had among its players in 1935 a pitcher named Cantrell Shines, better known as Bopeep because he called the batters he faced sheeps. That's bona-fide truth. I heard him say it a thousand times.

I guess you probably wondering if I'm ever going to get to me and him. I am. I do have one more little thing to tell you about the Negro Leagues first, though. It has to do with somebody who was opposite of Bopeep in some ways but just like him in others. Satchel Paige. He's in the Hall of Fame, the real Hall of Fame in Cooperstown, New York. Got his plaque thanks to Ted Williams, also known as the Splendid Splinter, a white man who, when he received his own Hall of Fame plaque—this would've been in the late 1960s, heady times in the country, what with the war over in the Vietnam revved plumb up and dog near another civil one bubbling up right here in the States because a lot of folks had finally done had enough of a lot of things, segregation being high on the list—who, the Splinter that is, added his two cents to the discussion by speaking up for Paige and saying a brave thing, a right thing. Said he hoped Satchel and some of the other great Negro Leaguers'd someday be elected into the Hall. Said they weren't there already only because they weren't given the chance. Meaning they was in the Negro Leagues and not the Major Leagues.

But that's all later than where we're going, which is the 1930s, a bad time, a dark time. It was like a sack has a wet bottom and can't hold the heavy groceries in it. Bottom falls out in '29, and if you're my daddy, you lose every bit of the little bit you have. He was just barely on the bright side of nothing to start with and now he gets throwed across to the other. Sawmill where he worked closed when I was I believe ten, and him having my mama and five other mouths to feed without steady and gainful employment put us in a bind. He picked up what he could here and there but it was rough. Me and my brothers was working like grown men out there trying to get something to come up out the red clay ground. By the way, one thing you won't never catch me cooking or eating or even being in the same room ever again with is a turnip. I ain't particularly fond of greens neither, though I'll choke a plate down long's I got a bottle of Tabasco to pour on them.

I said I hunted and fished the property. Well, it wasn't no sporting proposition for trophies to hang on the wall. Everything we done was for survival. By the time the Po' Boys' bus broke down that day and I saw a possibility other than being half-starved for the rest of my life, I was ready to take it. The funny thing is that Bopeep, who was playing *ball* for a living, was looking for another possibility too. I told him I'd give my eye teeth to be in his shoes and know what he said? He said, "I been thinking they's a better way'n even this."

Basically, what he was at that point in his life was a gambler. Not a con man try to cheat you but a gambler try to beat you fair and square. Hadn't been, he'd ended up famous as anybody who ever played the game. The tragedy of it is he was headed in that direction toward the end. We'd seen what was available and he was thinking he'd like to put on a uniform again. Not for the money. We had plenty of that. He was just thinking the way I look back and wish I'd started trying to get him to think long before I did. He was thinking about being part of the game again. But we were having us a time and the wheel was spinning a certain direction.

Sorry. I'm getting ahead of myself. Speaking of being half-starved, I move we go see about what's on the stove in yonder. Care for a bite?

And so the pattern was set.

"How'd you learn cooking?" Teddy asked.

"Cedric Vicknair taught me," Uncle Drew said. "Most of it anyway. I done told you that."

"Where at?" Teddy asked.

"Offshore," Uncle Drew said. "A few years after all this I'm fixing to tell you, the war broke out and I found myself in Europe, doing battle. After that I came back to the States and used the G.I. Bill to try me some more school and very quickly got enough of it to know I wasn't cut that way, so I went to work doing this and that, here and there, until I wound up offshore. First rig I was on Cedric was cook. I'd watched enough sitting at tables in the back of hotel kitchens and cafes traveling with Bopeep to've picked up a little bit and have an interest, something I most assuredly did not have in being out on that platform with the Gulf of Mexico lashing around down there. Found that out pretty quick and started hanging around the galley bothering Cedric, who never said nothing to me, not a word, until one day I went in there and he leaned back against the stove, crossed his arms, and says to me, said, 'Let's see you cook something.' Which I did. Fried some chicken for the hands. Next day, Cedric told me get an apron because he'd saved me from the platform. And that was that. Don't know who he talked to and didn't ask. I just put on an apron and started feeding roughnecks."

That day they had liver and onions, a dish Teddy had previously taken exactly one bite of. He had never had even that many of what was for dessert.

"Tell me what that is," Uncle Drew said.

"I was thinking blueberry, but it ain't blueberry," Teddy answered.

"You right," Uncle Drew said. "They close kin, but I always favored the huckleberry side of the family myself."

Teddy didn't disagree.

Chapter 10

Way it happened [Uncle Drew said] was the Po' Boys was headed south out of Arkansas. They'd been on a little tour playing against teams up there and over in Tennessee and their bus had been acting up for several days. Time they crossed the line back into Louisiana the thing had commenced to sound like Black Cats going off in a pipe. It finally broke plumb down out our way. I was fishing over at Mitchener's and was into a pretty good mess of bream. When I heard the commotion I walked across the field toward the highway to investigate. Left my pole and my fish.

Well, I got over there and what do I see but twenty or so colored fellows standing around a bus had smoke coming out the back end looked like a volcano erupting. One of them's fanning it with his hat, cussing like that'd do some good. Painted on the side of the bus is the words *New Orleans Po' Boys Baseball Club,* which I never heard of. I kept my distance but like I said I was close enough to hear the choice words from the one who's back there fanning the smoke. I can also hear what is a fairly animated conversation among five or six of the others has to do with one of them done had enough of everything, including the game of baseball itself. He's holding a suitcase by the handle and saying he's done, ain't no way he's riding another inch on that blankety-blank bus, and so forth and so on, and the others're saying come on now, ain't that bad, we be home soon, been a long trip, you our best player, and etcetera.

Of a sudden the one they're trying to convince to stay steps back, changes the suitcase from one hand to the other, and says he'll walk to New Orleans he has to, turns, and lights out. Like all the rest he's in a dress suit. It's dark but not as dark as him. He's about the blackest man I ever seen. Tall, skinny as a post, got feet on him look like pontoons, and I mean nighttime black. I watch him a minute and see that he ain't joshing them. He is what I'm talking about marching.

Now I was what by then, fourteen? This would be1935, so yes. I'm fifteen. Old enough to light out myself if I decide to. My brothers done already did. Folks glad to see them go too. Two less bellies to feed. I figure they probably'd welcome a third into that category. Just thinking, you know, daydreaming. So I take a little jog and catch up even with the skinny man, still keeping my same distance from the road. I get to some woods and have to hop along through the trees to keep up because he ain't slowing down. He's got his head aimed south and he's moving along right smart, carrying that suitcase like it's part of him. I don't think he's seen me but after maybe a mile or so he stops for a second. Then he starts back up walking. Goes forty paces or so and stops again. Course I'm stopping too ever' time he does. We go through this procedure a few more times. Walk a little and stop. Walk a little and stop. Well, you know what's coming. He's been aware of me ever since back at the bus.

He stops and puts down the suitcase and says—without looking at me, says, "I hope you ain't hunting for trouble because I ain't got you none."

I don't say nothing.

He says, "I know you there and I just want to walk on to the next town without no issue."

I don't want no issue neither. I don't even know what I want, tell you the truth. I'm just seeing something unusual.

So I say, thinking you know I might's well go ahead and quit acting like I'm not there, say, "You a Po' Boy?" meaning of course about the baseball team.

He lolls his head back and laughs a great booming laugh I ain't see how it's possible to come out such a thin little nothing of a chest.

"I'm that, all right," he says. "Po's a hobo. Am a hobo, I reckon, least for the time being."

Then he takes the suitcase back up and goes to walking again and me moving sideways through the trees.

"What you play?" I say.

"Play?" he says.

"On the team," I say.

And he says, "Don't play on no team."

"You just said you a Po' Boy," I say.

And he says, "That was a long time ago. I'm just a plain po' boy now, like probably you is."

And I say, "It wasn't no more longer'n fifteen minutes ago."

"Quarter a hour be a long time depend on what you doing," he says.

About that time the woods end at a fence that marks a hayfield. I climb over and have to move out in the open.

He says, "You got anything to eat?"

Which I then remember my pole and my fish back at the pond and say that, yes, I do. Tell him I got a mess of bream back yonder. Now he stops and looks at me for the first time. He ain't done that yet.

"Why you ain't say so before?" he says.

And I say, "Would have, you'd ask me."

"Well now I done has," he says.

And I say, "And I done answered. You want some, come on."

So he steps across the ditch, jumps the fence—just scissors it like nothing, suitcase and all—and comes over to where I'm standing there waiting. We look each other up and down. He ain't as old as I thought he was, but he's I figure five or six years older than myself.

"They pay you for playing ball?" I say after a minute.

"Not enough," he says.

And I say, "Pay you anything at all for that, you ought to be glad. I'd give my eye teeth to."

And he says, "Yeah, you would. I ain't get paid every day though. Just when I pitch. And I ain't like sitting. I especially ain't like not getting paid for it."

"You a pitcher?" I say.

"I can throw it," he says.

By now we done started walking again and are at the other fence, the one where the woods start. We climb over it.

"Snakes in here?" he says.

"Some," I say. "But don't bother to fret. We too big to eat."

"Ain't too big to bite though," he says. "Which be my concern."

I tell him no need to have it. But I can see he is sore afraid. He's got that suitcase by the sides, holding it in front of hisself like a shield and high-stepping through them woods like over ropes, like he thinks a old copperhead's fixing to come springing out from under the pine straw to sting him any time now.

"Ain't used to no woods," he says.

"Just hush and walk," I say.

When we come to the other field, he says he don't want his former teammates to see him. They're still broke down over there, but there's a couple of cars stopped to I guess see about helping them.

"How can you just walk away from them like that?" I say.

And he says, "Aw, they don't care. Much. We almost done finish with the season anyway. Probably won't be one next year. I just be getting a head start. Been studying on it for a while. Got me a plan about how to pitch and make money every day plus ain't have to worry about Mr. Landry—he own the Boys—about him telling us he short all time. Where them fish at?"

I tell him they're over at a pond across yonder. He says he ain't interested in getting back in there amongst the copperheads but also don't feel too much of a need to walk out in the open and be spied by any of the Po' Boys neither.

"Thought they don't care," I say.

And he says, "I said, 'Much.' They's a couple of them might do. Big old Delroy Shedrick—he my catcher—he be glad to see me go, but I know he love to give me a kick first to send me on my way. I stolen a gal from him up to Claybrook other night, see, and he been looking for a chance to get me back ever since. I say to him, say, 'Del, that gal ain't worth stealing. She just trouble.' And he say, 'Which you in, Peep.' Del asleep on the bus through all that racket while ago. Probably still is, but I ain't taking no chance him know I got away without him laying a good one on me. Thing is, we have three game since then and get along fine on the playfield, except once each inning he walk his big old self out to the mound for no reason at all other'n to hand me the ball and say he ain't forget me taking away that gal."

He don't even notice while he's talking that we've started back walking. We're edging the woods toward the pond, me a little ahead and him following. It's somewhat out of the way, but we get there in due time and none of the Po' Boys have spotted us. Which I didn't expect them to with their broke-down bus and everything. At the pond my pole is still there and my stringer. I check it and all the fish are too. But I realize we have a problem.

"Love me some breams," he says.

"How hungry are you?" I say.

"Got the ain't-ate-since-yesterday stomach grumbles," he says.

And I say, "Looks to me like you ain't got much of a stomach to grumble on you."

"I eat you under the table, boy," he says.

And I say, "Well, we ain't got no table for you to do that on. And we ain't got no skillet to fry these fish in neither."

Which is of course the problem. I tell him let me think a minute. I don't tell him why but it's because about a thousand things have gone to swirling around in my head, the primary one being that I have somehow gotten myself from daydreaming about lighting out to having took several purposeful steps in that direction. But I know I can't very well just up and leave home without telling nobody and fetching a few things to carry with me like, getting back to the problem, a skillet.

So what I decide to do is go back to the house, say what I have to say, and be on my way. I'm not exactly thinking that I'm throwing in with this runaway colored baseball player, but who knows? He said he had a plan, which I still don't know what it is. Don't know his name neither, except he said in the story about his catcher he's Peep.

I ask him can he wait there for me a little while and he sits down on that suitcase, crosses them long legs like a girl, the crossed-over foot just above touching the ground, and says he might as well if it'll get him a meal. I tell him it will and start away.

Then I stop and turn around and say, "What's your name anyway? Mine's Drew, short for Andrew."

And he says, "Had me a uncle down home to New Orleans once name that. He long gone to his reward ever since the bad flu done took him. Got him and my daddy too. I was just a mite at the time. Bad days, them was. Peoples be sick sure. Mine be Cantrell but they call me Bopeep or sometime just one part or the other for short—Bo or Peep."

I wonder how come that is and he says, "Batter step in to take what's coming and I think of him as a sheeps I'm herding back where he belong, to the dugout. I tell them about it too. People start calling me Bopeep I don't even remember when. I say it's okay long's you realize I ain't no little girl lost no sheeps. I know they always exactly sixty feets away."

And to that all I can say is, "Well."

At the house I pack me a gunnysack of some clothes and a coat even though it's hot summertime—this would have been in August of that year—because who knows what's getting ready to happen. I also pick up a black skillet and two forks. I already got a knife. Then last thing I ever do in that house is scoop up some lard in a can.

Mama's back in the patch hoeing weeds out of that clay and my sisters're with her. Daddy's gone to town. When Mama looks up and sees me standing there she just nods her head.

"Come give me a hug then," she says.

Which I do. She leans back away from me and looks me long in the eye. Hers are tired. She ain't forty yet but couldn't pass for a day under sixty. Sisters just keep weeding.

I say, "I'll send y'all any money I can."

"Take care, son," she says.

"I will," I say.

And that's it. I'm on my own. Me and Bopeep cleaned them fish and had the first of what turned out to be many meals together. He said the only thing missing was coconut pie and I said I'd see if I could catch him one next time I went fishing. He was a great fan of coconut pie.

"I guess that's when you really started cooking," Teddy said.

"Oh, I wouldn't call what I done then cooking," Uncle

Drew replied. "You got to do more than throw a fish into bubbling lard to call yourself cooking."

That day they had pork roast so tender it almost didn't even feel like meat in Teddy's mouth, mashed potatoes and gravy, green-bean salad, and homemade rolls with butter. Dessert was of course coconut pie.

Chapter 11

Bopeep had a plan [Uncle Drew said] that got my interest right off. He figured since he could throw a baseball with some authority why not make some money doing it.

"You already make some money doing it," I said.

And he said, "Not much's I decided I could."

We had this conversation walking. I had said we ought to go over to the tracks and jump a boxcar but he wanted to walk a while. This was after we ate them fish. The ones we didn't finish was rolled up in a shirt in my sack. Bopeep said it wasn't no way he was putting them greasy things in his suitcase. I told him that was a fine thank-you and he said he had too many good clothes he didn't want smelling like fish. Which he did. He had several nice white shirts, a couple of ties, and another suit coat. He also had an extra pair of brogans, his spikes, his Po' Boys uniforms and caps, and his mitt with an old brown ball in it. So I said I'd make him a deal and carry the suitcase if I could put my sack in there.

"I'll roll them fish up in here good so if they smell it won't be too much," I said. "They probably all we'll have for a while anyway."

And he said, "You'd said you carry my case first, wouldn't been no argument about them fish."

Then, like that, he switched to telling me his plan, which was kind of a hustle but not really. Hard to hustle somebody throwing a baseball. You got to set up a hustle, which you can do in a poolroom or at a card table, but you can either throw a baseball or you can't. Ain't no all-of-a-sudden-you-can involved.

It was a simple plan.

"They's always ballplayers around," he said. "Ones who is and ones who used to was. All of them's sheeps to me, same difference, but ones who used to was're what we be looking for, because they all think they still is, still can. It our job to give them they chance. I'm just thinking a straight-up bet every turn, so much a pitch, three pitches, and you can pick your umpire. Ump call it outside or inside or high or low, don't matter. Pitch ain't count. No arguments from me. I don't want no issue about that or nothing else. A called strike ain't bring the satisfaction of a swing and a miss anyway. Beside which, I throws strikes and plenty of them."

I thought about this for a second and then I said, "Sounds like a lot of trouble to me. I still don't see why you want to trade being on a organized team that pays you money and supplies you a bus to ride on to do it for being out here not knowing where you going to sleep or eat or even be from one day to the next."

And he said, "You know what I get paid?"

"No," I said. "How could I?"

"Not much is how much," he said.

To which I said the same thing I said earlier about anything at all ought to make him glad.

"How a dollar a game sound?" he said.

And I said, "Like robbery and you the robber."

"Shoot," he said. "Mr. Landry be the robber. He could pay every one of us fifty dollar a game and not never notice it. Could pay us travel days too. That old raggedy bus ought to be brand new. Least put us on a train. He the robber. Really is, I mean. He corruption in spats with a big old cigar. The Po' Boys just something for him to do. And Po' Boys is right. You ain't ever be nothing but that playing

ball for Mr. Landry. He tighter'n paint on a wall. I bet you
he could buy us into one of the big Negro Leagues right
now, get us in with them Crawfords and everybody. But he
ain't. All he do's count the money we make him and say
it ain't enough. I think he tired of it anyway and fixing to
close down the team."

And I said, "What do you mean, the big Negro Leagues?"

"They's colored teams all over the place," he said. "Some
of them up North is big-time organizations, play in the real
stadiums of the real teams."

Well, this is the first I ever heard of this. Not that I paid
much attention to what colored folks did with their time,
but I'd never thought about them playing baseball in big
stadiums somewhere.

So I said, "Why you don't just head up there and see if
they'll hire you, then?"

And he said, "Mr. Claybrook up to Arkansas said same
thing, said, 'Young man, you have an arm the likes of which
I have never seen. I think it could take you places.' He even
offered me a deal to leave the Po' Boys and join his outfit,
which I was studying when I ran into that gal, if you know
what I mean, and not only do I get myself into the position
of needing to keep my eye peel for big old Delroy, seeing's
how he run into her first, I now got to put some mileage
between me and Claybrook, Arkansas, soon's possible.
She have a beau, see, and I believe that is enough said."

He stopped talking for a minute and we just walked
along in silence. We were out somewhere between Oil
Camp and Pineview. A car or two passed us by. People in
them, I'd imagine, were scratching their heads over the
backward sight of a colored man in a suit walking along
with a ragamuffin white boy toting his load. But there we
are for them to think whatever they pleased to think.

"So anyway," Bopeep said. "By time we roll out of
Claybrook and into and out of Little Rock I have done

turned over and over in my mind what Mr. Claybrook say about my arm. And I know he right about it can take me places. But something else on my mind too and that have to do with I don't like traveling around with nobody and don't really care for playing games along the way. Don't mistake what I'm saying now. I loves the baseball. But then I ask myself serious what it is I most loves about it and the answer be me up against a batter. Herding them sheeps. That right there all I care about, and who need a team behind him for that? Dollar a game, shoot. How about a dollar a *pitch?*"

I interrupted him to laugh and say, "You ain't going to find nobody bet you a dollar a pitch, Bopeep. Ain't nobody got that kind of money. Besides which you ain't got it neither if they hit."

And he said, "Oh, I got me a little stake. And say they ain't bet a dollar. Start with a dime then. Throw ten strikes and you got you a dollar. That ain't even four full turns. You get four mens up there against you at a dime a pitch, you done put a dollar and twenty in your pocket. Then if they really biting you ease the wager up to two bits and so forth."

Well, sir, that lifted my eyebrows plumb back to my hairline. Wasn't much I could say against it. We walked along a little more, me thinking and Bopeep knowing exactly what I'm thinking. I glanced at him out the corner of my eye and he caught me doing it.

"Pretty good plan, huh?" he said.

"Is if you can pitch," I said. "Ain't if you can't."

"You want to see?" he said.

I said I did.

So we got his mitt and ball out the suitcase, which he sniffed when we opened it checking for fish stink, which there wasn't any of because I had them gents rolled up good and tight.

"Good thing for you," he said.

And I said, "Be a good thing for you when you get hungry later even if you could smell them."

"Take this mitt and wait right here," he said.

"This for a lefthander," I said.

"Just put it on and hold it out," he said. "You won't even have to move. All you got to do be to keep it in front of you so you won't get hurt. Ball be like a arrow to it."

He turned and stepped off an estimate of distance.

"This look about right to you?" he said.

I nodded, not that I ever caught before. But I'd batted, so I had some idea. He waved me to crouch. I hunkered down and put on the mitt, which made me feel off balance since it was on my throwing hand.

"Ready?" he said.

"Fire away," I said.

When he wound up, he kicked his right leg up so high looked like he done the splits in the air, while at the same time he took his left arm back so far I thought he'd scrape his knuckles on the dirt. He held that position just long enough for me to register it, then he unloosed himself forward like a catapult. I never saw the ball. I heard it right at the last, just before it hit the mitt with a sound like lightning striking a tree. The first time I moved was when I slung off the mitt and jumped up to rub my hand.

"God dog," I said. "God *dog.*"

I looked out at Bopeep, who was standing there with his hands on his hips grinning at me. I realized he hadn't even took off his suitcoat.

"You want to see it again?" he said.

"I ain't seen it the first time," I said.

"I do that all day," he said.

"I take your word for it," I said. "Ain't nobody hit that."

"That be the plan, Uncle Drew," he said. "That be the plan."

Well, our first stop was Pineview, as you can see in the first ledger, the 1935 one. I actually cheated a little bit on the first several entries, had to reconstruct them from memory after I got the idea of keeping a tally of our bets and balances. But that first evening in Pineview we found us a few old boys sitting on a store porch, moved the conversation around to baseball, and got six of them to try their hand against Bopeep out back. They went in for a dime each, three tries in the box, umping for each other. The store owner had a bat for us to borrow.

He said, "Y'all break that now, y'all find yourself broke by me later."

I caught—or rather, I let the ball hit the mitt and squoze down best I could. My hand was still stinging from that first pitch on the side of the road and it went plumb numb fairly quickly. The first two batters never moved. The third one swang once but by the time he did I was already tossing the ball back to Bopeep. When the fourth one came up, the ones gone before and the two left was crouched down behind me trying to see.

Bopeep would say, "Get ready, sheeps," do his windup, hold it, then let her go. Everybody but me and the batter was marching around howling and clapping their hands. Then they'd gather back in. Same thing.

"That ain't no pitcher," one of them said. "That man be a in-the-flesh bat dodger."

Six up, six down, eighteen pitches. Actually twenty-four. He gave them all one free chance just to be sporting. We took in a dollar-eighty in no more than fifteen minutes.

"See there?" Bopeep said to me once we collected our money and took our leave.

"I do," I said. "But one thing's for sure and that's this: I'm fixing to need to have me something other'n that lefty mitt on my hand, you want me doing this day in and day out. Plus, we need our own bat."

And he said, "I guess you think you all in with me then."

My heart dropped at that because he put a tone in

his voice like he been thinking it over and come to the conclusion he didn't need nobody in with him. I looked down and scrubbed the dirt with my foot, wondering if I ought to already head on back home or keep moving on my own and see what happened.

Bopeep let me dangle that way for a little bit, then he laughed that great booming laugh of his that always surprised me. I looked up.

"Come on now, Uncle Drew," he said. "Pitcher gots to have him a catcher."

He held out a hand and I took it.

"Partners?" he said.

"Partners," I said. "Uncle Drew and the Bat Dodger."

"The Bat Dodger, huh?" he said. "I like that."

I couldn't have been prouder.

"Or more relieved," Teddy said.

"Or more relieved," Uncle Drew agreed.

That day they had sandwiches made from the leftover pork roast. Uncle Drew insisted that Teddy try mustard instead of mayonnaise, which was what he said he wanted.

"Mayonnaise don't exactly kill the flavor of pork," Uncle Drew told him. "But it also don't bring it out. See what a coat of mustard'll do to it."

Teddy took his first bite tentatively. Uncle Drew watched him, his head cocked to one side and an eyebrow up. Teddy knew immediately that he had never fully tasted pork before. He nodded.

"From now on, don't even ask me anything about what I want," Teddy said. "I trust you."

"I'll try to live up to that," Uncle Drew said.

With the sandwiches they had thin-sliced potatoes battered and fried, squash boiled with onions, and English peas. Dessert was lemon icebox pie.

Chapter 12

First little bit of trouble we run into [Uncle Drew said] was at Shreveport. Got ourself in a situation in the railroad yard there that required some quick thinking when the bull spied us leaving the box we caught out of Pineview. We'd spent the night out in some woods not too far from the store. I wanted to buy some bread before we left but Bopeep said he'd rather be thrifty until we didn't need to. We made us a little camp and ate the rest of our fish. I kidded him about his fear of snakes and he said he was too tired to worry about critters. That made two of us being tired. I was wore plumb out. Slept like a brick.

Early next morning we slipped over to the stop and when the train started to move Bo asked me had I ever did this. I said I ain't and he said he ain't neither.

"Time to see what it's like," he said.

"After you," I said.

It wasn't much to it really, not that time anyway. We picked us a box and up we went. The Dodger first, his suitcase second, me third. Had to run a little more than he did but I swung a leg up and he hauled me in. The car was empty and it smelled like creosote and pine tar. We was on our way to I thought Minden but he said we ought to go on to Shreveport.

"Suits me," I said.

He said he'd been there the month before when they had the Negro Southern Association All-Star game. Told me all how he fared in that as the starting hurler for the South division.

"Only the best sheeps step up in that one," he said. "I mostly herded them right on back to where they come from, but the ump, he given this one of them a free pass. I's just fooling around with that sheeps, throwing down low three times to get him ahead in the count so I could stay playing a while longer. This was in the third, my last inning. So I went to work on that three-and-zero situation but then got me one called inside for the walk. Shoot, that throw'd sliced the plate in perfect two, you turn it to a knife and lay it down on there. Cut the sheep thigh high too. I just shook my head."

"You got any pitches other'n fast?" I said.

And he said, "Don't need none generally, but I be making it dance once you get used to be back there and trust it'll get to you without you need to go searching for it."

We didn't say anything else after that for a good long while. He was laying back with his head resting on the suitcase and his legs bent and one crossed over the other. I was up by the open door watching the pines slide by. It was still hot August out but this was early morning and the air was almost cool like it will sometimes be at that time of day even though you know it's fixing to get miserable later on. Just sitting there with nothing to do but get lulled by the chug and rattle of a freight train'll put you to sleep in a hurry.

Next thing I knew we was slowing down. Me and Bopeep looked at each other, thinking the same thing, which was that jumping down off a moving train promised to be a mite harder and more painful than jumping up onto one. So we decided to wait until we were at a stop. That was a mistake, because once you stop you might be able to step off in one piece but you're likely to run slam into a yard bull, which was what they called the railroad police. Course we didn't think about that until there he was. This one was a big old no-nonsense son of a gun, which he had to be given the kind of characters he was hired to deal with. He told us to get over against the fence. We didn't argue. I was sure we were done for.

"What's y'all's story?" the bull said.

You could tell it didn't much matter.

"We traveling mens," Bopeep said.

"Where you traveling, boy?" the bull said.

I thought he was talking to me but Bo knew he wasn't and said, "We on our way my mama funeral down to New Orleans."

He said it so sad I almost believed him myself. Took the bull by surprise too. But just for a moment. He looked at me.

"Why you going to a nigger woman's funeral?" he said.

I swallowed. My mind was racing and not getting nowhere. I was just about to say something, I don't know what, when Bopeep saved me.

"He deaf and dumb," he said. "Can't hear a word we saying."

The bull was still looking at me.

"What's he doing riding the rails with you?" he said.

And Bo said, "They's a home for his kind down where we headed. I work for his daddy up to Arkansas and be chaperoning him. When word come about my mama his daddy say I can go but I got to take the boy."

The bull tilted his hat back on his head.

"This don't make no sense," he said.

And Bo said, "That's what I been thinking. Nothing don't make no sense in this world. Why a man decide all of a sudden send his boy away like that, all the way to New Orleans? They surely a deaf and dumb home for him up to Arkansas somewhere. But even then, still. Shoot."

And the bull said, "No, no, no. I mean it don't make no sense under the circumstances why y'all in a box on a freight and not in a passenger car."

Bo shook and then hung his head.

"Yes it do," he said.

He looked back up and heaved him a lonesome sigh.

"How so?" the bull said.

And Bo said, "What happen is nobody won't listen to me say he can't be by hisself. They say they fixing to make me get in one car and him in another. Well I don't know how he know but the boy he sense something and start in having a thrashing-around conniption, and the conductor come up and ask me what the hell and I say he, the boy, say he have to be with somebody, me, and the conductor say he ain't putting no white boy in no colored car and no colored boy in no white car, and I say he won't even know he riding colored, and the conductor says he figure I got a point since deaf and dumb ain't much different than nigger, so what he'll do is he'll allow it for one leg but both us're getting off at the first stop. Which we do. And then we stuck in a bind and who knows where we even was? All I know was I just want to get to my mama done died and on top of that the boy daddy, my boss, he was expecting me to see the boy safe to the deaf and dumb home."

I was listening to all this just as amazed as the bull was. Bo was wound plumb up, creating a tale tall's a Georgia pine right straight out of thin air. Finally the bull held up a hand.

"Look," he said. "Y'all're still breaking the law here. That's the bottom end of it. But, Lord, you are in a situation. How much you got on you?"

And Bopeep said, "Mr. Cate—that the boy daddy, Mr. Cate—well he given me ten dollar for the trip, but these two mens at the depot in wherever we was at when they put us off saw us standing there not knowing what to do with ourself and said come go with them, they get us squared away. They looked trusty to me, but when they got us around the first corner, one of them pull out a pistol and say to hand him over all our money. Made my knees shake looking at that snub barrel pointed to my chest, and I think I ain't never getting that purse out my pocket fast enough. They'd probably took our bag too, but lucky thing was the boy here get scared and he don't stay. He turn and run off just 's I handed them mens my purse. I say I can't let him out my sight and take out after him, expecting to feel a bullet hit me any second. But it didn't. Guess the ten dollar in that purse be good enough to buy me out."

The bull shook his head.

"So you decided to jump the next train," he said.

And Bo said, "One after that, tell you truth. Took me that long calm the boy down. But we did hitch us a free ride, yessir, and here we is. Like I done told you, my mama laying down there done died and I gots to get to her, and Mr. Cate have put his boy safety in my hand to boot."

And the bull said, "If you wasn't dressed like you are I wouldn't believe a word you're saying. I ought not to anyway. The law is the law. What I ought to do is haul the two of y'all in for breaking it. But if any part of this is the truth, you in a fix, and I'd feel bad to complicate it any more'n it already is so ain't going to do it. Just do not ever let me see you or the boy either one in this yard again. Do and I'm coming after you under a black flag. You got that?"

I somehow remembered I was supposed to be deaf and dumb and didn't start nodding and thanking him. Bopeep began to ease away, walking backward. He laid a hand on my chest to get me to follow.

"You be a mighty kind soul," he said. "Mighty kind. My mama up in heaven with Jesus right now and they both smiling down on you. Yessir, they is."

We stepped along the ties up to the front of the train, then made our way across the tracks through the yard.

"Where'd all that come from?" I said.

And Bopeep said, "Don't ask me. Just be lucky it come from somewhere."

And I said, "What now, then?"

"Place to go here be the Bottoms," he said.

"What's there?" I said.

"Gals for one thing," he said. "Mens looking for gals for another. We was here two nights for the All-Stars. Went to Fannin Street the first, played the game, and then went back over the second. You interested in gals?"

"Not no particular one so far," I said.

And he said, "You ain't got to be particular on Fannin Street. All you need three dollar. Take you pick."

And I said, "You mean you can buy a gal?"

He laughed his laugh.

"Sure can," he said. "But we here on business. Least mostly we is. We looking for mens be looking for gals. They surely be some ballplayers down there."

He was of course right—about the gals and about the ballplayers, or at least some fellows who thought they's ballplayers. Now you way too young to know what a brothel is and I best not tell you, but let's just say that Fannin Street was all brothels and saloons and I mean gals everywhere. All sizes, all shapes, ones that was pretty, and ones that wasn't pretty. Like to scared me half to death being there once the sun went down that first night. But this was when I found out something I'd never thought about. It wasn't the people I was scared of after while, even though you'd think I might've been since I was the only white face down there.

What I took some time to get used to was all the activity. I never been in Shreveport before and it was one busy place. Thing I never thought about was, well, I already knew that a colored man needed to watch his back everywhere he went. That's just how it was. I didn't know the situation was entirely different for a white man—or boy, in my case. By which I mean I didn't all of a sudden feel like I had to start thinking something bad was going to happen to me just because I was down on Fannin Street standing out like the moon in the night sky.

They looked me over pretty good but mainly didn't nobody pay me much never mind. The ones who did treated me right kindly. Like Miss Audrey, big old gal who ran a saloon down there had rooms to let above it. Nice rooms. She took a shine to me right off. Some of her gals did too but that's a story like I said I best not tell unless I want your mama to skin me. Bopeep always introduced me as Uncle Drew, which everybody wanted to know was I his. And he'd say, "You know it," to much laughter.

Now all of this might've had something to do with the fact I was with him, because from the moment he showed up he had everybody fairly eating out of his hand. But I honestly don't believe it did. I believe there was something else going on. It was just plain human decency shown me, of a kind I know full well wouldn't've been shown to him if the situation was reversed.

We stayed a week and could've moved in permanent we'd wanted to. Left with over two hundred dollars in our pocket. And this was after paying Miss Audrey for her, let us say, hospitality. Some of those fellows down there just could not get enough of trying to get a hit off the Dodger. A few of them was real players too, from the Shreveport Acme Giants. They didn't do a whole lot better'n anybody else.

It was during that week I thought of keeping the records. Bopeep said he liked the idea and give me five dollars, the most money I ever held in my hand.

"This yours," he said. "Don't spend it all in one place."

And I said, "Ain't no way to spend five whole dollars."

"Shoot," he said. "You be surprise."

I walked over to Milam Street and bought that first ledger, a pen, and a bottle of ink with it at a store had for sale dog near everything you can think of, including sporting goods. I found me a catcher's mitt for a dollar-fifty and got that too. Right-handed. They had bats, but one of the Acme Giants had talked Bopeep into letting him put one up instead of money so we no longer needed a stick.

Just across the street was a movie house called the Majestic. Well, Bopeep said the money was mine and I wasn't on no schedule so I decided to take in a picture show. I'd only seen a handful in my life. This one was a dead-serious drama called *Woman Wanted,* with the great beauty Maureen O'Sullivan, who you might've seen. She's Jane. Anyway, it wasn't a Western, which I'd rather've come across, but what's the use being picky when it's the middle of the afternoon and you're sitting in the movies?

After that I figured I better head on back over to Miss Audrey's, but I got to watching the trolley cars on Texas Street and came to the conclusion that I better ought to take a ride on one because first I had the money to do it and second I'd never been on the trolley. Cost me seven cents to go down to the river, make the turn around, and come all the way back to where I started from. It was one keeper of a day, I tell you that.

When I got to Miss Audrey's, Bopeep was sitting at a table with her and one of the Acme Giants talking about maybe he ought to sign on with them. He said he'd probably best decline, seeing as how he'd made more money throwing strikes in the alley in three days than he could make in a season throwing them on the diamond. The ballplayer stroked his chin, pooched out his lips, and said he saw his point. Later on the Dodger asked me how far five dollars had took me and I told him a right smart way.

"We just getting started, Uncle Drew," he said. "Just getting started."

"Sounds like y'all were off to a pretty good start," Teddy said.

"I'd say so," Uncle Drew agreed.

"You said I might've seen who was in that movie. Jane."

"Right," Uncle Drew said. "Jane. That's the best one. Maureen O'Sullivan."

"What do you mean?" Teddy asked.

"What do you mean what do I mean?"

"Jane who?"

"Jane Jane, I guess. Don't recollect a last name. Tarzan's gal."

"Oh. I only ever saw a cartoon of it when I was little."

"Good land, boy. You still little. But yessir, that's the best Jane. Maureen O'Sullivan."

That day they had cornbread and cabbage boiled with a hambone. The cabbage tasted considerably better than Teddy thought it was going to while it was cooking. It was the first thing Uncle Drew made that didn't smell good. Dessert was fudge with peanuts in it.

Chapter 13

One thing Teddy hadn't been doing lately was saying anything much to his parents about the stories Uncle Drew had been telling. He was keeping those to himself because he was working on an idea about them. It was just the beginning of an idea and he wasn't sure if it was even a good idea, but he thought that it might be and wanted to carry it out on his own. All he had done so far was write down some notes about what Uncle Drew had been saying. Everything matched what was in the first ledger. The stops in Pineview and Shreveport were right there. He even knew the exact amount of money they left town with. The old man had said it was over two hundred dollars. It was in fact two hundred seventy-five dollars and twenty-five cents, and according to the next few sheets they were headed for Texas.

Teddy's parents did know that he was spending a lot of time at Uncle Drew's house, however, and they were pleased by it. His mother was particularly pleased because she hadn't been too keen about his staying by himself in the first place. His father enjoyed the leftovers Uncle Drew occasionally sent home with Teddy.

"I'm going to have to go over there myself and get some of his recipes," his mother said.

"He don't use no recipes," Teddy told her.

"Sounds like you're picking up some bad English habits over there," his mother said. "Say that correctly, please."

"He doesn't use any recipes," Teddy replied.

"I don't think most really good cooks do," his father said.

"Are you saying that I'm not a really good cook, Mr. Caldwell?" his mother asked.

"I said 'most,' Mrs. Caldwell," his father answered. "That don't mean 'all.'"

He winked at Teddy to acknowledge the usage error and pointed at his mother, who was shaking her head.

"Why does everybody around here have to talk like they work in the oilfield?" his mother asked.

"Because most of them do," his father said.

"Why're you always so worried about how people talk?" Teddy asked. "You and Mr. Sherman. Uncle Drew wouldn't sound as good if he didn't say things the way he does. I like the way he talks."

"Well, just don't get such a crush on it that you forget it's incorrect," his mother said. "Your teachers won't be amused. And neither am I. Mr. Weems can speak as he pleases."

"I ain't fixing to talk like that in front of none of my teachers," Teddy said.

His father laughed.

"I certainly hope not," his mother said.

Later that evening, when his mother was taking a break from her work, he sat down at the computer and typed *Bopeep Shines* into the search box. Several citations of the same article Mrs. Delhomme had given him appeared. He scrolled through them and was about to give up when he saw something that caught his eye. He clicked on it. The piece contained the same information the other one did, except for one additional tidbit. He was reading it when his mother returned.

"Can you print this for me?" he asked. "It's about Bopeep Shines."

"Mr. Weems has really got you interested in that character, hasn't he?"

"He's not a character," Teddy said. "He's real."

"It's a figure of speech," his mother said.

"Okay."

He was preoccupied with the article, which was now emerging from the printer. When it stopped he picked it up and immediately began walking toward his room.

"You're welcome," his mother said.

Teddy turned around.

"Thanks," he said. "Sorry."

In his room he took out the 1935 ledger and opened it to the last entry. He focused on the place that had been rubbed out, studying it more carefully this time than he had before. It had been written in ink, like everything else, so that whoever rubbed it out had probably used spit on a finger to do it. He ran his finger across the paper. It was rough in the rubbed-out place. He held the page close and squinted, trying to make the words appear. All he had to go on were the few letters that were still visible. The line looked like this:

y   *b*   *so*   *a*   *t h*

Teddy stared at the letters for a long time before giving up. They were smeared and ragged, but he wasn't imagining them. Still, he knew he would never figure out the sentence, if it even was a sentence, they were a part of. The new information he'd found changed his mind about whether the place that was rubbed out mattered. When he first saw it he didn't think so. Now he was certain that it mattered a great deal. He went to bed thinking that he would ask Uncle Drew about the "all/auto" bet the next day. But maybe he wouldn't. That would be a big jump in the story. They still had to go to Texas and back through Louisiana, Mississippi, Alabama, and Florida before they even got to Georgia.

Teddy was impatient to know about the car and the possibility that Bopeep had won it in a bet—a bet, if the new information were true, that might possibly have been with one of the greatest players who ever lived! That really did seem unlikely, except for the fact that they were driving a car in the story the old man in Jonesboro had told his father. And it was a Hudson. Who ever heard of a Hudson anyway? They didn't make them anymore. But according to Mr. Bilberry, Uncle Drew's car was a Hudson. What if— Teddy didn't allow himself even to finish asking himself that question. He suddenly stiffened his back and kicked his feet up and down. He shook his head to clear it. The whole thing was crazy. Nobody would believe what he was thinking. He wished he could confirm it all right now. But he couldn't. There was no reason even to think about it.

One of the many things he was learning from the old man that summer was that letting things unfold on their own time is not a bad way to go. It's frustrating to have to wait but not nearly as frustrating as having a dozen theories and no way to test them.

Chapter 14

Interesting thing about Shreveport [Uncle Drew said] is here it is not an hour's drive from where we sit and I'd take it right now over everywhere else we went, with the possible exception of New Orleans. That's likely because it was our first stop and the place where we got our traveling stake in pocket. I learned some things in Shreveport too, tell you that for a fact. I come *that* close to settling there when I headed back this way in the winter. But I seen how much it's grew and decided against it. Plus also I had a hankering to be home, by which I mean where I come from. I left here and never looked over my shoulder until not too long ago. Then of a sudden I found myself for some unknown reason wanting to be all the way around to where I started.

You said your grandmother lives over in Shreveport these days. Next time y'all go see her have your folks take you to the Bottoms. It's registered historical now. St. Paul's Bottoms. There you'll see Fannin Street and can walk over to Texas Street and where all I told you about. It'll have changed but there it all was.

Anyway, Lord, we left out of there riding high. Had new haircuts and new clothes, all that money, and a regulation catcher's mitt instead of that turned-around southpaw contraption of Bopeep's I'd been using. Had us a good bat too, courtesy of the Acme Giants, and of course them ledgers to keep our records in. We got us a couple of tickets on the train to Dallas, Bopeep in one car and me in the other, naturally. I almost wasn't going to do it but he got me settled down enough to.

"Aw now, Uncle Drew," he said. "We ain't going to fix how things be just by you refuse to ride. Let's get on here and ease over and see we can't do us some damage to some of them Texans. No use to just fight and lose, which you will. Might be a day come you can scrap and that be message enough even if you lose, but this ain't it."

I didn't like it but he had a point. I just hated seeing him and all those other people spent good money on a ticket not being able to sit where they wanted to on the train. I ain't too sure I would've made much of a black man myself, tell you the truth. I'd probably said something smart and got myself hided or worse. But I saw it time and again, him just taking what came. Bopeep and others. Just taking it. Pushed and shoved and called all kind of terrible things. Not accepting it, mind you, at least not in the sense of somehow putting an "okay" stamp on it. But just, you know, enduring, casting their mind somewhere else till it passed, waiting till the time was right to rise up—unlike some of them that had a more "I want things set straight now and not after while" outlook. That would've been me. I'd most likely've fought it hard and, as Bopeep said, most likely've lost the battle for my trouble. I don't know, though. Lose the battle, win the war. Which if it ain't won, compared to once upon a time it might 's well be. No, it ain't won and may never be. Maybe Bopeep and them who didn't seem to be fighting it actually was. Everybody fought in their own way—them that endured the humiliation that got thrown at them no less than them that stormed the barricades, endurance being a kind of fight in itself if you shine a certain light on it.

It's like a fellow with a handicap. Say he's got him a gimp leg or a deformity of some kind or other. Maybe he's blind. He don't have to necessarily think it's right but he knows

he is going to have to put up with it because that's the way
it is. Some can, some can't. Some it drives crazy. A man's
pigment ought not to been a handicap, though, by God.
Not then, not now, not never. But it was. It surely was.
And I have to say still is to a degree. But back then? Back
then makes me so mad I could spit thinking about it. Our
supposedly Christian nation lived as shameful a lie as ever
was lived. Men hid out under hood and sheet of a Saturday
night and then turned around to don a choir robe on
Sunday morning. They'd quote the Good Book in their lap
chapter and verse. Sat there saying, "Love one another,"
with a straight face and no more willing to practice it than
a bunch of rattlesnakes. Makes you wonder what in the
world.

And that right there is probably enough preaching to
hold you a while. Take it for what it's worth. Let's see here.
Dallas was where we was headed, Dallas where lay the Deep
Ellum. It was like Fannin Street times ten. A lot rougher
place. I never felt like I needed to keep my valuables in my
brogans in Shreveport but in Dallas I was always little bit
on edge. Maybe it was because we was out of the South.
You can't call Dallas the South. I wouldn't call it the North
neither I don't guess, but it definitely wasn't the South.
I don't know what it was, tell you the truth. Everything
moved faster. You had to think in a bigger hurry. I got
no different treatment on a face-to-face basis, understand.
I was just feeling a considerable leerier. Matter of fact,
except for this one incident I'm fixing to tell you about that
had some real tension in it, we got along without a scrape.
Didn't stay but two days. The Dodger wasn't all that fond
of it neither.

Now it was in the Big D that a batter got ahead of us for
the first time. So far everybody who'd lined up to step in
either went out on three whiffs or hit only one. This time
Bopeep'd thrown two that came right back at him. Went

over him actually, over him and everything else. Left the bat like a rocket ship. Went well up and away.

We'd set up in a lot behind one of the buildings down there in the Ellum and had gathered a pretty good crowd of takers and onlookers. This was our second and last night there. It was early evening, folks just beginning to make their rounds. I'd say we'd gone through maybe a dozen hitters—course you can look that up—when this fellow steps in and Bopeep says, "Ready to be herded, sheeps?"

To which the fellow just sort of snorts like a bull. He's a big old wide son of a gun with a set of shoulders on him look like the tailgate of a pickup. He stands in and Bopeep winds up. But then he steps out. He just holds out a ham of a hand and steps back. That threw Bopeep off, which was undoubtedly the point. He had to arrest his motion midway, which ain't good for the muscles.

I stood up out of my crouch and said, "Hey now."

To which the batter turned to me and said, "I will cutcho' th'oat, boy. *Git* back down."

He said it real quiet but his voice was like a rumbling roll of thunder. I got back down.

Bopeep, who didn't hear what he said, looks in and says, "Come on, sheeps. Let's play us some ball."

Batter steps back in—we had a dollar a pitch going here, understand—and Bopeep gives him a screamer that he lifts clean out of sight. I mean he just uncoiled on that ball like it was tossed underhand by a girl. Swatted it like a fly.

"One dollar," he says. "Make this next'n double?"

And Bopeep says, "Make it five, you want to."

Course we have to wait a while for some kid to go find the ball. Batter just stands there like a statue. Don't say a word. I don't neither. Bopeep's of course talking a mile a minute.

"Got you a big bat there, sheeps," he says. "I like seeing that. Do a man good to have him a challenge. Maybe I return the favor this next time coming up here."

And so forth and so on.

Batter just waits.

"We two or five?" Bopeep says.

Batter holds up his hand with his fingers spread out look like a fan from the Orient. Little kid hands Bopeep the ball.

He says, "You sure?"

Batter says, "Pitch the ball, blankety-blank."

Calls him a terrible name.

Bopeep just grins and says, "No need to be ugly front of these chilrens, sheeps."

Then he winds up and—same thing. Batter uncoils and the ball sails away. Bopeep stands out there grinning big and clapping his hands.

"I likes this one, Uncle Drew," he says. "Got hissef a eye on him."

Now I ain't stood up since the batter told me to get down but I figure maybe I ought to go out and have a word. I didn't walk in front of him when I did it neither. Made my mark in the book, another circle, and got up backing out of there. Took the long way around.

"I guess he can see it," I said.

Bopeep gave me a little smirk.

"You think I ain't know what I'm doing?" he said. "Big old elephant like that I ain't riling. Got to give him a peanut make him think he the boss, Uncle Drew. Course he see it. Don't you?"

I thought a second and said, "Well, I guess it don't hurt as much as usual, now you mention it."

Bopeep nodded.

"Get ready for this one to," he said. "I ain't playing no more." Then he called down to the batter, said, "You six to the good, sheeps. Want to make this here next one for ten?"

And the batter says, "Name you price, blankety-blank."

Called him that same terrible name again.

Bopeep didn't grin this time.

"Fifty," he said. Then *he* used the terrible name.

I thought, Lord, we are going to have to tangle with this monster before we get out of here. But as I'm walking back to my place, I see the batter do one of those frowns and tilt his head like it ain't really a frown but more what you'd call just making a thoughtful face, like saying, "Well, all right then," like there's some respect been earned by Bopeep calling him that name.

The crowd, which is considerable, picks up on what has transpired between the two of them, and they start making a racket. I'm sure plenty of side bets are being made because now they're yelling out serious encouragement, some for Bopeep, some for the batter.

"Make him miss, Traveler!"

Course they don't know Bopeep's name, only that he's from out of town.

"Hit it again, Big-Big!"

That's when I found out the batter's called Big-Big. Fit him, that's for sure. He was some kind of big. Looked like a mountain standing there in the twilight, especially from my vantage point crouched down behind him.

"Last chance you to save your money, sheeps," Bopeep says.

And Big-Big says, "Ain't no saving yours, though, is it? Fifty fixing to leave out your pocket with the next ball you throw."

He digs in. Bopeep winds up. The crowd noise rises to a peak. I swallow hard. Bopeep brings the ball forward. It hits my mitt. Big-Big don't even budge. Half the crowd goes silent. Everybody else howls. They're dancing around clapping each other on the back. They're laughing and pointing and leaning back with their hands on their foreheads like they can't believe what they just seen. Or didn't see. That third pitch was invisible as the wind. I make my slash in the book and stand. Big-Big's still right where he was.

It was my job to collect and pay out, which I rarely had to pay out, and I usually had the bet money in hand. But I realize I ain't got Big-Big's fifty. We owe him six, he owes us fifty. So I need to get forty-four dollars from him and he don't look no more happy about having to hand it over than I probably look having to get him to.

"We need to settle," I say.

And he says, "Too dark out here for a fair bet."

"But you made it," I say.

I'm trying not to look at him but I'm too scared to look away so I focus just above one of his eyes, where there happens to be an ugly scar like maybe a knife made. About this time a woman comes over to us out of the crowd very close to near about large as he is.

"You the dumbest mans ever was, Big-Big Watts," she says. "Fifty dollar on a baseball pitch."

And Big-Big says, "But I done hit two, Inez. Odd on my side."

Quick as a snake she whacks him over the head with the flat of her hand like he's a little kid. Has to go up on her tiptoes to do it but she gets it done.

"This baseball, fool," she says. "Ain't no odd in baseball. Give the boy they winning."

And Big-Big says, "Aw, 'Nez. Maybe I fight him for it."

Course she whacks him again for that.

"Pay off you bet," she says. "And don't expect no attentions from me this evening."

Then she looks at me and says, "He mean to give up them first two shots, child?"

And I say, "Might've the second one. First was all Big-Big, though."

For some reason I feel the need to get him a little bit off the hook with her.

"Should've bet his fifty right then, then," she says. "Wish the good Lord'd give him half's many brain He give him muscle."

Later that evening we run into Big-Big out on the street and he says he wants a chance to get his money back.

"Maybe you shoot me a rack of nine-balls for it," he says.

And Bopeep says, "Would if I ain't left my stick in Louisiana. Maybe you give me a raincheck till next time I'm through."

And Big-Big says, "Do the boy play?"

I look at Bopeep, who shakes his head just barely enough for me to say I don't, even if I do. So I shake my own head, which ain't a lie because I never shot a stick of pool in my life.

Well, up to that point old Big-Big has seemed in a neighborly mood but I can see that his face is changing into something let you know he means business about getting his money back. Gone is that respect frown he had on earlier. This is just a plain frown, a scowl. And to make things seem even worse that scar is throbbing from the vein beating underneath of it. I'm hoping to see the woman who helped us out earlier but Inez ain't in evidence.

Bopeep nudges me, then he points past Big-Big and says, "Hey, Inez!"

When Big-Big turns, Bopeep nudges me a little harder and says, "We gone."

And we was. Slipped in behind some folks on the sidewalk, eased our way into the crowd, and left old Big-Big standing there looking for Inez. Didn't run, just walked at a good clip, turned the corner, and went around the block back to the place we had our room.

"That right there be some trouble, Uncle Drew," Bopeep says. "Look like he one of those folks be everywhere. Best us not be nowhere. I say we say bye and see you to Dallas."

And I say, "How you know her name was Inez? You couldn't've heard any of what we said earlier."

"Whose name?" he says.

"His woman," I say.

And Bopeep says, "Inez just the first name pop in my head. Old trick to do. Shoot, he'd look I call out for Eleanor."

He pauses a second, then he says, "That big old gal whacked him upside the head name Inez?"

I tell him she is.

He laughs his laugh.

"He probably run the other way then," he says.

We started putting our things together. Talked about heading back to Louisiana and going the other way ourself but decided that since here we are at the doorstep of the West and ain't neither one of us ever seen it we ought to go on out that direction a little bit. We're in the money, see. Comfortable. Have plenty enough to ride passenger to any destination we choose but we know they'll just split us up again so we talk ourselves into hopping. Figure we'll be fine, long's we make absolutely certain ain't no yard bulls nearby. We done learned that lesson.

And so we did that. Free rode the freights clean across Texas, which ain't scenic. It's flat and hot and fairly miserable. Got off to round up takers in Abilene and Odessa and Pecos and then went all the way on over to El Paso, where we tried to stay in the Hilton Hotel. We was thinking maybe we'd gone far enough some of the race rules might not necessarily been in effect no more. But they was in full effect. Man at the desk told us I's welcome but Bopeep was not. Said the usual thing about Bopeep right to his face. I near about climbed plumb over his highly polished counter trying to get at him but he stepped back and Bopeep hauled me down.

"We just be on our way then," he said. "Thank you kindly, mister."

On the way out of there—and I was kicking mad, I tell you that, partly at what happened, partly at us being stupid enough to think it wouldn't—the doorman pushed the door open as we passed and said to us, "Y'all go on round back, ask for Bess. She give you a plate you won't regret. Tell her you there on Jimmy word."

Which we thanked him for and did. Sat down to a feast of the best cooking I ever tasted. Never had salmon before or potatoes au gratin neither. But Bess could cook them. Busy place, the kitchen of a hotel like that. You heard of Hiltons I reckon. This was the original one. Reason we went there in the first place was as much how tall it was looming over El Paso and wanting to see it up close as thinking what we thought about the rules. I guess we knew we wasn't going to no more get to stay there than a couple of stray dogs but it was so big and nice and new, just a few years old, that we got carried away. Least we ate good. Had coconut pie for dessert.

"My old mammy can fix her a coconut pie make you cry," Bopeep said. "Never thought I'd taste a rival."

"Pleased you like it," Bess said. "Something special in there."

"What it is?" Bopeep said.

"I done told you all I will, hon," Bess said. "Something special."

"It do the job," Bopeep said. "Have mercy."

I been trying to figure out what it was ever since. Lord that pie was something else. I've throwed ever' logical thing I can think of into my coconut but have never quite hit the exact taste Bess at the El Paso Hilton did.

After we was done she told us where we could get a bed. I was ready for one, tell you that. We been sleeping out on the ground for a while with the hobos in what they called jungles. Sometimes they was like little towns. Other times it was just me and Bopeep and a couple of other fellows. They was almost all white but other'n a couple of exceptions they didn't seem to mind Bopeep being black. He was just another hobo far's they were concerned. Little did they know he had a stack of money on him would've made their eyeballs pop out. We never made any bets with them, though. What we'd do is camp, then walk into whatever town we was near and see if we couldn't find a few hitters. What we found, as usual, wasn't hitters. They was just batters. Nobody could hit Bopeep. I think you'll see in the ledger that we went several weeks after our run-in with old Big-Big in Dallas without having to write a single circle. It was all in our favor for a good long while.

"You ever get scared being out there like that?" Teddy asked.

"Not too bad," Uncle Drew said. "Dallas made me a little nervous, as I said. And I fretted about our money quite a bit no matter where we was. I kept it flat and tucked in good underneath the cardboard bottom of that suitcase, which I got to where I wouldn't leave behind. Carried it with me everywhere we went if we stayed somewhere any length of time. But we got to where we wouldn't mess with the big towns. We kept to smaller places. In some ways that was a lot easier."

"I thought hobos was thieves," Teddy said.

"Hobos just like any other group," Uncle Drew replied. "Some're honest, some ain't. We just didn't give the ones who wasn't trusty much of a chance to prove it. Kept that suitcase close and slept with one eye open. At least I did. Bopeep always slept like he didn't have a worry in the world."

"Didn't y'all get dirty?" Teddy asked.

"We was filthy 's pigs most of the time," Uncle Drew said. "Sweat and dust equals mud and there was plenty of both in Texas."

"Everywhere else too, I imagine," Teddy said.

"Wasn't many dust-free places," Uncle Drew agreed.

Teddy thought for a minute. Although Uncle Drew's habit was to tell him one sustained story each day, this might be a good time to nudge him in the direction of another, specifically the one he had become most interested in hearing.

"So," he said. "Texas was as far as y'all went out that way."

"That's right," Uncle Drew said. "Should've went over into Mexico but didn't, which I always about half-regretted. It was right there to do. But after El Paso we figured the West was just more of the same so we headed back thisaway. Returned through Beaumont and on into the Deep South via Lake Charles. Took a few dollars away from them Acadian batters around Lafayette and New Iberia. Ate tremendously well down in there too. Went all the way across Louisiana at the widest part but stayed above New Orleans. Got clean over to Covington and there's the lake, and right across it yonder's the big city. I told Bopeep, said, 'You pretty much home,' and he said home'd be his last stop and he wasn't ready to go home yet."

"Was all this on trains?" Teddy asked.

"We walked and hopped trains the rest of that year. Well, almost the rest of it."

"What happened to get you off the trains?" Teddy asked.

"Something I still almost don't believe myself," Uncle Drew said.

He seemed about to continue but didn't.

"You playing on a ball team this summer?" he asked.

Teddy was surprised and a little disappointed by the abrupt change of subject.

"We start first of next month," he said. "I ain't much of a player, though. I just like being part of baseball."

"What's your position?" Uncle Drew asked.

"Right field when they let me play," Teddy said.

"Not too busy a place in the small leagues even if you ain't got a pitcher—and who in the small leagues does? They'll pull it out left every time except for the lefties, who'll knock it your way. Wake up that right fielder. You ever pitch?"

"Never have. Never have done much of anything. You know something funny? Me hitting that ball through your window is funny. That's probably the hardest I ever hit one."

Uncle Drew nodded.

"Must've been fate," he said.

That day they had chicken and dumplings, green beans, and biscuits. Dessert was strawberry shortcake.

Chapter 15

Thing about the small towns in those days made it easier [Uncle Drew said] was that the lines was clear. They wasn't exactly blurred in the big ones, except for later on in New Orleans, but you didn't have to go looking when you landed in some of those places along the Gulf Coast. Blacks here, whites there. Simple as that. And out there was the big salt water. If you weren't where you could see it you could always smell it on the breeze. Amazing to see for the first time, water that didn't meet nothing but sky in front of and on both sides of you. Made me appreciate what I was standing on. Little did I know that the day would come when I'd be out there where water was all there was, no matter which way I turned.

We used the sand for a bed several times, one or two of them bringing us to the unwelcome attention of John Law and the local cutups. Wasn't as much money to be taken but we had got well ahead in that department anyway, so collecting nickels and dimes here and there didn't seem like too much of a move in the wrong direction. They spent just fine and they returned a whale of a lot more than they do now. Course folks took exception to seeing the pair of us together sometimes and it got to where I was picked on for it just as much as Bopeep was. He always dressed in a suit but I stuck to my overalls, then same's now. So we looked out of whack. Law'd see us and here we go. All kind of questions and sometimes it didn't matter what we answer, it ain't right. Got harassed fairly regular for nothing other'n just being who we was. Where we was at was the wrong place. When we was there was the wrong time. That was the situation.

Jumped off just outside of some wide spot in the road through Alabama one afternoon for instance. All we was doing—and I mean we ain't even brought up who can hit and who wants to prove it yet—was minding our own business on a store porch when here comes our old friend John Law. He stops and gets out his cruiser, looks us over a minute, and then for no reason at all says to Bopeep, said, "Come on, boy, we need to have us a word."

Naturally I felt compelled to put my two cents in, said, "He ain't been here long enough to get into anything he needs to have a word with you about."

And John Law said, "I appreciate your input, son, but shut up. You with him?"

I told him I surely was and he said he thought he told me to shut up. Then he added that I must be half-nigger, like he thought I'd take it as a insult. Which I did but not in the way he expected. I was fairly instantaneously hot up under the collar and so I told that redneck son of a you know what I'd rather be all nigger than even a drop of white if being a drop of white gave me any connection whatsoever to him. The five or six fellows sitting there on the porch with us just about fell out over that, which it probably goes without saying didn't set too awful well with Mister John Law.

He said, "You boys erase them watermelon-eating grins off them soup coolers you call mouths right now, else y'all all going in too."

Then he looked at Bopeep and said, "I hope one of y'all's got money, Sambo. Like, oh let's see. A hundred each ought to cover me. You ain't got a hundred, we fixing to spend some quality time together."

Well, I wasn't in no mood to put up with that kind of bull crap—sorry. Ain't no other description for what he done, him to just drive up out of nowhere and, for no reason other'n he's sporting a uniform and a badge he thinks gives him the freedom to do whatever pops into his gumball of a brain, decide to offer us the choice between getting robbed or threw in jail.

So I said, not exactly thinking it all the way through, and certainly not consulting Bopeep about it, said, "We wouldn't piss on your face if you's dying of thirst in the Sahara Desert, much less give you two hundred dollars."

Which little speech got me a pretty good love tap just above knee-high on the side of my leg with a billy club and secured for the pair of us a night in a brick cell didn't have nothing but a stinking hole hardly big enough to spit in for us to do our business into. I told Bopeep I was sorry every three or four minutes or so and he said he was already as good as hauled in before I said anything and was glad to have the company.

Besides the fact that wasn't nobody else in there with us, the only thing good about our time in jail was the food, which was a genuine surprise. I figured we'd get grits and water but they served us a nice fried-catfish supper that evening and some kind of a good country breakfast with just-right eggs next morning. After we ate that, long about nine o'clock, Bopeep got to talking to the sheriff. I was sitting on the cot rubbing my leg, which still smarted from where I'd got tagged. I'd saw that coming and stepped away from the brunt of it, though, so it wasn't as bad as it could've been. Anyway, as you might recall from our run-in with the Shreveport yard bull, the Dodger had a golden tongue on him when it came to putting folks at their ease.

"Ever heard the one about the two snowmen, sheriff?" he said.

Law said he ain't.

Bopeep said, "Yeah, one turned to the other and said, 'You smell carrots?'"

Just, you know, easing things a little bit.

Said, "Gal come up to me in Helena, Arkansas, one time and said she'd do anything I wanted her to for two bits. I said, 'Fine. I got a house over town needs painting.'"

Well, they got to jawing back and forth a little bit.

Law said, "Couple of old boys decide they'll buy theyself a bottle and whichever one dies first the other'n is to come to his gravesite and pour the whiskey on it. Sure enough, one passes and the other'n shows up at his resting place bottle in hand. He's about ready to pour it out but then he thinks to hisself, says, 'Be a shame not to run this through one time.'"

Not the best jokes ever, but the point is that John Law has done rose to Bopeep's bait. Before long he asks which one of us is the ballplayer, says he figured one of us bound to be after going through the suitcase, which finding out he done that made me just about come out of my skin worrying did he pull up that bottom and discover our money. We were well up over a thousand dollars by then. Bopeep tells him he used to play a little ball before he tore his arm up.

"Can't hardly throw from the mound to the plate no more," he said. "But I tell you what, sheriff. I bet you I can still strike out any batter you pick to stand in against me."

Sheriff laughs and says, "Boy, you can't even strike me out."

Now you never can tell about a man's ability with a bat by just looking at him. It's like trying to pick a racehorse that way. One might look like Pegasus hisself going to the gate and then just trot around, while that old nag over there grows wings and takes flight soon's the bell sounds. Nevertheless, I'm fairly certain that our sheriff ain't no hitter. Might once've been but he's looking a little too stately now.

So Bopeep says, "Shoot, sheriff, I'm thinking we might've just done landed on a way to clear up this misunderstanding we be finding ourself in. You know I ain't done nothing to be in here for and you surely also know Uncle Drew mouth just went and got the best of him, which it will do to a certain kind of youngster in a czertain kind of situation. He didn't mean nothing by what he said. Did you, Uncle Drew?"

Course I'm thinking I meant every word and might would say it again. But I know that'd be the end of us sure enough, so I apologize up and down like I done committed a mortal sin and the sheriff is the pope holding my pass out of it. I go on so long about it that Bopeep has to interrupt me to say, "Point's I do believe thoroughly made," then turn to Law and ask him, said, "How about we go out yonder and I'll give you three chances, sheriff? You hit one, we yours to do with what you wish. You don't, we walk. That gives you three times the opportunity I got, and me with a damage arm."

Law considers it a minute, kind of rolling his shoulders. Then he says, "What if you don't throw me nothing to hit?"

And Bopeep says, "You be your own ump. Don't like the pitch, fine with me. I'm talking three in the zone according to your eye and nobody else's."

No use to prolong what happened except to say it's a funny thing about small towns. Time we got set up back there a good little audience was gathered around, white on one side and colored on the other as always. White folks're yapping like fools, calling Bopeep the usual names trying to get his nerves in an uproar. Colored don't make no noise at all. They just watching and waiting, abiding. I bend and stretch my leg out good and get settled into position. First pitch Bopeep throws is a curve I've not yet seen from him, and the sheriff falls all over himself moving away from it. But it drops right into my mitt without me having to budge.

Sheriff says, "Thought your arm was dead."

And Bopeep says, "Some days better'n others."

Sheriff says, "That was high anyway."

Bopeep shrugs. I don't make a mark. Second pitch comes

in slower than cold-morning syrup but right straight down the middle. Sheriff swings and misses. I make a slash. The white folks really start up now. Colored folks is still quiet but they see what's happening and show a few teeth. Third pitch is another curve. Sheriff like to kills hisself bailing out again but all I got to do to catch it is squeeze. My hand is liking this. Sheriff calls it outside. I look at Bopeep and he nods just barely, telling me he's through fooling around.

Next one's invisible. Sheriff's still swinging when I take it out of my glove. I toss it back and make the second slash. Sheriff's red in the face and puffing. He touches the ground with the bat, brings it up, digs in. White folks're screaming at Bopeep. They look like the dogs of Hell over there. Colored folks're showing a few more teeth and elbowing each other. Bopeep winds up and comes over with one on a path looks like a bee'd make. It's here, it's there, and then it ain't nowhere until it hits the mitt. I lean over to make the third slash, pick up the ledger, and start walking before I'm full stood up.

Bopeep has our suitcase out by where he was pitching from and he's got it in hand. He's leaving too. Sheriff swang so hard he sat down. He's probably still on the ground but I ain't looking around because I know we just caught a break and if I do look I'll say something I better not.

One of the fellows from the store day before says, "Y'all come go with me. Ain't nothing here but all them crackers and they friend of the sheriff. Y'all don't want none of that now you done embarrass him."

We didn't argue. He had a pickup and drove us out to his place, where his wife packed us up some dinner—pork chops and cornbread and a couple of roasting ears apiece. After that he took us over to the Florida state line. When we got out we thanked him for the food and the ride and he said he enjoyed the show.

Said, "Don't reckon I know which part I like better, the youngster here saying what he say over to the porch yesterday or y'all putting that peckerwood on his big old rusty dusty while ago. How that leg doing anyway?"

"Better'n it'd be if he'd made solid contact," I said.

"Shoot," Bopeep said. "No more better a bead than he drew on them balls while ago. It a wonder he made any contact at all."

"Ain't it the truth," the driver said. "Well, I best get. Y'all do be careful now."

We watched him turn around and drive out of sight, which reminds me that I ain't said it was getting over into the late fall by this time and was about half-chillsome out. I was glad I'd thought to put my coat in when I packed up back in August. We started walking and Bopeep said it was maybe about time for us to start thinking about another mode of transportation.

"Here we is walking around with enough money on us to put ourself in a vehicle, Uncle Drew," he said. "That make any kind of sense to you?"

I said that it did not.

We'd been wearing our shoes out and risking life and limb hopping trains since hot weather and now into cold. Done had Thanksgiving a couple of weeks back with a group of fellow riders under a bridge in Mississippi. I always kept up with what the date was so I could maintain my records accurate in the ledger, but we didn't know it was Thanksgiving because of that since Thanksgiving ain't never a specific date like Christmas or your birthday. We knew it was because the old boy who was mixing the mulligan out there that evening said he'd put a turkey in it if he had one but didn't so we was going to have to settle for rabbit. We ate a lot of rabbit. Also turnips. I mentioned how much of them I ate back home, I believe. I's tired of them when I left out and got to where just smelling them pulled and ready to go in the pot like to made me gag. Lord, if I ever was starving I might have to just go ahead and do it if all I had to save me was a turnip.

Ever since Uncle Drew had told him what Bopeep had said about changing how they got around, Teddy had been waiting for his chance to get the old man to elaborate on the subject. This wasn't the day for it, though.

"Been over to the pool lately?" Uncle Drew asked.

"Ain't in a while," Teddy said.

"Maybe you ought to. Shame to spend your whole summer sitting on a porch with a wore-out old man."

"You don't seem wore out to me."

"Oh, I get a little tired sometimes."

That day they had pinto beans and cornbread with slaw. Dessert was blackberry cobbler. The top crust was light and flaky, the bottom thick and doughy.

Chapter 16

Teddy decided to take Uncle Drew's advice and return to the swimming pool that afternoon. He and his friends played baseball with a beach ball, they raced each other using different strokes, they lay in the sun eating snow cones and talking about the upcoming season, they got back in the water for more baseball, and they performed a can-opener/cannonball parade off the high board, moving up the ladder like cats, running as fast as they could off the plank and pedaling out into the open air, pulling one or both knees to their chests halfway down, ka-whumping into the water, swimming over to the side ladder, and hoisting themselves up to do it all over again, slowing their pace only when a lifeguard blew her whistle and told them not to run and not to fake not running but to walk or she was going to sit them down. They all saluted her and continued—up and down and back around—until each one in his turn was winded and they flopped on the warm, wet deck to catch their breath, the pool water still in turmoil from the parade.

"One of my favorite things about summer is you can just do stuff," Lonnie Williams said. "You ain't got to sit in no desk all day. And you ain't got to read. I ain't reading nothing all summer."

"You ain't reading nothing all winter, spring, or fall neither," Mike Medders said.

They all laughed.

"What's the use of it?" Lonnie asked.

"You can learn stuff," Teddy said.

"I don't need no book to learn what I need to know," Lonnie replied.

"Whatever," Chris Mayfield said. "I guess you already know everything."

"What I need to I do," Lonnie said.

"What about just knowing stuff that don't matter?" Teddy asked.

As always he heard the voices correcting his usage.

"Like what?" Lonnie asked.

"Like statistics in sports or something," Brandon Jenkins said. "But them do matter."

"Like how many feet're in a mile," Teddy said. "Or yards. It's just something you know for no reason. Like the capitals of the states. What good is that going to do you? Like what a yard bull is."

"Never heard of a yard bull," Lonnie said.

"What is one?" Chris asked.

"It's a railroad policeman," Teddy said.

"How you know?" Lonnie asked. "Why is a policeman a bull? My daddy calls them bears sometimes."

"That's state ones," Brandon said. "They wear those hats like Smokey the Bear."

"Like what mulligan is," Teddy said.

"That's stew," Lonnie replied. "We have squirrel in it all the time in hunting season."

"Hobos made it," Teddy said.

"Hobos are bums," Lonnie declared. "Thieves and bums."

"Some are," Teddy said. "Some ain't."

"How you know anything about hobos?" Lonnie asked.

"A friend told me," Teddy said. "He told me a lot of things."

"Who?" Brandon asked.

"My next-door neighbor," Teddy said.

"It's just a old man lives next door to y'all," Lonnie replied. "And the Waldrons other side."

"The old man's my friend," Teddy said. "His name is Mr. Weems. Uncle Drew. He's telling me a story."

"What kind of a story?" Mike asked.

"Ever heard of Bopeep Shines?"

All of the boys shook their heads.

"He was a baseball player in the Negro Leagues way back when," Teddy said. "Well, not really for long in them. Just a year. Then he decided he could make more money pitching on his own."

"The Negro Leagues, like they was all just nigger players?" Lonnie asked.

"Why you have to say that?" Teddy asked.

"Why not? You think you can stop me? I can say whatever I want to."

"Come on, Lonnie," Teddy protested. "It's stupid."

"Niggers say it to each other," Lonnie said.

"So?" Teddy asked. "It's still just as stupid."

"You calling me stupid?" Lonnie asked.

The other boys had withdrawn from the conversation and were now watching to see what was going to happen.

"It's stupid," Teddy said. "I'm saying it's a stupid word. It isn't right for anyone to say it if you ask me."

"Listen to Teddy, y'all. 'Isn't right.' He sounds like a sissy. He's a sissy that hangs around with a old man who probably everything he says is a total lie."

"Uncle Drew doesn't lie. Take that back."

"What?" Lonnie demanded. "That you're a sissy, which I ain't going to, or that the old man is a liar, which I ain't going to neither because he ain't even your uncle."

Lonnie was considerably bigger than Teddy, but he was quick and athletic, and he got to his feet almost as fast as Teddy did. The other boys scooted themselves back. Lonnie was obviously ready to fight, as was Teddy. But unlike Lonnie. Teddy was no veteran scrapper. He was angry, though, furious past talking anymore. A rush of adrenaline surged through his system. He felt almost weightless.

"Come on, Teddy-boy sissy," Lonnie said.

He faked a punch but instead of getting the reaction he expected, which was for Teddy to jump back afraid, he received a blinding shot to the nose and fell to his knees, skinning them on the concrete.

By now one of the lifeguards was blowing his whistle and hustling down from his chair. The others began blowing their own whistles, sharp blasts of sound that indicated serious trouble. Everybody in the pool began either treading water or standing still. Mr. Belcher emerged from the pool office and jogged around the deck.

Lonnie's nose was broken and bleeding profusely. Still on his knees, he held the tent of his hands against his face. Teddy stood over him, his own hands still fists. He was breathing hard, less from the exertion of punching Lonnie than from the adrenaline that continued to flood his system. He was exhilarated.

"What's going on here?" Mr. Belcher demanded.

"Lonnie called Teddy something and Teddy hit him," Mike said.

"Is that right, Teddy?" Mr. Belcher asked.

Teddy nodded. He watched two of the lifeguards ease Lonnie onto his back and have him tilt his head so that the bleeding would stop. Lonnie was groaning.

"Lonnie started it, Mr. Belcher," Brandon said. "He swang at Teddy first."

"Teddy ought to not be in trouble," Mike said. "Lonnie asked for it and Teddy gave it to him. Pow!"

Mr. Belcher knelt beside Lonnie.

"You okay, son?" he asked.

Lonnie mumbled something and nodded. His eyes were watering so much that he appeared to be crying.

"Well, let me see," Mr. Belcher said.

He took Lonnie's hands away from his face.

"Just relax now," he said. "I need to take a look."

When he touched Lonnie's nose, Lonnie howled in pain and brought his hands back to his face.

"Be tough," Mr. Belcher said. "It's broke and there ain't but one way to fix it. We got to put it back in place. I've done this a thousand times when I seconded fighters in my army days and I've had to do a few here at the pool. It's going to hurt real bad but just for a little. Then it'll be fine. Think you can trust me and stand it?"

Lonnie opened his eyes wide and nodded. He removed his hands and clasped them on his chest so tightly that the knuckles turned white. Teddy leaned in and saw what he'd done for the first time. Lonnie's nose was bent to one side and his face was wet with blood, which had run all the way down his front to his swimming trunks.

"Try not to move your head," Mr. Belcher said.

He took Lonnie's nose between the sides of his index fingers and snapped it back where it belonged. It made an awful grinding sound. Lonnie kicked his feet and released his hands to slap them on the concrete, but he somehow managed not to howl this time. He just made a sound like people make after they've been throwing up. Mr. Belcher and one of the lifeguards helped him into a sitting position and then to his feet.

"You boys come go with me and we'll get this sorted out," he said.

Teddy paced the deck between one of the lifeguard chairs and the pool-office door while Mr. Belcher spoke with Mike, Brandon, and Chris. Lonnie leaned back against the wall, holding an icepack a lifeguard had given him up to his face. They didn't speak to each other. Teddy knew he should at least ask how Lonnie's nose was, but he was still angry and he was still waiting for Lonnie to take back what he'd said, especially the part about Uncle Drew. Lonnie didn't even know Uncle Drew.

Directly, Mr. Belcher opened the door and told them to come in and have a seat. The only place to do it was on some baskets the lifeguards had stacked for use during their breaks. Mr. Belcher moved his stool over from its place by the cash register. He wasted no time getting to his point.

"We can't have fighting at the pool, boys," he said. "Y'all know that."

"Yessir," Teddy said.

Lonnie nodded. He now had the icepack balanced on top of his head. His nose, which had stopped bleeding, looked as sore and tender as it must have felt. The skin beneath his eyes was beginning to turn purple.

"Well, now," Mr. Belcher said. "I need to see if everybody's story lines up here. According to the other boys, you brought this onto yourself, Lonnie. What say you—yes or no?"

"It was me the one, yessir," Lonnie answered. "Teddy didn't do nothing except hit me for egging him on."

His voice sounded as though he had a bad cold. Teddy had expected him to try to argue his own side, even if he didn't have one. His honesty was admirable. Teddy felt his anger begin to release its grip on him.

"Appreciate you being truthful without me having to dig it out of you, Lonnie," Mr. Belcher said. "That's what the others said too. Now you boys need to realize that I am aware of how much easier it is for me to sit here and preach you a sermon about fighting's a last resort and so forth than for you to put the idea into practice. Every boy I ever knew can get into a scrap pretty quick if the stars are lined up just so. I got there myself more than I can count when I was y'all's age and even older. These things happen. Somebody says something and somebody else takes it wrong and fists fly. But none of that makes any difference here at the pool because the rules're the rules and there can be no exceptions. You get in a fight, you lose the privilege of coming here for a while. I'm the judge and I'm the jury when this happens. So. I don't want to see you over here for a week, Teddy, and you for the next two, Lonnie. Understand?"

Teddy and Lonnie nodded.

"Well, I guess that's it, then," Mr. Belcher said.

He stood and indicated for the boys to do the same.

"Let's have y'all shake hands," he said. "Patch this up."

Teddy and Lonnie turned to face each other. Teddy offered his hand first. Lonnie took it and they locked eyes.

"Sorry about what I said," Lonnie told him.

"Sorry about your nose," Teddy replied. "You okay?"

"Feels like at the dentist when you're waking up from numb," Lonnie said. "It kind of hurts and don't at the same time."

That made Teddy smile. Lonnie looked down, then up. He was also smiling—or trying to. He seemed to be hurting pretty bad. Teddy almost felt sorry for him. But he knew he had earned his respect. That was plain. Lonnie wasn't going to be calling him or anybody else names again for a long time, if ever, and Teddy couldn't wait to tell Uncle Drew all about it. He was in considerably less of a hurry for his parents to hear the story. But Mr. Belcher took care of that for him. They already knew when he brought it up at the supper table that evening. Mr. Belcher had called his mother at Builders Lumber and she had called his father on his cellphone.

"How much trouble am I in?" Teddy asked.

"None," his father said.

"I don't like fighting, but Mr. Belcher convinced me that you were in the right this time," his mother told him. "He even said he wished he didn't have to kick you out of the pool for a week."

"Lonnie got two," Teddy replied.

"I think old Lonnie learned him a lesson today," his father said. "His daddy won't mind you whipping him either. What he will mind is Lonnie going down after one lick. O'Dell Williams played a whole football game one night, both ways, after breaking his thumb on the opening kickoff. He just had Coach Crews pop it back and tape him up. I don't guess Lonnie's made that way."

"Probably lucky for me," Teddy said.

After supper he walked over to Uncle Drew's house but the old man had gone somewhere. Teddy climbed the mimosa in his backyard. He looked at the place where Uncle Drew parked his truck, which always seemed to be gone in the late afternoon and early evening. He wondered where Uncle Drew went. Probably to the store. He had to get all the food he cooked sometime.

Teddy called it a day earlier than usual that night because he was worn out. He still had a few pages left in the second Hardy Boys book, but he was too tired to finish even one. Frank and Joe were going to have to spend a little longer in the water tower with Hobo Johnny, who was definitely somebody Bopeep and Uncle Drew would have tried to avoid when they were out on the road.

He turned off the light and lay listening to the racket of bugs and frogs outside his open window. The night world was a busy place. He drifted toward sleep thinking that it had been a good day, all things considered. He was proud of himself, not for breaking Lonnie Williams' nose but for standing up to him for saying such terrible things. It was like something Uncle Drew would have done.

Chapter 17

Ain't no other way out of it [Uncle Drew said] except to go ahead land you a punch in a situation like that. Call the other fellow's hand. Most of the time a good hard lick's all it takes. Don't always work out that way, though. Occasionally you'll run into somebody who all hitting him does is wake him up. Then you're in a position of getting ready to find out about yourself, because you are fixing to get hit back. Best to avoid that if at all possible. Bopeep had that gift. I didn't and would've got myself into plenty of jams if he wasn't with me. Course the fact that we was together was what generally brought attention our way. Blacks and whites weren't supposed to associate in public. Rules was different in the hobo camps, as I've said, least for the most part. But just about ever' time we got in a situation elsewhere, it wasn't fighting going to get us out of it anyway. It was either John Law we was dealing with, who might fight you as I learned but who you do not fight back unless you aim to lose fairly immediately, or else a crowd of peckerwoods had numbers on us. It was always at least three against two and usually a couple more.

But Bopeep was a talker, not a fighter. Oh, I seen him give as good as he got when there wasn't no other resort. Skinny little old thing was quick. He'd scrap when necessary, but except for this one time I'm fixing to relate, I never saw him start out with a physical response to a situation. He was a peacemaker, like I said. You'll remember one of if not the first thing he said to me was he didn't want no issue. And

141

he didn't. What he wanted was for things to run smooth amongst folks.

Don't know if I've presented you much to go on by way of describing him other'n to say he was tall and rail thin and black as pitch, which I guess is all you need for a picture. Had them big old feet too. And hands to go with them. Wasn't so much big as they was long. Fingers looked like tentacles dangling down there at the end of his arms. If ever anybody didn't look like a athlete it was Bopeep. What he looked most like was a scarecrow. Except for dressing too nice, he could've been one.

So. Once he got to trusting me with different pitches and quit always hurling that invisible screamer, he'd hold the ball all kind of different ways, them fingers allowing him to set the seams in particular ways so that when he came over with it the thing was about as predictable from him to me as a fly. It always found the mitt, though. We didn't need signs because of that, though I was to find out later that he did have a system of numbers he used in his mind. He said there wasn't no use in him telling me what he was going to throw because all I had to do was give him a target and he'd hit it. We drew a plate in the dirt, by the way, or let whoever was standing in draw one. Course they always made it smaller'n it ought to've been since they thought that'd give them an edge. Bopeep said they could put a silver dime down far's he was concerned. He could split a Mercury head just as easy's he could split a barn door.

And, you know, we never had much trouble with the calls. We always offered everybody the option of picking somebody to ump for them or else they could do it for their-self, like the sheriff in Alabama. Bopeep was like a cobra out there. He fascinated them with that slow, high-kick, bent-back windup of his and next thing they know they're hearing the ball smack my mitt. They usually called it what it was, and more often than not what it was was a stee-rike.

Now you don't normally associate Florida with cold weather and I ain't saying nobody'd ever confuse it with Alaska. But we spent some mighty chilly nights down there in the Sunshine State and neither one of us liked it just too awful much. Don't take very low of a Fahrenheit to get into your bones when you're trying to sleep, which was what we was doing one of the few times I remember being called to task in a camp. This was also the one time I saw Bopeep behave in a violent manner without it being retaliation for same.

There was five or six of us out there that night. Had a nice fire going and was all of us fairly content in the belly. This old boy showed up after we'd ate and talked and drifted off. He was what you'd call a bum, the kind of no-good tramp who gave hobos a bad name. Come in there about half-cocked on the hooch, squatted down by the fire, and immediately took up the spoon to inspect what was in the pot, which wasn't but a little bit of scrapings. Didn't say a word, just busted in there and woke us all up like he owned the trestle we was under and wanted something in return for us staying there.

"Got a name, fella?" one of the hobos said.

He was the mixer. It was his pot and his spoon and he'd fixed our supper.

New man said, "What's it to you?"

Mixer said, "Just being friendly. Ain't nothing to me really."

New man said, "You trying to tell me something about manners there, buddy?"

Course by now we're all awake and sitting up, bleary of eye and cold. I threw a log onto the fire, stoked it up.

Mixer said, "I ain't trying to tell you nothing. I's just asking your name, as in mine's Jackson. Mack Jackson from up to Kentucky. Folks call me Mack-Jack."

And the new man said, "I don't give a blankety-blank what your name is, Jackson, and I give even less of a one who calls you what or where it is you from."

Mixer said, "What if I told you that's my stew you're eating?"

New man said, "I'd say your stew tastes like blankety-blank."

Mixer said, "Well that's a fine hidy-do. These boys found it right nourishing, if not tasty."

New man looked around at us. When he saw Bopeep he said about what you'd expect a man like that to, which was, "What's the nigger for? Y'all looking to have some sport later on?"

And the mixer said, "Now see here, mister. We don't need none of this kind of talk. That boy right there ain't no different from me and you. He's just looking for a bite and a flat place to rest his bones."

The new man snorted.

"Speak for yourself, Jackson," he said. "I ain't got nothing in common at all with no nigger."

I looked over at Bopeep, who as usual I could tell had already got hisself rose above the matter. He huddled a little tighter and kept his eyes on the fire. Me, though, I wasn't interested in rising above nothing. I was, as was usually the case, interested in flying right straight into it.

"Why you maybe don't just eat you a bite, thank the man for it, and be on your way, mister?" I said. "We all doing just dandy here without your like come in stirring things up."

And he said, "Who the hell you think you are talk to me that way, boy? You ought to be home in your cradle."

I started to stand up but Bopeep laid a hand on my shoulder and kept me from it.

New man said, "Nigger ever touched me'd be the last thing he ever done."

He took a bottle from his coat pocket, uncorked it, and had himself a couple of long gulps. Wiped his mouth with the back of his hand.

"Any you boys like a snort?" he said. "Except you, nigger. And you, baby boy. When y'all reckon we might can get all these black blankety-blanks back to Africa where they come from anyway? It was up to me we'd go ahead and send this one on his way to Hell right now. String him up from one of them ties yonder and peel him like a tater."

I ain't sure who he thought his audience was, but I figure without a doubt he was as crazy in the head to start with as he was drunk. I mean he kept going on like that, talking about how they had a free chance to erase a nigger and why was they just sitting there.

Said, "Look to me like y'all'd be jumping at the chance. Ain't but one of him and all of us. We could rope him and the boy up together, make them smooch. Hate to think y'all afraid to taking a nigger and a nigger lover out. It'd make the world one step closer to a better place. Hold that black blankety-blank's hand in the fire a minute, watch him beg us to spare him. Done it once. Hoo, boy! Had to raise my voice over his screaming to tell him we all was fixing to be better off him dead. Him because his struggles'd be over, us because one less nigger."

All the time he talked he was swigging from that bottle. None of us said a thing. Wasn't no need to really. It was like watching theater, like he wasn't a real person saying real things but an actor reciting words somebody'd wrote. Awful, awful things.

Finally he said, "Well, if ain't nobody going to help me here I reckon I'll just have to do it myself. You ready to meet your Maker, boy?"

I swear, I think he thought we was going to let him kill Bopeep. He had things all out of order. It wasn't Bopeep was just one against everybody else. It was him. So he started trying to stand up, and that's when Bopeep come undone. He was up and on top of that son of a you know what faster'n I can tell it. New man tried to go upside his head with his bottle, but Bopeep arrested him at the wrist in them tentacle fingers of his and caused him to drop it. Had him pinned down with one of his bony forearms at his throat, the new man bucking and twisting and trying to get himself some leverage to hit with his free arm. But it wasn't no use. Bopeep just pressed tighter and tighter up against his throat until he had him gurgling.

We all sat there watching without too much concern for his health. I was mostly amazed to learn that Bopeep had such a level of scrap in him. Shouldn't've been but was. I realized later that this was him just being fed up and through for the moment with enduring being done wrong to. It was like he took everything been handed him out on that bum, made him pay for all of it.

"Reckon he deserves it if he strangles," one of the hobos said.

"Reckon so," another one said.

When the new man stopped struggling Bopeep loosened his hold and, with every ounce of his weight, punched him in the mouth. Then he stood up.

"Think this the last thing I ever do, you ofay blankety-blank?" he said.

New man probably didn't hear him he was so busy spitting out teeth and trying to bring some air into his lungs. He rocked from side to side and kicked his legs like something having a fit. Bopeep came back over to where I was. He was breathing pretty hard hisself.

I said, "What's 'ofay' mean?"

He took a couple of deep breaths to get steady and said, "It mean enemy. Closest thing to nigger you can call a white man."

And I said, "I see."

The intruder left shortly after that just like he come, without a word. Didn't fetch his bottle neither. Wasn't much left in it, but we passed it around a couple of times and wound up sleeping sound as logs out there in cold Florida. Nobody said anything to me about being a little shy on years to be drinking hooch neither.

Next day me and Bopeep headed out. We somehow got ourselves going north and wound up in south Georgia, where the thing that's still hard for me to believe happened.

"I don't know how much you've browsed around in those ledgers," Uncle Drew said, "but if you ever looked at the last thing I wrote in the 1935 one, the one has all of what we been talking about so far in it, you've seen an unusual entry. The bet is 'all' against 'auto' and there's only one mark there, a slash, of course. The winning column says 'auto.' You seen that?"

"I have," Teddy said. "I been wondering about it. You or somebody wrote something else after that. It's rubbed out."

"Kind of a mystery, ain't it?" Uncle Drew asked. "Something like your Hardy Boys might find theirself in the middle of. Got any theories?"

"Not about what's rubbed out, but I found another article on the Internet and it said something about Georgia."

"Did it, now? What'd it say?"

"It said that of all the stories told about Bopeep, this one was the most unlikely."

"You read it?"

"I did. Reckon how come the other story didn't have it."

"Whoever wrote that'n probably ain't heard it. Or they found it so outlandish they thought there wasn't no point putting it in there."

"Did it happen?"

Uncle Drew nodded.

"Like I done said," he replied. "It all happened."

"Well?"

"Tomorrow," Uncle Drew said.

That day they had fried chicken, rice and gravy, butter beans, and biscuits. Teddy told Uncle Drew he used to think he'd never see the day anybody could fry a chicken better than his grandmother did.

"You still ain't," Uncle Drew said. "Never forget that."

Dessert was ice cream with peach slices that still had the skin on them.

Chapter 18

One thing needs to be clear at this point [Uncle Drew said] and it happens to be something you have no chance of understanding. You will one day but right now it's a concept as foreign to you as why women act the way they do. Well, that ain't a good analogy. Nobody ever understood that, including them, so it's likely you won't neither. Good luck anyway. What I mean is that you're just too young to understand getting older. A youngster thinks he's always going to be young. He looks at a old man like me and ain't no way for him to imagine him another way. If I showed you a picture of myself in my prime you'd have a hard time reconciling the image with what I've became. Not that I was ever going to have some movie director spy me at the grocery store and whisk me off to Hollywood, now, but believe it or not I used to have smooth skin and dark hair.

The point I'm trying to make is that age takes its toll. Man used to could run like the wind progressively loses a step or two as the years add up and gets to where he'd be hard pressed to run at all. Man used to could see twenty-twenty finds himself having to squint, either at what's right in front of him or what's out yonder a ways, sometimes both. You said you's nine. At nine none of this applies. Lord, at nine, you ain't got the first sense of yourself yet. Be a while before you know what's at stake here.

Reason I bring all this up is you have to realize that the man who made this bet with us wasn't who he'd once been. He was forty-eight years old, he was just a hair shy of a decade out of the Major Leagues, and he had no business doing what he did. Wasn't no use us trying to talk him out of it, though, because his mind was made all the way up. Said he knew a good deal when he saw it. Said he'd take as many dollars off Bopeep as Bopeep had pitches to throw him. Said wasn't no nigger alive could get a ball past him. Said he'd take every dollar he had and put him in a hole he'd never get out of. Said he'd make him his slave. That was his attitude. Tyrus Raymond Cobb was as eat up with pride and hatred as any man I ever encountered. Perfect match, him and Bopeep. Two exact opposites.

"We can do it a hundred a pitch, boy," he said. "Or we can do it a penny. Either way, I aim to clean your blankety-blank black butt *out.*"

Bopeep just shook his head and said, "Tell you what, Mr. Cobbs"—and I am here to tell you, him adding that s on there like to drove Cobb plumb around the bend—said, "I done face sixty-two mens already and ain't but four stood in found a pitch with they bat. I got to be well over five hundred dollar to the good, which, way I see it, give me plenty reason to walk away right now. I be done got a little tired, tell you the truth."

And Cobb said, "You scared of me, nigger?"

"Nosir, I ain't," Bopeep said. "Fact is, I just don't want to take advantage of a old man out here in front of all his friend."

And Cobb said, "I ain't too old to hit you, boy. Let's get to it."

Where we was at was out in a field by a roadhouse somewhere between Waycross and Valdosta. This was a Sunday afternoon and it was chilly. Kind of like Florida, you don't generally think of Georgia as a place where you can get just too awful cold, but you're liable to need a wrap don't matter where you at once the short days come. It wasn't bitter, just nippy. Anyway, how Ty Cobb—who just oh by the way would be the very first man voted into the

Hall of Fame the very next year—how he came to be in our midst that afternoon is one of the mysteries of Fate. He just happened to be out on that stretch of highway, just happened to look over when he passed, just happened to register that the crowd gathered over there was watching a pitcher and a batter, and just happened to decide to stop and take himself a closer-up look. I don't know how long he'd been there before he'd seen enough.

It was an all-comers kind of day, everybody in a pretty good mood I guess because it was right around Christmastime and folks were feeling charitable. A little of the John Barleycorn probably didn't hurt. They were gathered in the usual alignment, colored here, white there. The batters was coming from both sides. One man'd strike out, he'd hand the bat to the next one, might be white, might be black. They was all united in the cause of trying to send one back Bopeep's way and wasn't none of them getting the job done. We even had us a all-time ump back there after a few stood in.

Old boy said, "I ain't wasting my time going against him but I'll sure call for y'all you want me to."

I said I'd be obliged and looked at Bopeep.

"Fine with me," he said. "Long's you give me the same truck you give them sheeps."

Old boy said, "I'm honest."

And he was. Course I don't believe he could see what Bopeep was throwing about half the time. I mean, to say he had his good stuff that day's redundant because Bopeep always had his good stuff. But it was particularly good on this occasion. Ball was coming in there hard and straight, hard and up, hard and down, hard to this side, and hard to that side. Sometimes it was coming in there hard and all the other ways on the same pitch.

He started out with his sleeves down and his tie up, but chillsome as it was he worked up a lather after while, so up come the sleeves and down goes the tie. Folks was having a time. I'd like to've had a piece of the side action because they was passing the bills in both lines after every pitch. At least at first they was. Wasn't long before that stopped because nobody'd back the batter. We was making a good run. Man take the stick and hand me whatever he wanted to wager, now a coin, now a bill. Except for those four hits got scattered through there, I didn't have to hand any back and all I had to do pitch after pitch was throw the ball back and put a slash in the book. It was a lot of whooping and hollering going on for half an hour or so but then things got a little quiet. All you'd hear was the ball coming and slapping into my mitt, the grunt the batter made swinging, and the old boy umping saying, "Stee-rike!"

Black folks was first to start to clapping. Then, surprise, the white folks got to joining in. They'd make a racket after every pitch, then they'd get quiet and wait to clap again. Bopeep just kept delivering. Up they came and down they went. Then even the clapping stopped, like everybody realized they was seeing something miraculous and nobody wanted to make a sound. This lasted until right after the sixty-second batter took his third swing and a voice came out of the crowd.

Said, "Good God almighty damn. What the hell? Can nobody hit this blankety-blank nigger?"

We all looked around trying to see who it was. Couldn't at first, then the crowd on the white side parted and here he come, throwing his shoulders from side to side to move the last couple of folks out of his way. He was a good-sized fellow, not huge, but plenty big enough. And well built. Looked like an athlete who'd just gotten a little long in the tooth for hard play.

I turned to the old boy umping and said, "Who is that?"

He looked down and said, "That's Ty Cobb, son."

Course I knew who Cobb was, least who he'd used to've

been. Son of a gun was maybe the greatest ballplayer who ever slid his feet into a pair of cleats—rumored to be filed cleats in his ornery case. Don't know how much you know about him but any all-time nine you put together had better have the Georgia Peach in the outfield. Nobody'll ever conclusively settle the debate over who was the absolute greatest of the great but you definitely wouldn't be wasting your vote if you was to cast it for Cobb because he'll always be in the running. No need to unscroll the entire list of accomplishments since for our purposes the one that matters most is that right now, as we sit here today, he owns the highest lifetime batting average ever achieved. Weigh that for a second or two and see if you ain't impressed.

He wasn't a power hitter like Babe Ruth but that's partly due to how he held the bat. Took it in a spread grip because he was interested in making contact, putting the ball into play. He wanted to get on base, which is where he did a good deal of literal and figurative damage. They say he'd scrape his spikes into blades and maybe he did. What he'd definitely do is come in high, so that if you was covering a bag you'd have to think twice about putting yourself in his way. He'd tear your uniform and your skin with them things. He believed the path belonged to the runner. Even taught himself to bat left handed so he'd be closer to first when he hit the ball. And he was I'm talking about one fierce son of a gun who considered losing a kind of death to the spirit. He'd do anything to win. It's all there in the books if you want to look it up.

Other thing about him is he did not—and I mean let's put no sugar on this—he did *not* like black people. He certainly didn't think they belonged on the baseball field and I think you could make a case that he didn't think they belonged on the planet. So even though he'd disappeared over the hill in terms of being a baseball player by 1935, he was not about to spend too much time watching Bopeep mowing down batter after batter without standing in hisself.

He walked about halfway between where I was and where Bopeep was and said, "You know who I am, boy?"

And Bopeep said, "Nosir, I don't believe I do."

And Cobb said, "My name is Tyrus Raymond Cobb and I will send as many balls as you care to throw me right straight down your blankety-blank black throat."

And Bopeep said, "Why, I be dog. Pleased to meet you, Mr. Cobbs. My name Cantrell Shines."

And Cobb said, "It's Cobb, not Cobbs. Perfect name for a shine, by the way. Shines. Ought to be all niggers' last name."

And Bopeep said, "I know who you is, Mr. Cobbs. What bring you out this way on a Sunday afternoon?"

And Cobb said, "That brand-new car yonder brought me, if it's any business of yours. And it's Cobb without an s, dammit."

Which was when they got into the exchange I mentioned earlier that ended with Cobb saying, "I ain't too old to hit you, boy."

After that, he said, "And these ain't my friends. I ain't got no friends."

And Bopeep said, "That a shame, Mr. Cobbs. Man ought to have him some friend."

And Cobb said, "You call me Cobbs again, nigger, I'll take that bat upside your head."

And Bopeep said, "Ain't no sense us standing here fussing, Mr. Cobbs. You already too old and I be done got too tired for it. Also it ain't no sense us standing here rest of the day trying to take each other's money. Let's come to terms. Like I said a minute ago, I figure I be five hundred up easy. Don't know how much you pay for that new car of yours but man like you seem to me like he be willing to put a dollar against a doughnut for belief in hisself.

What say we make your dollar that fine automobile and my doughnut what I won so far this afternoon and put them up on one pitch? You don't like the pitch, I give you another'n. You don't like that, wait till one come you do like. You hit it, you take home everything Uncle Drew back there holding. You miss it, I take the car."

Cobb didn't say a word. He just turned and strode back to where me and the old boy umping was standing.

"You call a strike on me I'll beat your face with a chain, mister," he said.

Then he looked at me and said, "You his uncle, kid?"

I swallowed hard. He had eyes on him looked like two fires burning. Meanest face on a man I ever saw. Wasn't that way earlier. I'd even say he looked almost genial when he first appeared out of the crowd. Now, though, now he was getting ready to compete and he looked about like what I'd reckon the devil might if you was to see him up close. He shrugged out of his coat and started rolling up his sleeves.

"Cat got your tongue, kid?" he said. "I asked you a question."

I shook my head.

"Nosir, Mr. Cobb," I said. "He just calls me that."

And Cobb said, "I wouldn't let a nigger call me nothing didn't have 'Mister' in front of it. You travel with him?"

I nodded.

"You're a disgrace, kid," he said.

Then he fished a key out of his pocket and handed it to me.

"I'll be taking this back here in a minute," he said. "But what the hell? We might as well act like this is a bona-fide bet. It ain't, though. This is just the old Peach fixing to rob a skinny nigger boy in broad daylight."

He picked up the bat and began stretching. I looked out at Bopeep and he motioned to me with his head.

When I got to him he said, "Get everything you got back

there in close so soon's this done we out of here. These peckerwood ain't fixing to probably like this none."

I glanced over to where Cobb's car was parked. It was sitting a little away from the others, maybe a hundred yards from where we'd set up.

"He give me the key," I said.

I showed it to him.

"You drive?" he said.

I nodded.

"You?" I said.

He spat and shook his head.

"Never have," he said. "Maybe you can teach me."

And I said, "Ain't you getting ahead of yourself?"

He shook his head again.

"Not really," he said. "We at the formality stage here regarding all that. Car good 's ours already. Now look. Ump been fair all day. Might not now, though, so I'm throwing him a dancer be fixing to drop the bottom out of it just past the mark. It'll be slow so he have too good a look at it not to swing. Ain't no way he hitting it. You just snag it, get you book, and we be gone. Have that key ready."

He said all this dead serious. There was going to be no fooling around whatsoever. I handed him the ball.

"Good luck," I said.

"Ain't no luck necessary, Uncle Drew," he said. "This a test of *skill*. Ty Cobb just another sheeps to herd. I'd feel sorry for that old man he wasn't so ugly with his mouth to me."

Meantime, Cobb is stretched and ready and has commenced yelling at us about how this ain't the damn World Series, dammit, and he'd like to go ahead and hit so he can get back on the road to Atlanta, and so forth and so on.

I trotted back to my place, slipping the key into my pocket on the way. The crowd was in close like a gallery at a golf tournament. Whatever respect Bopeep earned from the white side earlier was long forgotten now. They was yelling all manner of awful things at him and of course not missing the chance to direct some of it at the blacks across the way. Cobb stepped out and held his arms out like Moses parting the Red Sea to get everybody to move back and give him some room.

"Don't care if I crown a nigger with this," he said. "But if I pull it, I might hit a human being and I don't want that to happen."

Everybody obliged but not by too much. There was maybe fifteen yards between the lines of people, who'd gathered three or four deep to I'd say three-quarters the length of a football field out. I wrote *all/auto* in the book and closed it over my capped pen. I eased it in beside my foot and hunkered down. Figured I'd write the result later. Cobb took a couple of easy practice swings and stood in. The crowd was making a kind of shriek by now. I held out the mitt. Wasn't sure what to expect from the pitch because of what Bopeep'd said about the bottom dropping out of it but I assumed I'd see it and that it'd find where it was supposed to go.

"Ready, Mr. Cobbs?" Bopeep said.

"I'll tie you up and drag you to Atlanta behind my car for keeping on calling me that, boy," Cobb said. "Just pitch the blankety-blank ball."

And Bopeep said, "You lefty against lefty, Mr. Cobbs. Sure you wants to go through with this?"

And Cobb said, "Don't make me laugh, boy. You just a left-handed nigger, not a left-handed pitcher."

Now a man my age has a lot of memories crammed into his head. Some are clearer in the mind's eye than others but I don't believe I have a one that's stayed as intact and focused to me as the one I carry about the next couple of minutes. First thing happened was everything slowed down, seemed like. Next thing happened was the volume of all the noise that surrounded us changed. I know those voices was loud and getting louder but when Bopeep went into his windup, which itself seemed even slower than usual, they all them voices just sort of receded. I could still hear them but it was like they was now coming through a baffle. I never took my eye off the ball. I watched it from the moment Bopeep started back with it, to the moment he brought it over and released it, to the moment I realized that Cobb had come up with the extraordinarily intelligent idea of bunting it and was squaring himself to do so, to the moment just before it met with the bat, when I thought we was surely done for. Then the thing literally dipped beneath the wood and rose back to its original path, something like a dog going under a fence, and smacked into my mitt.

There was a heartbeat of absolutely no sound or movement before the old boy umping said, "I believe that was a strike, Ty."

And Cobb said, "I realize that, dammit," at which point everything went back to normal speed.

Cobb took to beating the ground with the bat. He'd hit it and cuss, hit it and cuss. He stopped and looked at me, his eyes still blazing.

"You got to the count of three, kid," he said. "After that I aim to kill me a nigger and then I aim to thrash you and then I aim to be on my merry way. One . . . "

I didn't hear the rest of the count. I grabbed the ledger and my coat, put the mitt with the ball still in it under my arm, and took off sprinting toward the car like a scalded ape. Bopeep was already almost to it. The black folks was still clapping and cheering and the whites was still stunned into not knowing what to do except stand there and stare. I looked over my shoulder and saw Cobb in hot pursuit. He had the bat over his head, shaking it. Several others joined him and I thought again we were done for. But Bopeep was in the car reaching across opening the driver's-side door.

Since both my hands was full I couldn't get the key out

of my pocket, so I thought ahead. When I got close enough to do it I'd throw my things in, pull out the key, and have it ready soon's I was seated. I had just enough time to get all of that done and push the starter before Cobb and what had by now turned into a gang of folks chasing me reached the car. We fishtailed out of there and hit the road with a squeal, Bopeep laughing his laugh the whole time. I must've looked in the mirror a thousand times between there and where we finally stopped, which wasn't until we'd drove over two hundred miles and was in Jasper County, South Carolina.

Thing surprised me was nobody chased us. I's shaking in my brogans every time we saw John Law. Figured Cobb'd have an all-points bulletin out to put us under immediate arrest for stealing his car. Didn't happen, which made me think that in the end he played the bet honorably with us. We stayed a few days with some tenant folks up there outside a place called Ridgeland whose kids I recall just could not get over that vehicle.

"So I guess y'all never had to jump trains after that," Teddy said.

"Nosir. Cobb's car got us off the trains. And other'n the minor detail of the registration being absent—we turned that car inside out looking for it—and in his name to boot, plus the fact that neither of us had a license to drive it, we was in fine shape."

"What'd y'all do about all that?" Teddy asked.

"Not a farming thing," Uncle Drew said. "Figured we'd drive her till somebody told us we couldn't."

"Weren't you worried about a fine or having to go to jail?"

"A little, I guess. But not enough to park her."

"Whatever happened to her?"

"Come here, I'll show you."

They walked around to the shed. Uncle Drew lifted the door. The car, originally a deep red that had faded over the years, was partially covered with a tarp, but Teddy could see the rear end with the winged Hudson insignia. Uncle Drew walked ahead of him, removing the tarp as he advanced. Teddy stood looking at the vehicle as though he had happened upon some magnificent creature long extinct, a dinosaur not reconstructed in a museum but still very much alive, if sleeping. Uncle Drew opened the driver's-side door.

"Come get in," he said.

Teddy hesitated.

"What're you waiting for?"

"I can't believe it," Teddy said.

"Needs a lot of work. I've kept the inside in fairly good shape but you can see that the outside could use a little rub. The engine's another story entirely. She has sat for quite a while in her life. Had to have her hauled up here when I moved. Been tinkering a little late at night, though. She'll run but I wouldn't want to depend on her to get me out of another jam. Maybe one of these days I'll have her able enough for a short spin."

Teddy stepped forward and scooted under the wheel but kept his hands in his lap for fear that if he touched anything the car would suddenly come to life. The interior was immaculate, well rubbed and smelling of leather. Everything looked heavier and more substantial than what he was used to from riding in his mother's car and his father's pickup. There was also more space. He felt as though he were sitting on a sofa.

"I didn't know they had radio back then," he said.

"Had some good music come out of it too. I never was partial to any particular kind myself. Whatever was on was fine with me. Bopeep liked the country so that's mostly what come out of that box there."

Teddy looked at the old man, who stood bent at the waist with one arm on the roof and the other on the door.

"Is this really it?" he asked.

"This is really it," Uncle Drew said. "Straight-six Terraplane originally owned by the great Hall of Famer Ty Cobb."

"I been wondering," Teddy said. "Mr. Bilberry said there was an old car back here, and my daddy heard a Bopeep story from an old man in Jonesboro who said he saw him pitch in Mississippi one time."

"Drove her through Mississippi, sure did. Lots of fish fries over there."

Teddy reached out and took the wheel in his hands. He worked the slack in it. There wasn't much. He looked at the speedometer, which was shaped like a football and went to 100.

"How fast will it go?" he asked.

"Fast enough," Uncle Drew said. "Manual says keep her at sixty after she's broke in, which she wasn't when we got her. But I drove out of there doing well past that. Had to. Least I thought I did. Never had been in charge of anything like this before, but you drive some of them old jalopy trucks and tractors I got put behind the wheel of as a kid, there ain't nothing you can't make go."

Teddy sat up straight and looked through the dusty windshield past the car's long hood at the back wall of the shed, which in his mind temporarily vanished to become an open Georgia road on a long-ago December day. He suddenly felt exhilarated, lifted, elsewhere. When he returned to himself, he noticed that Uncle Drew was sitting beside him.

"Thought you'd went to sleep on me," the old man said.

"I was just thinking about y'all. What it must've been like."

"I see," Uncle Drew said. "What'd you decide?"

"Like a dream," Teddy said. "A perfect dream."

The old man alternately shook and nodded his head.

"Sure seems like one now," he said.

"This car is probably worth a fortune."

"What's that?" Uncle Drew asked.

Teddy repeated his observation.

"Car's worth exactly what anything is, which is what somebody's willing to shell out for it," Uncle Drew said. "I'd imagine there's a fellow or two probably open up a good-sized wallet for her, though, if he's convinced of her background. Another 'if' in this case'd be her being for sale, and I can put that one to rest with two words. She ain't."

Teddy was satisfied about all but one element of the story.

"What was in the ledger somebody erased?" he asked.

"I done that years later," Uncle Drew said. "When I originally wrote it was the next morning after our first night with them tenant folks in South Carolina. I suppose you ain't ciphered it out."

"Not yet," Teddy said.

"Want me to save you the time?" Uncle Drew asked.

"That'd be fine."

"Says, *Ty Cobb is a son of a bitch,* is what it says."

Teddy laughed.

"Well, I guess he was," he said.

"And you'd guess right. But I showed Bopeep what I'd wrote and he surprised me, as he often did. He said, 'Aw, Uncle Drew, old Mr. Cobbs he just being how he be.' Can you imagine that? After the way Cobb talked to him out there and him to be big enough to say something like that? Downright amazing. Anyway, I read a lengthy story about Cobb in the paper upon his death some years later and course got to thinking about all what I just told you. Newspaper story didn't pull no punches about what a scoundrel the Peach was, but it was made clear that like everybody else there was more than one side to him. Turned out he was almost as good a businessman as he was a ballplayer. Made millions of dollars and put a good bit of it toward charitable causes, particularly the education of poor kids. Well, I read all about it and recalled Bopeep's generous statement and got to feeling bad about what I'd wrote in the book now that Mr. Cobbs, as the Dodger called him, was dead. So I went in there and rubbed it out. Most of it anyway. I still thought of him as a s.o.b., just maybe a little bit less of a one. Made me feel better too, like I'd lived up in a small way to Bopeep's good nature."

That day they had macaroni and cheese sprinkled with bacon bits. Dessert was banana slices and halved strawberries covered in whipped cream.

Chapter 19

By now Teddy had finished the second Hardy Boys and a Tarzan book called *Tarzan of the Apes,* which he'd checked out because of the conversation he and Uncle Drew had had about the actress who played Jane. He was now midway through the next Tarzan, titled *Tarzan the Terrible.* Although the second one was full of the high adventure Mrs. Delhomme had promised it would be, Teddy preferred the first. In it Tarzan did not end up getting Jane, even though he could have. Teddy was disappointed, but he admired the honorable way Tarzan handled the situation. In the second, Tarzan was once again searching for Jane, who was now his wife and who was being held captive by a man who needed her help because he knew nothing about survival in the jungle.

There were plenty of gaps in Teddy's knowledge of the overall story, and it was this—in combination with the fact that Uncle Drew's tales had left little room in his imagination for anything else—that made what he was doing less reading than simply moving his eyes across the lines of words. He would come to a place in the book and realize that he had no idea what had been happening. The first few times that he caught himself in this, he went back and reviewed. After a while he quit doing that and just continued, looking at fewer and fewer sentences on each page. This actually allowed him to focus on the story better. It also allowed him to finish the book in record time.

Teddy knew that what he was doing was a form of cheating,

but he didn't think of it as the kind of cheating that made him a bad person. It wasn't as though he planned to put a book on his list that he hadn't at least skimmed. If Mrs. Delhomme quizzed him, he would still be able to tell her the basics of the plot, which ended when Tarzan and Jane were saved from what seemed an impossible situation by their son, whose name was Korak.

He realized that he had just stumbled on a way to achieve his summer goal of reading a book a week. He would speed-read, making certain to turn every page, if not look at every sentence there. The idea was a relief. It made him feel lighter to have that little problem solved.

Meanwhile, he had finally told his parents about Uncle Drew and the Bat Dodger, as he had begun to think of Bopeep after hearing of the pitch that got past Ty Cobb. That one was too much to keep to himself, and as he told it he added in bits and pieces of the other ones, going all the way back to the broken-down bus. He substituted an *n* sound for the word itself when referring to it was unavoidable. Before he finished, he interrupted himself to go get the ledgers out of his bedroom. His parents leafed through them while he was talking.

"So I guess that's the car they were driving in that story the old man in Jonesboro told me," his father said.

"And it's the car that's sitting over there in his shed right now. Look on the last page of the 1935 one."

His mother was holding it. She turned to the place. Teddy and his father got up and stood behind her. They all three looked at the writing that was there and at the letters that remained from where Uncle Drew had rubbed out what he'd written about Ty Cobb. His father pointed to it. Teddy hadn't told that part yet.

"It's cussing," he said.

"Does Uncle Drew cuss in front of you?" his mother asked.

"He just says the little bad words. The big ones he'll say

'blankety-blank' for. Like this here. He said it once the way it was: 'Ty Cobb is a . . . ' The other time he said the initials of it, 's.o.b.' And don't worry. I already know all those words anyway."

"How?" his mother asked.

"School," Teddy said. "Lonnie mostly. He says them a lot."

"Figures," his father muttered.

"The only thing Uncle Drew ever said that I don't know was 'brothel.' He said I was too young for it and that he'd get in trouble if he told me what it is. I looked it up and still don't know. What is it?"

His parents exchanged a look.

"First of all, good for Uncle Drew saying that," his mother answered. "You are too young to know what it is."

"It's a place where men pay women to spend time with them," his father said.

"Uncle Drew said he learned a lot in them."

"Oh, I would imagine he did," his father replied. "Those kind of women have quite a bit of knowledge to pass on."

His mother punched his father on the arm.

"Or so I've heard," he said.

"That's enough," she warned.

"Well, it sounds like you're getting quite an earful over there, son," his father said. "It's kind of amazing. Somebody ought to call Rayford Kennedy to interview Uncle Drew for the paper. Let him tell his story for the record."

Teddy had been thinking this ever since Uncle Drew began telling his stories. But as his own notes added up, he had begun to consider the idea of trying to write something himself—with Uncle Drew's permission.

"Might as well ask him and see anyway," his father said. "Say, why don't we have him over to supper one night? I'd like to hear some of these tales myself if he's willing to tell a couple. Reckon you could cook him something satisfactory, Mrs. Caldwell?"

"I reckon I surely could," his mother said.

She emphasized the word "reckon" with playful disdain.

"I reckon it'd be great," Teddy said.

"Oh, for heaven's sake," his mother protested.

Teddy wanted to go over and invite Uncle Drew right then, but he knew that the old man would be gone wherever it was he went in the evening. There was, of course, an even better way. He excused himself from the table and wrote his first note in a while.

You're invited to our house for supper tomorrow. Don't know what we'll have but my mama's a real good cook.
                                            Your neighbor,
                                             TCaldwell
                    P.S. We eat at six o'clock.

He slipped the note into an envelope, walked over and attached it to Uncle Drew's screen-door handle, and returned home.

"He'll answer in the morning," he said. "Like we did at first."

"Interesting system y'all have," his father said.

"I'll assume he'll accept and cook that way," his mother declared. "If he doesn't, we'll just have some leftovers."

"He'll accept," Teddy said.

He had no doubts about that. And sure enough, as Teddy expected, Mr. Bilberry brought Uncle Drew's response with the next morning's mail.

I bet she is and I accept the invite. Look forward to meeting her and your daddy.
                                            Your neighbor,
                                             AWeems

"Been a while since I had one of these to bring," Mr.

Bilberry said. "It's kind of like old times. Everything's all right, I trust?"

"Everything's fine," Teddy said.

"Any new news on your ballplayer?"

"Lots of it. Uncle Drew traveled with him."

"Uncle Drew?"

"It's what I call Mr. Weems. Bopeep did too."

"You don't say. Andrew was a ballplayer?"

"Not exactly. It's kind of a long story. Maybe he'll tell you sometime."

"I'd like to hear it. What I'd really like is another one of his pie samples. Always smells good over there."

"Except the day he made cabbage."

"Cabbage will foul up a kitchen. But it's some kind of good eating. You take care, now."

"Will do. You too."

For the second time in recent days Teddy felt lighter, as though something unpleasant had been lifted off him. He was glad to officially be back on good terms with Mr. Bilberry.

The house smelled like a café when Uncle Drew arrived, promptly at six, carrying a bouquet of flowers in a vase. He was dressed not in his usual overalls but in a suit and tie. The suit was brown, the tie burgundy. Teddy's mother set the flowers as the centerpiece on the table.

"There," she said. "What a thoughtful gesture, Mr. Weems."

"Call me Andrew," Uncle Drew said. "Better yet, call me Uncle Drew."

"Well, Uncle Drew," she said. "Welcome to our home."

"Much obliged," Uncle Drew said.

Teddy's father excused himself and told Teddy to come with him.

"I need to change and you do too," his father said. "I should've realized he'd dress up, man his age. They're more formal."

"Think we need ties?" Teddy asked.

"Not a bad idea," his father said.

When they returned to the kitchen, in fresh shirts and ties, Teddy's mother nodded approvingly. She herself always looked nice, no matter what she had on, and tonight she had on pressed tan slacks and a sleeveless white blouse.

Uncle Drew was sitting at the table holding a glass of ice tea. He was saying that, yes, the car in his shed was in fact originally owned by Ty Cobb, the famous ballplayer, that, no, he'd never thought of looking into how much it might be worth to a collector because wasn't a figure nobody could name would match what it was worth to him, and that, well, there wasn't much way Teddy could possibly be enjoying listening any more than he was enjoying talking.

Teddy and his parents joined Uncle Drew at the table. Teddy's father said a short blessing and they passed the plates around.

"So," Teddy began. "Yesterday y'all had won the car and were in South Carolina. It was almost Christmas."

"Must've been nice not having to worry about transportation," his father said.

There was a long pause.

"I mean, after y'all got the car and everything," his father said.

Teddy had wondered about this. Uncle Drew's habit, he knew, was to eat without talking. He did it every day during dinner at his house, and now it looked as if he was going to do it during supper at Teddy's. The old man took a bite, chewed it, and swallowed nodding. He sipped his tea. Teddy was trying to think of a question to get him talking, but that turned out not to be necessary.

Certainly was [Uncle Drew said], since we was now on the road on our own terms. Had Christmas dinner in the kitchen of a hotel in Savannah. Couldn't have it in the dining room out front for the usual reason, but much like what happened to us over in El Paso and other places I ain't mentioned, we got the royal treatment out back. This become a fairly regular occurrence. We'd try our luck at the desk, get told no soap or worse, and find ourselves back on the sidewalk or, as Bopeep called it, the banquette. After a while we hit on the idea of having him act like my servant, but all that achieved for us was to get me welcome and him dismissed or at best offered other quarters. Not a single farming desk clerk at a single farming hotel we presented ourselves in where white people lodged ever just said, "Yes, we have a double-occupancy room available. How long will you gentlemen be staying with us?" It was always, "We're pleased to offer you a room, sir"—meaning me—"but the boy"—meaning Bopeep, naturally, even though I was the only boy in our pair—"the boy ain't welcome."

Course "boy" wasn't the way they put it most times, as you can imagine. Only good thing about it was afterward we'd more often than not be directed on the sly by a doorman or a bellboy to a friendly table or even a few times a friendly hotel. Folks that ran them didn't blink an eye at me, didn't look at Bopeep and say, "Nice to have you with us, sir, but the ofay needs to move along." Generally speaking, whites treated Bopeep like a diseased dog. And blacks, generally speaking, treated me like a human being. Generally speaking, now. There was a few to turn their mouths down at me. And I swear I's almost glad to see it happen, because it allowed me to think I knew how Bopeep felt.

One time I said this to him and he said, "You ain't. You can't." Which brought that discussion to a quick conclusion. I was embarrassed for thinking it. How could I have any idea how it felt to everywhere you went without exception be reminded that the majority of a entire race of people looked at you like you wasn't worth the time it'd take them to spit in your face? But Bopeep kept whatever he thought in return to himself. He literally could've bought and sold 90 percent of them people but he never argued, never protested, never called their hand—except as I've already told Teddy here there was once upon a time in a Mississippi hobo camp he put a fellow deep into his place.

Anyway, all of these other folks we was told to look up would have a bite for us to eat. Some had places for us to stay too but some didn't, which when that happened we always had the car. The old gal give us shelter many's the night. And it was about this time when my education in cooking got full speed under way. Had a lot of cooks in a lot of kitchens show me how they done things. I always liked eating just plain old Southern "batter it and throw it in some lard" best, but there's a world of flavors to put together if you know what you're up to, like Bess back in Texas did, and we run into some folks who knew exactly her kind of what they was up to. I didn't realize until later how much of it I absorbed. Had no idea how well it'd serve me neither.

We made kind of a square with a *x* through it—up to the North, across to the Midwest, back down into and across the South, then up again going diagonal, back across opposite how we done it the first time, and finally another opposite cross headed for New Orleans, which was where Bopeep said all along'd be the last stop and was, though not in the way either of us expected. Had us a bad run-in on the way that changed everything, ended it, in fact. But that's still to come and I'd rather not spoil everybody's meal here—fine meal, by the way, just awful good. Best not to ruin it.

Now I'd told my mama the day I left that I'd send money home if I ever made any and I had the good intention of doing just that. Problem was twofold. First, except for them five dollars Bopeep give me in Shreveport, I hadn't had any in hand. Second, I never thought to ask him for any even though I was technically speaking in charge of it. I took it from the batters, I counted and logged it in the books, and I secured it in the suitcase. Well, sir, come Christmas night in Savannah, what do you know but he up and says to me, said, "Believe it's time I put you on salary, Uncle Drew. Couldn't be doing none of this without you."

"Shoot," I said. "You could find anybody to catch you, Bopeep."

And he said, "Ain't could find no better friend, though," and handed me five brand-new one-hundred-dollar bills.

Now that was a frightening amount of wages for a kid from Oil Camp, Louisiana, never had two dimes to rub together other than that day in Shreveport to find hisself all of a sudden holding. I didn't know what to say and, after I caught my breath enough to, said so.

"Ain't no need to say nothing, Uncle Drew," Bopeep said. "Money yours. You earn it."

"Thank you, Bopeep," I said. "Thank you, thank you, thank you."

He held up a hand, them long fingers of his looking like spokes on a wagon wheel, and said, "Believe I'm thanked. Do believe I thoroughly be appreciated."

I wired half of it home along with a message saying no need to worry, I's fine. Course there wasn't no way for them to get in touch with me and there wasn't no way for me to know what was going on back here in Oil Camp. Made me a little homesick to think it but I was having too much of a time to let that get any kind of a hold on me. I started wiring an amount regularly, keeping in touch from my side even if they couldn't from theirs. Made me feel good, proud of myself. I knew it was a big help. Little did I know that they never saw a penny of it because things had changed considerable since I threw in with Bopeep. But that's another not-for-now story that I'll leave dangling. You have the bottom-line detail, which is enough.

What we done was I drove and the Dodger rode. He

pitched and I caught. I kept the records, as y'all've seen, down to the penny, and he trusted me to. I also kept our clothes cleaned and our shoes shined. Bopeep wore a suit at all times. Never changed that habit. I tried a set of dungarees we bought in a store in St. Louis for a few days but I didn't care for them and went back to my overalls for good. Worn them regular every day of my life other'n ones involving a special occasion such as this evening.

And that's how we traveled all throughout the next year and into the next. We slowed down the wagering a little bit after while, got to where we'd land someplace and just see the sights. Went to some ballgames too. Saw Satchel Paige play. Saw Josh Gibson play. Saw Buck Leonard play. One time up in Pittsburgh I asked Bopeep why he didn't go talk to somebody about a tryout. Without hesitating a beat he eased one of his big old hands into his trousers pocket and tweezed out just enough of a roll of bills for me to see.

"I know all that," I said. "But don't you want to prove you can play with these people?"

He shook his head.

"No need to, Uncle Drew," he said. "You know I could. I know I could. What I need to for?"

But I knew he also knew that that kind of knowing ain't really good enough in the end. So I started working on him, dropping in a comment about it ever' once in a while. He wouldn't say nothing at first but after while I could tell I was beginning to get to him a little bit.

Then one morning—don't recollect exactly where we was, somewhere out in Ohio—we was driving along and he says to me, said, "What'd you do if I was to go back to the uniform, Uncle Drew?"

And I said, "Why, I'd be there every time you took the mound."

"No," he said. "I mean, what'd you *do?* Man can't just go to ballgames every day."

Well, I was immediately mixed. I's glad to hear him toying with the idea on the one hand but on the other I took his point about where it'd leave me, which was on my own.

"Maybe I could get me a job with whatever team you'd be on," I said.

"Pretty sure the colored clubs wouldn't hire no white boy," he said. "And I be more than pretty sure ain't no white clubs hiring no colored players."

I thought about that a minute. He was of course right. I had no prospects in baseball, least not Negro League baseball. Then I realized that what we was talking about, if we was really talking about him getting back into the organized game, was the end of something, about heading our separate ways. I'd thought about it off and on along the way, knew the day'd eventually come, and here I was might actually be looking at the beginning of it.

"We really talking about this, Bo?" I said.

"I think maybe we really is," he said. "Been studying on it ever since other day I showed you that wad of money at the game. We done had ourself a time out here, just about the best time I ever had, but I'm starting up to wondering if maybe I might be selling myself short just herding these has-beens and never-wases. I'm wondering if maybe I ought not to go back and find out what I could do when somebody be a right-now-is ballplayer stand in."

"You already know that," I said.

"Know what I think, is all," he said. "It a start, but thinking and doing be two different things."

"I'd hate to give up being on the road with you, Bo," I said. "But I sure would love to see you herd some real sheep for a change."

Well, it's something we'll just have to wonder about because it didn't happen. Couldn't happen. Never seen a man throw a ball like he did. Nobody else never did neither. That's a fact. I sincerely believe he would have become a legend like Paige or, shoot, how about Feller or Koufax? A real legend, I'm talking about, and not just a tall-tale legend or like what they call in Teddy here's article a footnote, which is all he'll ever be. He walked away from the bus that day and never got back on.

"What if somebody was to interview you and set the story straight in the paper?" Teddy's father asked.

"It'd still be the same story," Uncle Drew said.

"But it wouldn't be apocryphal anymore," Teddy replied. "We have the record."

"No," Uncle Drew said. "I don't suppose it would. But except for that one episode early on—and, course, his time with the Po' Boys—he never faced what nobody'd consider legitimate competition."

"That's beside the point," Teddy's father said. "Who knows what some of those batters he did face might've been handed under the right circumstances? Who knows how many people could have been great ballplayers, great artists, or great what-have-yous under different circumstances? There are a lot of batters in those books, hundreds of them, and from what I can tell only a handful even got the stick around before you were throwing the ball back to him, much less made contact. It might've been some of them could've become household names too if they'd played ball instead of whatever it was they did do."

"It's a consideration," Uncle Drew said.

The supper they'd eaten, cooked by Teddy's mother, was veal cutlets on rice with cream gravy, Brussels sprouts, and buttered rolls. Dessert was carrot cake.

Chapter 20

Instead of telling Teddy another story the next day, Uncle Drew had something else in mind and had him go fetch his baseball.

"Spent the night thinking about a couple of things," he said. "One of them is what your daddy had to say about sitting down with a newspaperman. Don't believe I'll do it."

Teddy started to protest but Uncle Drew held up a hand.

"I'm calling it this way for now," he said. "I'm giving you the story and like I done told you, I'm giving it to you because you like baseball. You're a safe place for it. Do with it what you will. Other thing I thought about last night is I'd like to put the idea of being able to move out of the field and onto the mound in your mind. I picked up quite a few tricks catching for Bopeep and ain't never had nobody to pass them on to. Seems to me it'd be a shame to let them go to waste. Interested?"

"Sure," Teddy said.

"Course I'm too old to squat down and catch you. But we ain't going to have you throw just yet anyway. All I want you to do right now is be holding the ball in your hand."

And so Teddy's education as a pitcher began. First the high kick, which was awkward at first but became more comfortable after he'd done it a few times. Next the backward lean, which seemed even more awkward than the kick and took longer to perfect. Finally the delivery. Kick, lean, deliver. Uncle Drew had him practice each element separately. The kick—again and again Teddy bent his knee and then extended his leg like a ballerina. The lean—again and again Teddy bent himself back until his knuckles were almost touching the ground. The delivery— again and again Teddy brought his arm up and over so that his entire weight would be behind the ball when he threw it. He practiced in exaggerated slow motion with Uncle Drew's hand against his back when he bent, then he practiced at regular speed.

After a few mornings of this, Uncle Drew said it was time to look at different ways of gripping the ball. He adjusted Teddy's fingers in various combinations and in various ways on the seams.

"There's names for all this," he said. "But Bopeep preferred those numbers of his, which I didn't even know he had until one day he just up and started saying to the batters, 'Got a three for you, sheeps,' or 'Ready for a five, sheeps?' I went out and asked him what he was talking about and he said, 'Them be my pitches, Uncle Drew. Different number, different throw.' And I said, 'Why didn't you never tell me this, and besides that, why don't you just call them their names?' And he said, 'Ain't know they name. Just know what the ball do. Number one go thisaway, number two thataway. Ain't told you because I just ain't. Never thought to. Ain't no need I can see.'"

"They won't let us throw curveballs yet," Teddy said.

"Figures. I swear before all's said and done, if we keep on protecting ourselves from every possibility with rules and regulations, there won't nobody be able to do nothing, ever. We'll all be sitting with our hands on our knees staring straight ahead."

About the only time Teddy didn't have the ball in his hand was when he took a shower or ate. He actually did try to eat with it but he had to put it down to cut his meat and he didn't like the awkward way the fork felt in his left hand. At night he read (or scanned) with it and it was with him when he drifted into sleep. After a while the ball had begun to feel like it was a part of him.

One day Uncle Drew took him to his backyard, where he'd rigged up a pillow between two stakes. The pillow was in a white case that had a red circle about the size of a grapefruit drawn on it.

"Don't have no mound for you," Uncle Drew said. "But you don't need no mound. Bopeep never had one neither. Imagine the speed he could've come at them with throwing from a mound. How far y'all away from each other in the small leagues these days?"

"It's sixty feet between the bases," Teddy said. "That's all I know."

"Well, let's make it fifty from pitcher to catcher, then," Uncle Drew said. "Won't be no further'n that."

He took a tape measure and had Teddy hold one end of it below the bottom edge of the pillow, then he walked it to its length, which was thirty feet. Teddy moved to that spot and Uncle Drew went back another twenty feet. Teddy found a brick by Uncle Drew's shed to mark the location.

The next lesson was devoted to accuracy.

"We ain't interested in nothing but hitting the target," Uncle Drew said. "Don't even need to find the circle yet, just anywhere on the pillow'll do. Don't aim. Throw. And easy does it right now. Hold it however you want to."

Teddy quickly discovered that he had a knack for placing the ball. He would throw it, the pillow would block it, and Uncle Drew would return it to him. Each time he got the go-ahead to throw a little harder, he was pleased to see that his accuracy did not diminish. Finally Uncle Drew let him cut loose and he was just as accurate throwing full speed as he was throwing easy.

"Well, now, there you go," Uncle Drew said. "I thought we might find a hidden talent in there somewhere if we looked hard enough. Your call whether you want to reveal it or not. Won't bother me a bit if you decide to stay in the outfield."

Teddy had never thought of himself as a pitcher before. Nobody else ever had either. The men who coached his teams always came with their minds made up about who would play where, and since he'd always been in right field, he assumed that's where he'd be this season. He knew he could pitch, though, so maybe he'd give it a try—if the coaches would let him.

"Thanks, Uncle Drew," he said.

"You're welcome, Teddy."

They walked around the house and took their seats on the porch, Uncle Drew in his rocker, Teddy in the lawn chair.

"Do I look like Bopeep throwing?" he asked.

"Impossible to look like Bopeep throwing," Uncle Drew said. "Unless you're Bopeep."

"Been a while since you told me anything else about y'all," Teddy said.

Uncle Drew nodded.

"Maybe what I ought to do is tell you that we parted the ways with a handshake and that everything turned out just dandy," he said.

"But you already told me enough for me to know that even if y'all did, there was a lot of leading up to it."

The old man stared across the way deep in thought for a moment, as was his habit before he began talking. Teddy watched him, waiting.

He was one of a kind in several ways [Uncle Drew said] and how he threw a baseball qualifies for that category. That way-back lean of his looked funny but wasn't nobody laughing when he delivered. Now like I was saying the other evening, we got to where we wasn't working too hard scaring up people to try their luck ever' day. We'd earned a sizeable amount of money and I could tell that Bopeep was beginning to go through the motions a little bit. You can look in that last book toward the end and see that he even gave up quite a few more hits than he normally did. Don't know if this was on purpose or if he had his mind on our conversation about calling our travels finished or just what was going on, but something was. I decided I'd rather let him say what it was than press the matter. Finally he spoke up. I remember it clear as day because it meant we wasn't just talking no more. After nearly three years we'd reached the homestretch, marked by the bridge over the river around Ashland, Kentucky. We's about halfway across it when Bopeep raises up and says, "Let's go to the house, Uncle Drew."

He was in the backseat, which he done the first time as a joke but then got to where he liked being able to stretch out back there. I never did teach him how to drive, by the way. By now, course, I had a license. Got it up in North Carolina— no test. Talked our way into a registration too, said the car was a gift left me by my granddaddy's will that had burned along with all his other papers, including the original bill of sale and registration, in the fire that killed him. Had the man so upset he started filling us out a replacement before we got the story all the way told. So now we was legitimate, which meant we didn't have to keep our eyes quite so peeled for almighty John Law on the highway.

I looked at the Dodger in the mirror. He was leaned back against the door with his legs on the seat. Wasn't looking at me but out the window, just watching that pretty Kentucky country go by. We'd come a long way since those days on the train out in Texas.

I said, "Been wondering when you was going to say it."

And he said, "Yeah, I don't know. I mean we could do this for the rest of our life if we wanted to, but me, I ain't be all that much wanting to. You?"

"Your call, Bopeep," I said. "You the moneymaker of this

organization. You decide not to keep on with it, what else can I do but go along?"

He thought a minute, then he said, "I wouldn't quit just yet you don't want me to, Uncle Drew."

I said I appreciated that, said, "We been pretty good partners, ain't we?"

And he said, "Sure has, Uncle Drew. Sure has."

We rode along for a little while before he said, "All this time we done spent out on the road together and here I am ain't never tell you about my gal."

Course, I laughed at that, said, "Bo, you have done told me about so many gals I lost count a long time ago. Believe one of the first things you ever told me was about some gal in Arkansas."

And he said, "I mean my real gal. All them other ones just sporting gals see me while I'm in town. Wasn't nothing serious. Shoot."

"I thought you was just thinking about really pitching again," I said. "Not being tore up about some gal."

"Oh, it about a even call betwixt the two," he said.

I looked at him in the mirror again, and if it was possible for a fellow black as Bopeep was to blush, he was blushing. It was like he was embarrassed, which I couldn't imagine. Bopeep had a way with the gals. Never did myself, not like him anyway. I always liked them plenty and a few liked me back but tell you the truth I had two things going against me. First, I was shy. Second, I wasn't the settling-down kind, which is why I never took a bride. Now on the surface of it you'd think it was the opposite, that I's the one who'd wind up wanting to leave off rambling due to pining for a special gal and Bopeep'd keep moving on from town to town and gal to gal. Wasn't the case.

"You been in touch with her?" I said.

"Ain't been but should have," he said. "Think she'll still have me, Uncle Drew?"

"How should I know?" I said. "I ain't heard tell of her till two minutes ago."

And he said, "Lord, Lord."

We drove on through Kentucky and into Tennessee. Had the radio out of Nashville tuned in, which you'll recall me telling you that Bopeep was partial to the country music. We pulled it in ever'where we went, heard Roy Acuff and Bob Wills, Gene Autry and, course, the Carter Family. I reckon "Right or Wrong" was his favorite number. It'd come on and he'd sing along, beginning to end. Couldn't sing a lick neither, which I always got a kick out of. That day we had the WSM going and it come on.

"That you in this song, Bopeep?" I said.

"I sure do hope it ain't," he said.

If you ain't never heard it, it's about a man done lost his gal but still loves her and always will.

"Tell me about her," I said. "Like what is her name?"

"Name Dolores," he said.

Then he started to talking and didn't stop for a hour. Dolores Capanel was of course the best-looking and smartest gal ever put on lipstick. He'd known her all his life, couldn't remember not anyway. And on and on. I just let him talk. I guess it was one of them things happens to a fellow sometimes. He ain't been home in dog near three years, ain't mentioned that gal a single time, and now getting there and finding her was the one thing on his mind.

"Yeah," he said. "You know, me and her might get wound back up together and start us a family. I got enough money we already way ahead. Tell you what else, Uncle Drew. I lately been thinking hard about them games we seen. Didn't let on how much they got to me at the time. Po' Boys drew some folks out to the game but nothing like that. Might be a thing I'd like, playing with one of the big clubs."

And I said, "All you got to do is get in touch with the

right folks and arrange you a tryout, show them what you can do. They'd be lined up to sign you."

"Might just, Uncle Drew," he said. "Might just."

"We could go to Memphis right now," I said. "Find somebody associated with the Red Sox."

He didn't say anything for a few minutes, so I knew he was seriously studying the idea. I wish now I'd took it on myself to head us that way without even saying it, but I didn't.

Finally Bopeep said, "Naw, I better find Dolores first. There be plenty of time for the baseball."

I should've at least kept driving. If I had, everything might've went the way I was seeing it in my head, Bopeep finding his gal and getting settled in one way or another with her and then getting back to situated with a club again. It's what he was meant to do. Watching him throw and catching what he throwed all that time we traveled around convinced me that he had greatness in him and just needed to understand that the only way to tap into it was to step back on the bus and play some real ball. Wouldn't be but a matter of time before somebody saw him and he'd have a place up there in front of the big crowds against the big players in the big stadiums where he belonged. But we was tired of driving and needed to get out for at least a bite, if not a nap.

Stopped in a town south of Nashville called Columbia, which had a history we didn't know nothing about and would've passed right on through if we had. Bad things'd happened there in the past and bad things was fixing to happen there in the future. Bad racial things, I'm talking about. Lynchings and riots. Well, one riot. Happened just after World War II, when a black man and his mother got into it with a white man. Turned ugly in a hurry and wound up in the national press. It was mayhem. Took everything a future Supreme Court justice by the name of Thurgood

Marshall could come up with in the courtroom to get the black folks acquitted that went on trial for attempted murder, which they was charged with though all they was doing was protecting their homes and businesses from being destroyed by a mob that come into their section of town and just about tore it all to pieces.

The lynchings was still recent memory. Same old story— black men wrongly accused of attacking white girls and didn't get punished enough to suit certain people, never mind that there wasn't nothing to punish them for—and those certain people taking matters into their own hands. Vigilante justice, it's called, like in the Wild West. What it is is inexcusable behavior, and me and Bopeep seen it up close and personal. I didn't lose him the way the friends and family of Henry Chote and Cord Cheek lost them, with a noose around their neck, but I did see him get pretty bad hurt over nothing but walking down the street. Took a beating myself because I happened to be with him.

Now this was early in the morning when we pulled in there. We parked and got out and stretched good. Wasn't nobody about yet so we just took a stroll thinking we'd eventually kill enough time to where somebody'd open and we could get a bite of breakfast. Then we'd be on our way. First folks I noticed was these three fellows about Bopeep's age headed down the other side of the street. I caught one's eye and nodded. You know, just a nod like a how-you-doing tilt of the head. He didn't nod back and I thought nothing more about it until a couple of minutes later I realized we was being followed. I turned my head and it was them three fellows.

They caught up to us and one of them said, "You say something to me back yonder, nigger?"

"Just keep walking, Uncle Drew," Bopeep said. "Anything happen, you get on out away from here and don't look back."

And I said, "I ain't going nowhere."

Then I hear one of the three fellows say, "I'm talking to you, boy, and you best look here and give me a answer. What was it you said back there?"

Bopeep stopped and turned around. I did the same. Two of the fellows looked alike enough they had to been brothers. Had oiled hair and eyes sunk in looked like shadows around them. Faces was sharp like blades. They was stout fellows, wide at the shoulder like their buddy.

"Niggers belong in Mink Slide, boy," the buddy said.

"Why, we's just headed there," Bopeep said.

"But you ain't made it yet now, have you, boy?" the buddy said.

Now this was the one time of everything that happened to us I was genuinely scared. These fellows wasn't going to be put off by no show like we done for the yard bull in Shreveport and they wasn't going to stand in and let Bopeep pitch to them like the sheriff in Alabama. They meant to cause us some trouble. All three had a mean look about them, and you could tell when they talked they wasn't the brightest bulbs on the string, which being both mean and stupid is the worst combination you can run into.

I said, "Why don't y'all just tell us where Mink Slide is and we'll be on our way."

And the buddy said, "Your nigger friend just said y'all was headed there, stranger. I reckon he must've been lying if y'all need directions."

And Bopeep said, "Way I figure it, y'all want us to head on over there, we say we appreciate the tip and be headed on over there. Wasn't no lie. All we need to know is which way the fastest to get us to it."

"I believe we got us a uppity nigger here, boys," the buddy said. "I don't much care for a uppity nigger myself. Y'all?"

The other two looked off for a second. One of them started scraping the sidewalk with the toe of his boot. The other one spat.

"Nope," the first one said.

And then, like they was responding to a cue of some kind, their buddy moved around behind me fast as a snake and grabbed me in a bear hug, while the other two, the brothers, began pushing Bopeep—not hard enough to make him lose his footing, just enough to get him going backward. I started kicking at the one was holding me, but that just made him tighten his grip. He moved one of his arms up around my neck.

"Be still, blankety-blank," he said. "You don't I'll strangle the nigger-loving life out of you."

My heart was hammering. This wasn't no situation like we'd ever been in. It was serious trouble and I didn't see no good way out of it. Meantime, the brothers had moved Bopeep around a corner and into an alleyway out of my sight. Like I said, this was early in the morning so wasn't nobody around to help us. Not that anybody in that part of town would've necessarily taken up our cause, but my eyes was peeled just in case.

After giving me a good long squeeze I thought for a second was fixing to be all she wrote, the one holding me sort of half-picked me up and half-dragged me over to where the brothers and Bopeep done disappeared around the corner. When we got there, I saw something made me sick. Bopeep was down on his knees and one of them had Bo's arm bent up in the air behind him. His left arm, the one he threw with. The other'n was slowly circling him and pausing to give him a kick every so often. Full force. He was kicking him wherever he took a notion—back, sides, stomach, face. I yelled at him to stop but the one holding me put his hand over my mouth.

"Y'all save me some of that," he said.

"Get on over here then," the brother holding Bopeep's arm said.

Just as he said it the other'n lifted his knee up to his chin, launched himself off the ground, and came down with his entire weight on Bopeep's shoulder, which caused him to make the most godawful sound I ever heard come out of a man. It was pure screaming agony.

"Look, Cecil," the one holding him says. "You done tore this monkey's arm clean off."

Then he twisted it and I could see that Bopeep's shoulder had to've been completely ripped out of its socket. It was like a doll's arm. About that time the one holding me pushed me away and so hard I didn't have time to get my hands out in front of me, so that the first thing to hit the ground was the side of my face.

"He's a baseball player," I said.

The one who'd come down on him said, "Is that a fact? Well, I don't believe niggers deserve to play the great American game of baseball."

I scrambled to my knees but the one who'd pushed me down kicked me in the ribs and I buckled. I bunched up into a ball trying to protect myself. Wasn't nothing else to do. The kicks kept coming. Then one landed just behind my ear. There was a flash of pure white light, and the next thing I remember clear I was getting my head dabbed with cool water.

I opened my eyes and immediately closed them against the sunlight coming through the window of the room I was in. I tried to sit up but couldn't for the pain in my ribs and elsewhere. I heard a voice say, "There, there. You rest now." I opened my eyes again but the sunlight was like a stabbing dagger so I knew I needed to keep them shut.

"Bopeep?" I said.

But there wasn't no answer.

"Was he all right?" Teddy asked.

Uncle Drew shook his head.

"Was he . . . did they—"

Teddy couldn't finish the question. He looked at Uncle Drew, who was staring into the distance as he had been since he began talking. The old man seemed shaken by his memory. Teddy watched him, feeling sick. It was like the first wave of fever settling in before the flu, when everything becomes dreamy and strange. Uncle Drew looked as though he felt the same way. Teddy stood up and put his hand on the old man's shoulder. He stayed that way for a long time before he returned to his chair.

"Appreciate that," Uncle Drew said. "I needed me a second there."

"I ain't in no hurry," Teddy said.

Chapter 21

Answer to your questions [Uncle Drew said] is to the first, no, and to the second, they did not. Son of a bitches like to, though. Sure did. Sure did. But they didn't.

House we was in belonged to a woman called Mama Pearl and her husband, June, last name of Clifton. They insisted on me calling them Mama Pearl and June, and I got used to it even though I considered it disrespectful at first. It was June found us in the alley and carried us out there. Literally loaded Bopeep up like a dead deer in the bed of his truck. Had me set up against the door riding shotgun, but I tell you that not from memory but because it's what he told me. I have no recollection of anything from the time that kick hit the side of my head and I entered that flash of white light till I woke up in a place smelled like fried food and smoke and turned earth. It was a strange odor but by no means unpleasant.

June said he thought he'd come upon a murder scene when he saw us. We was busted all to pieces and out cold. Him and Mama Pearl put me in their room. They just completely gave up their bed for me. Bopeep they settled in the one Mama Pearl used when folks would come to her for their healing. She was a midwife and she knew some rudimentary medicine. Had her some cures stored. Roots and leaves, that sort of thing. Home remedies you eat and drink that work out from the stomach into the blood and on to the necessary places. Awful-smelling broths that tasted even worse, what of it she had me take down. She

191

said things too, musical things in a language I couldn't understand and she wouldn't translate.

"Can't be English," she said. "English ain't got power like this do. These old, old words go back across the waves. They clean words from before here."

Being a farmer, June had a knowledge of animals and how they move he could apply to humans. Between the two of them they got Bopeep put back together enough to satisfy theirself that he wasn't going to cross over. His arm was ruined, though. Those three fellows really did dog near tear it off. Imagine pulling apart a chicken wing to eat it. That's what they done. Muscles, tendons, cartilage, the ball in the socket, nerves—all of it was traumaticalized. He should've had surgery but who'd perform surgery on a black man? June did best he could to arrange everything back to where it was supposed to be and fixed it between two slats he tied in place with rags. And Mama Pearl had those remedies. They said he'd be all right in the sense of not dead but he'd most likely never be able to use his arm for anything more than something to fill a sleeve with.

I learned all this from June the afternoon of the second day when I was up to talking a little bit. Still could hardly keep my eyes open against any kind of light at all. Headache I had was the worst I ever experienced. We both had cracked ribs and Bopeep's face was a mess of cuts and bruises. His nose was of course broken too and several of his teeth were gone. June said he'd considered taking me over to the hospital because he knew they'd admit me but figured me and Bopeep was somehow together and didn't want to separate us.

He said, "I guess they might've took him down to the basement maybe, bad hurt as he was, but wasn't no use letting them do that and him have to wait for them to get around to taking a look. He needed some care right away. Shame about that arm."

And I said, "He's a baseball player. He pitches like nobody you ever seen."

"Which arm do he throw with?" June said.

There was a kind of hopeful note in his voice when he said it. But when I opened my eyes and told him he just shook his head.

"That mean he through then," he said.

The reality of that didn't register on me. It was just something you hear but don't think about, like on the news when they say this many thousand of folks have died in a earthquake or that many hundred went down in a plane. You can't get your mind to it because your mind knows if you did, the sorrow of it would destroy you. I even had the thought that maybe Bopeep could somehow learn to throw with his good arm, his right one. That's how far away from the here's-what's-been-dealt fact of the matter I was, how far away from it I had to be just then. Even if he could do that impossible thing, a right-handed Bopeep would make about as much sense as a map showing the state of Louisiana turned the other way.

The hell of the whole thing—and I mean this in the literal sense of what you think Hell might actually be—the hell of all this is that there was nothing we could do in the way of obtaining justice. We was victims of a crime and victims was all we'd ever be. Wasn't a thing in the world ever going to bring them fellows before a judge and a jury. And even if there was, the judge and the jury wouldn't have nothing to go on except what the three of them said and what the two of us said. Not much of a mystery whose side they'd've took. We'd most likely've wound up in trouble for making a false accusation. This wasn't my thinking at the time. I wanted to go to the police. I wanted to see them boys suffer somehow, not for what they done to me but for what they done to Bopeep. They would've left me alone if I'd been alone. Him too if he'd been white. But that's some mighty big ifs. I wasn't alone and he wasn't white. It was when I mentioned this that June and Mama Pearl told me about the lynchings they'd had in Columbia, the last one just a few years before.

"We knew them boys," Mama Pearl said. "Sure did. They ain't done a thing and the shame of it is they come a hair from everything turning out all right. Ain't how it work out for them, though, and I pray to the Lord Jesus every night since they threw poor Henry off the courthouse for things to be different. Then they went and done the same thing to poor Cord."

And June said, "Jesus know He done give us everything we need for it not to be like it is. All we got to do be to make use of what we has. Be easy's that for us to get along. Peoples just don't want to."

"But I could identify them," I said.

Mama Pearl smiled a sad little smile at that.

"Sure you could, child," she said, "but it ain't make no difference. All they do'd be say they's on the river when it happen. They say they sorry's can be about it. They say they wish you well finding out who done it."

Later, when he got to where he could sit up and talk, Bopeep said almost exactly the same thing, said, "Uncle Drew, one of these days you be fixing to learn it ain't how it ought to be that turn the world. World turn on how it do be. Was just you they swarm maybe you got a case. Wasn't just you. You with me. They ain't nobody on your side. I hate it just much as you is. But look here. We fine."

And I said, "You ain't fine, Bopeep. You ain't never, ever going to pitch again."

Which was when the full truth of the situation hit me like a shot cannonball. I knew it was true all along but I knew it like a idea. Saying it made it a fact. He really wasn't going to throw a baseball ever again. I looked at him laying up there in that bed with his arm between them two

boards and his face still swole up and leaking blood out
the ragged stitches Mama Pearl had done her best to sew
him up with and then came the tears in a rushing flood.
I couldn't stop them. I sobbed to where I couldn't get my
breath.

Mama Pearl knelt in front of me and held out her big old
arms. I leaned over so she could put them around me. I let
myself go limp and she hummed and rocked me back and
forth until I was finally cried out.

She said, "It a mean world, child, sure is. It a mean,
mean world."

"Is that," June said.

"Why?" I said.

"There now," Mama Pearl said. "Just rest a spell."

I guess we stayed with them good folks for three weeks.
Shortly after we got there June and a man he knew had
went into town and picked up the car for us. I don't
remember telling him about it or giving him the keys but
I must've done both. My head wasn't clear for a few days.
The car was unharmed, which surprised me. I figured them
fellows'd most likely either taken hammers to it or else
drove it away for their own. Guess they didn't associate
it with us. When we was finally able to be on our way
Mama Pearl and June sent us off with a basket of enough
food to feed Communist China. We had pork chops and
chicken, biscuits and beans, two pies and several jars of
well water and tea, all of it packed with what you couldn't
call nothing but love. Mama Pearl also put in some bottles
of remedy and told us to be sure to take it all down, which
we promised to do and did. How could you not? Tasted a
little worse every time but we figured she knew best.

Before we left we tried to pay them for their trouble.
Wasn't too much laughter during our stay but we heard
some then. Mama Pearl said she ought to whip us both for
suggesting such a thing.

And June said, "Y'all boys ain't owe us nothing. We just glad we able to offer y'all a hand in your hour. Don't be no need to start in arguing about it neither."

Which we didn't do. We did pay them though. Left them a couple of hundred dollars to find under one of the pillows on Bopeep's bed. That wouldn't near cover what all they done for us—no amount could—but we agreed they'd come upon it and understand our gratitude. I always wondered about the conversation they had when they stripped off the sheets Bopeep'd been resting on and discovered it.

Now, of course, Bopeep was by no means fully recovered. He was in a great deal of pain and he had a hard time getting comfortable. The other problem was, since it was his left shoulder giving him such a time, he had to lay with it away from the back of the seat—with his head behind me, in other words. I didn't like not being able to glance into the mirror and catch his eye every once in a while like I normally did when we was on the road talking. All I could see was his knees sticking up. But we made do. And he slept quite a bit anyway, which left me to my thoughts. I knew we was coming to the end of our travels and I wasn't sure what I was going to do once we got him home and, we both hoped, back into the arms of his girl Dolores. As you know, I'd completely lost contact with my family. Didn't have no idea the funds I'd sent their way never made it to them because they was gone, which I'll tell you the details of in due time.

I was also seventeen years old by then and unlike Bopeep had lost all sense of my ties. Coming back here didn't seem like too much of a viable alternative. Maybe there'll be something for me in New Orleans, I thought. Or maybe I'll light out on my own. I felt like I could take care of myself. In some ways it'd be easier, which to think that made me feel bad, because I knew I wasn't thinking it except in terms of him being black and me being white.

Economically it made no sense at all. I didn't make a dime out there. He made it all. If you know what irony is you'll understand how ironic this whole thing was. Here it is the slap middle of the Great Depression and people are standing in lines to get a bite to eat. Black folks are treated like criminals. Their prospects, to say the least, are severely limited. Yet me and Bopeep had more money than we knew what to do with. We was rich by any standard and all because people who didn't have anything to start with were willing to play a game of chance. I probably should've felt bad about that but I didn't. We wasn't making them stand in for them pitches. They chose to do that on their own, just like a fellow goes to the racetrack and buys a ticket on a horse. Nobody hauls him to the window by the scruff of the neck and says he has to. He does it because he's willing to take a chance. Never mind that he'd be better off keeping his money in his pocket ninety-nine times out of a hundred. But he keeps going to the window, believing in that one time. Them fellows that came up to bat against Bopeep was laying odds on themselves being able to connect.

Funny thing about all that. Wasn't but that once with Ty Cobb I ever seen anybody think about employing the bunt. We might've been in a different story altogether otherwise. Anyway, all in all, I considered what we done a legitimate enterprise. We played a fair game. Only trick we had was what Bopeep could make a baseball do. Lord, I look back sometimes and wonder what would've become of him if he'd stuck with the Po' Boys. Wonder what my own life'd been like, which I suppose everybody does at some point. They look in the mirror and say if this and if that then what? Well, who knows? Only thing for sure is, what happens happens.

"Like me breaking your window," Teddy said.

"Like that."

"Where do you go every day in your truck?" Teddy asked.

"Riding," Uncle Drew said.

"Riding where?"

"Here and there. Go by the store and pick up a few things for our dinner. Go out by where our place was. That's all erased now but I can remember. I can show you the exact spot where the bus broke down. Something happened everywhere you look. I also go down to the hospital in Pineview, visit folks need visiting. Take the leftovers I don't send home with you to folks look like they might need it."

Teddy felt better than he had earlier now that he knew the outcome of Uncle Drew and Bopeep's encounter in Tennessee. It was bad but it easily could have been much worse. He studied Uncle Drew. It was well past noon and telling the long story, reliving it, had taken something out of the old man. Normally at this point in their visits they would go inside and eat dinner. Teddy wasn't sure that was going to happen this time and wouldn't have minded if it didn't.

"Well," he said. "I guess I better get going and let you rest."

"Hate not to serve you a bite before you leave," Uncle Drew said.

"You feel up to it today?" Teddy asked.

"I always feel up to setting a plate in front of a fellow," Uncle Drew said. "Let's us go see what we can put together."

That day they had grilled-cheese sandwiches and potato chips. Dessert was frozen green grapes.

Chapter 22

A sequence of dreams troubled Teddy's sleep that night. He awakened from each with a start, the details already either gone or fading. He did recall a piece of the last dream. In it he was climbing a ladder made of baseball bats. Somebody was pursuing him but he wasn't sure who or why, only that they intended to do him harm. This left him unable to return to sleep. He lay prone listening to the earliest morning birds and thinking, his chin resting on his stacked fists. It was still dark out but dawn was near.

Uncle Drew's most recent story bothered Teddy more than anything he'd ever heard or read. He felt as though something vital had been lost and this made him deeply sad. Bopeep was getting ready to rejoin organized baseball. He was too good not to. Once he found Dolores and learned where the two of them stood, once winter had passed (or maybe before), once he was fully settled, he would have made his way to a diamond somewhere. He would have talked to the people in charge and shown them what he could do with a baseball. He had every chance of becoming one of the greats who set standards for those who followed him. That he'd wound up not being able to pitch at all struck Teddy as monumentally unfair. It was an injustice far worse than being called names or not allowed to ride on a certain train car.

Teddy wished that there was somebody he could appeal to across the years, that he could somehow change the course of things so that Bopeep could be what he was supposed to be. He thought about saying a prayer but he was obviously too late to help that way. All he'd be able to do was ask, "Why?" which always seemed to be a useless question. Prayer itself was mostly useless. It made you feel better sometimes but things happened because they happened, not because somebody prayed for them to. The same could be said about things that didn't happen. Mama Pearl had prayed after the first lynching for an end to such horrible behavior, but that didn't stop the second. Teddy liked June's idea about people having all they needed to make the world run better. Why couldn't they see that? Maybe they did and just ignored it, which was worse.

He also liked Bopeep's way of dealing with situations that went against him. There were many things he admired about Bopeep, but this topped the list. He remembered the story about the new man in the hobo camp. There was no hesitation on Bopeep's part. He took care of himself, as he would have done against the three who attacked him in Tennessee if only he'd had the chance. But those were violent physical confrontations that left him without options. It was the other times, when he did have options, that his response impressed Teddy. Trouble was always present, of course, especially in those days for a person like Bopeep—but it wasn't usually right in his face like that. Teddy admired his courage against the new man in the camp. He also admired his cleverness against the yard bull in Shreveport and the sheriff in Alabama, even against Ty Cobb that day in Georgia. But it was his overall attitude that made Teddy think of Bopeep as a special person. Uncle Drew had mentioned it several times. He had shown Bopeep saying again and again that things were what they were and then simply dealing with whatever had happened by refusing to let it knock him off course. He'd even done this after the attack took who he might have become away from him.

Being only nine, Teddy was still some distance away from having a clear idea of who he might become or, for that matter, might *want* to become. Most people who lived in Oil Camp were connected in some way to the industry that gave the town its name. Others were in the timber business. Once there was a glove plant but the company had closed its Louisiana operation before Teddy was born. Choices were limited, in other words, unless you were a professional of some kind—a doctor, say, or maybe a lawyer or even a schoolteacher. Teddy thought about what he would do if he had to choose right then what he wanted to become. He wasn't sure but that didn't matter because this was not a real decision. What was real was that Bopeep had decided that he wanted to become a baseball player and then couldn't do it. Not because he got sick or had an accident. Not because of something he could have avoided, something normal. He couldn't do it because of who he already was.

What if I was good at science? Teddy thought. What if I was good enough at it that I already knew I was going to become a doctor? What if I *was* a doctor but I decided to do my job in an unusual way? What if after a while of that I started thinking about returning to the regular way and then when I was almost there three people broke my hands or put my eyes out just because the world they lived in allowed them to believe it was okay to do that to somebody who wasn't like them?

He couldn't imagine it, hard as he tried. The idea was beyond his comprehension. It was insane. It made him tired. It gave him a headache. It reminded him of the time a few years before when he saw some older boys douse a chicken snake with gasoline and set it on fire. As it writhed and lashed in a vain attempt to escape what was happening, the boys rocked with laughter. They added to the creature's torment by poking it with a stick. Teddy got away from there as fast as he could. He remembered that Bopeep was afraid of snakes. He was too, but his fear of them didn't keep him from being any less sickened by what he'd seen done to one that was no more harmful than a frog. Although he'd done nothing, he felt ashamed. It was as if he'd helped and joined the laughter. He sensed that something was terribly wrong with anybody who would do such a thing, and that idea took him to a thought he understood but couldn't possibly express. Had he been able to, he would have said that seeing those boys burn the snake alive indicated to him that there was something fundamentally wrong with the entire human race. He realized that he'd carried this knowledge like a burden ever since. It wasn't that he went around thinking about it all the time; he just knew: people were cruel. They tortured animals. They tortured each other. Teddy wished he could swing in on a vine like Tarzan and put a stop to wrong, to evil, whenever and wherever it happened.

The sky outside was beginning to lighten. Teddy listened to the sounds his parents made as they got out of bed and prepared for the day. He heard their showers. He heard their voices, their laughter, their footsteps. He heard the coffeepot and the dishes. He heard the front door open and close. He heard his father's pickup start, back out of the driveway, and leave. He heard the front door open again and close again, followed by the turning of the deadbolt. He heard his mother's car start, back out of the driveway, and leave. All of these sounds made him feel better, as did the breakfast way the house smelled. He breathed it in and knew the other, better thing about people: they were also decent. They worked hard. They loved each other.

Later that morning, Teddy sat down with a pencil and the notes he had been making. There was a lot of information. Uncle Drew seemed serious about not wanting to tell the story to anybody but him. He'd said from the beginning that he thought it would be safe there. But what did that mean, exactly? Maybe it meant that Teddy was free to do with it as he pleased. Maybe it meant that he could tell it himself. But who would believe him? And how could he possibly get it across the way Uncle Drew did? But worrying about being believed was not important or even pertinent. The ledgers were sufficient proof that the story was true. Even the part about Ty Cobb was there if you knew how to put it together. Too bad Uncle Drew had rubbed out what he'd written beneath that entry. But even that had its place. It was part of the story. No, the important question had to do with Uncle Drew's voice. He was the only one who could tell all of this. It was something like his wanting Bopeep to go back to organized ball and wishing he'd pushed his case harder than he had. It was like Tarzan finding Jane at the end of the first book and not taking her back to Africa with him. It was like any situation when somebody has a chance to do something and doesn't. Sometimes it all turns out fine anyway but sometimes it doesn't.

Teddy wanted more than anything for things to turn out better than they had for Bopeep. There wasn't anything he could do about what happened in Tennessee. That was a fact of history. But it wasn't necessarily the final word.

He turned to a fresh sheet in the notebook and wrote a letter. When he was done he clipped it to the notes he had been making and put the pages into an envelope that he addressed to Mr. Rayford Kennedy in care of the *Oil Camp News*. He attached the letter to the mailbox with the clothespin that was there for the purpose. Mr. Bilberry would pick it up in a couple of hours. Mr. Kennedy would find it in his mail the next day. The only question Teddy had was whether he would tell Uncle Drew what he'd done or not. It didn't really matter. They were going to be hearing from Mr. Kennedy soon.

Chapter 23

Never much liked endings [Uncle Drew said] because they always carry the reminder that the clock is ticking. I bet you watch one doing just that while you sit in your desk at school ever' day. Look at them hands and wish they'd get on around to the bell that lets you out. We're a funny species that way, humans, wanting during so much of what we do for it to be over with so we can move along to the next thing, whatever that might be. If nothing else, at least it's not whatever it was we was just a while ago wishing was over. Strange business, our wanting time to pass—which of course it's always in the process of doing. We want Friday to come, or Christmas. We want that bell to ring, or that quitting-time whistle to blow. I bet if you was to add up all the time we spend wishing for whatever we was doing to be over you'd have a percentage'd amaze you. Like sleeping. Nothing against sleeping because few things're better, but your view of it does change when you consider that you use up a full one-third of your life doing it. In the end you'll most likely find yourself wishing you'd paid a little more attention to time right here and now and not time done been or yet to come. The bell'll ring, guaranteed.

So anyway. Me and the Dodger was headed directly toward another ending. Done already seen the end of his baseball career. Them blankety-blanks in Tennessee took care of that for him. Arm was ruined. I don't know what I was sicker about, that or not being able to do a farming thing about making them pay for it. Tell you truth I ain't never fully got over the second part of all that. I knew Mama Pearl and June was right about the futility of trying to, but telling all this lately, I been prone to wonder what if we had. What if *I* had. An idle thought to be sure but there it is, nagging me like a fly you keep hearing and can't get the swatter down on him fast enough. Oh well. Ain't nothing to do except hope they come to some kind of a reckoning somewhere along the line, that bad befallen them. I hate to think like that about a man, but them three wasn't men. They was snakes, and the trouble with snakes of their stripe is they ain't generally all of a sudden fixing to grow theirself a conscience and be able to put two and two together close enough to see the connection between what they done and how they ought to feel about it. Shoot, I'd prefer running into a bad snake than into that bunch. Snake mind his own business. He ain't looking for trouble—well, I've seen a moccasin or two who might've been. But your average serpent, he's going to have a reason for coming at you. Fact of the matter is them boys had no motive other'n pure meanness and it's highly doubtful any of them ever give a second thought to what they done.

In between times of running all of that back and forth there was two other things on my mind as we drove. First was, what was Bopeep going to do? Second was, what was Uncle Drew going to do? I assumed we'd get to New Orleans and that'd be that. He'd go his way and I mine. And that's what turned out to be the case, just not immediately. Once again I was about to be the beneficiary of some real fine hospitality on the part of black folks, namely Miss Liz-Beth Toups. Not E-lizabeth like one word. It was two, Liz-Beth, hyphenated, Bopeep's mama's given name.

She was a great big woman, just the exact opposite of string-bean Bopeep, who they told me took after his daddy, Marcel Shines. Liz-Beth give up her first married name when she threw in with Chesterfield Toups four or five years after Marcel died in the flu epidemic of 1919, same one that took Bopeep's uncle Drew, which you may recall my mentioning way back when this first started. He was my nickname-sake, you might say. I guess when they died would've made Bopeep about your age, maybe a year different one way or the other—old enough to have had it affect him to lose his daddy anyway, and certainly old enough four or five years later to have had it affect him to see his mama marry another beau. He got over that quick, though, because Chesterfield was just too likeable a fellow. Plus, he was the one put Bopeep in touch with his ability to throw a baseball.

Most of the time we was out on the road we didn't have no serious particular place to go. We just followed the breeze, went wherever we got blew to. Now we had a specific destination in mind. New Orleans, Louisiana—home for Bopeep and near to it for me. I'd already just about made up my mind to get on back up Oil Camp once I got the Dodger settled down there, but things didn't work out like that as you will see, least not right away. In fact it took me until last February to make it all the way back up to where I started from. You can figure out how long that is yourself if you're so inclined. I'd just as soon not think about all them years—speaking of time passing. Gosh a-mighty! It moves. Course, you ain't to where that makes much difference.

Well, seems like I'm having trouble getting started with my ending here. I'm rambling off about this and that, and what you bound to want to know is what happened next. Let's see here then. First, there was New Orleans herself. Different kind of a place, New Orleans is. For one thing, the black folks kind of just lived all over. Wasn't many streets you wouldn't find some on. They had their primary areas, but this wasn't like Shreveport and Dallas and everywhere else we went, where the boundaries were clear. Shoot, it wasn't like our town is right now and probably will still be until the last ding-dong. It was a little hazier, which I came to think of as making sense because everything in New Orleans is a little hazy. Don't bother asking for directions because what you'll hear won't make a lick of sense, at least once you start trying to follow them. You just about have to be from there to know where somebody's telling you something is—and why in that case would you be asking? Just keep moving if you ever go there. You'll come upon something of interest, that's a fact. Might not be what or where you was looking for but you might as well take a minute for it because it'll generally be worth your while. Also, what's the hurry? In New Orleans, there ain't one. If nothing else, you can stand there and imagine how deep under water you'd be if you were right there in that spot after the big hurricane a few years ago. But that's all lately. We need to get back to Bopeep. It's the river that does it, by the way. The river makes a curve at New Orleans and because of that, directions are generally out of the question as far as making any kind of sense.

So that's something about where we was headed, which the closer we got to it the more excited Bopeep became. I swear if a city could ever be said to heal a man, New Orleans healed the Dodger. Course, we're talking about home now, where the heart is. They say you can't never go there again but that's a lie. Bopeep did and I firmly believe it saved him from despair. He was hurt on the inside of his mind as he was on his body. New Orleans couldn't give him his arm or the career he might have had back, but what he found there was in the long run maybe even better. Dolores Capanel. She wasn't exactly pining away the hours waiting for him but she was pleased enough by his return to welcome him with open arms. And let me tell you something: his description of her stood up. I ain't never seen a prettier girl before or since. I'm talking movie-star good looks. You could tell right off that here was somebody special. Be honest with you, I thought a little less of Bopeep when I initially laid eyes on her, first for ever leaving her behind and second for ever having anything at all to do with other gals. I wouldn't say I judged him, but I did wonder if something was wrong with his head. Told him so, too. He said he wondered the same thing.

Miss Liz-Beth and Chesterfield lived on Dryades Street, where Bopeep directed me to after we was off the ferry across the river and got into the city proper. He was pointing out everything we passed. Oh there's the this and there's the that and there's the other thing. Old so-and-so runs that pharmacy, used to anyway, and look yonder at old such-and-such's insurance company. I can read all of this for myself, of course, but I don't say nothing except I do point out the Cinderella Shoe sign when we pass that because it stands out to me.

"There it is with that high heel," Bopeep said.

He was going a hundred miles an hour, sliding back and forth on the backseat like a dog with both windows down can't decide which one to stick his nose out of, everything smelling so good.

"You recovered back there?" I said.

"Hometown, Uncle Drew," he said. "Hometown."

I glanced into the mirror and saw him bring his good hand up to his face and dab at the corner of both his eyes with an index-finger knuckle. Under regular circumstances I would've thought he was being theatrical for my benefit, but these wasn't regular circumstances and he didn't know I was looking. It wasn't many of them but they was genuine tears—equal parts regretful ones about what had happened to him and grateful ones about being once again surrounded by New Orleans. I like to teared up my own self.

Well, as you can imagine, Miss Liz-Beth had a walleyed

fit when she opened the door to us that evening. It was well after dark when we pulled up to her and Chesterfield's house, which was not at all what I'd pictured colored folks living in. Not that it was a mansion, but it was about four times the size of what I grew up in—and nice, I mean, flowerbeds and shrubbery and great big old oak trees like seem to be everywhere down there. Chairs out on the gallery, all of it painted crisp and clean. Which right there you have got yourself an example of prejudice in its purest form, a already made-up mind. I tried not to let on I was surprised, but Bopeep noticed me gawking.

"Come on now, Uncle Drew," he said. "You didn't think I came out a hole in the ground, did you?"

"You came out a bus, first I knew of you," I said.

"I see how you looking," he said.

"Sorry, Bo," I said. "It's just—"

"I know what it's just," he said. "I'd been surprised too if I was you. Actually do be a little anyway, place all fixed up like this. Course I have been sending a donation every now and then. Let's give them a surprise."

He hadn't been as lively in a while. I was happy to see it.

"Go up, knock on the door," he said. "Ask whoever answers, say, 'I'm a friend of Cantrell's. He home this evening?'"

"Well, Cantrell obviously ain't home this evening," I said. "And he obviously ain't been home in quite some time. Don't you think that'll irritate them—a white boy come up out of nowhere to ask after their long-lost son?"

And Bopeep said, "It's just a little joke. Don't fret. I got everything under control. You'll see."

So I went up there and rapped on the door. I could hear the radio playing inside, some jazz most likely but I don't recollect. There's a little bit of a bustle and then there stands as big a woman as I believe I ever saw in my life. She would've been sizeable in any ensemble, but what she had on was a house robe so she looked something like a pup tent with a head. Took up the entire doorway.

"Is you planning to state your case, or do you just wish to gaze at me all night?" she said.

"Yes ma'am," I said. "I mean, no ma'am."

She turned her head and called over her shoulder, said, "Come see something, Chester. We got us a escapee from the sideshows on our gallery. He giving a free look out here."

I looked back toward the street but Bopeep was nowhere in sight.

"Chesterfield!"

"Coming, coming," Chesterfield said.

And then there he was, in an undershirt and khakis, a section of newspaper folded under his arm. If the Dodger's mama was big and soft, Chesterfield was—well, he was big and *big,* nothing soft about him. Except his eyes. They had that light in them of the kind lets you know ain't going to be trouble unless you insist.

"Well?" he said.

"Y-yessir," I said. "I'm a friend of Bo—I mean, Cantrell's, and I was wondering if he's home this evening."

"Don't you be joshing, boy," Bo's mama said. "Cantrell left out of here three years ago and ain't been back since. Who you fooling?"

Chesterfield lifted his eyebrows and cocked his head just the least littlest bit.

"Maybe I got the wrong address," I said.

"Who Cantrell you looking for?" she said.

"Cantrell Shines," I said. "He's a ballplayer. Was one, anyway. We call him Bopeep."

At that she shifted her weight and brought the back of her hand to her forehead. Then she took a deep breath, exhaled it slowly, brought her hands together before her, and said, "Young man, as you can see I am ready for bed.

The hour is late. I have no time for any shenanigans. So I am going to kindly ask you one last time to state your business."

She all of a sudden sounded like a schoolteacher, as you probably noticed. Don't know about you, but schoolteachers always intimidated me. And there I was, already feeling about a inch tall for being there, interrupting these folks' evening. I couldn't think of a single thing to say. She shook her head exasperatedly. Chesterfield lifted his eyebrows even higher.

"You said 'was' a ballplayer," he said. "Ain't he still one?"

Well, I guess Bopeep had been watching and listening and knew I didn't need to get tangled up in having to explain why he was "was" and not "is" in relation to being a ballplayer, because just when I was about to start to try to I hear his voice out on the sidewalk, which I think I might've mentioned he wouldn't call a sidewalk but a banquette.

"That you, Drew?" he said. "Hey, Mama. Pops."

By now he's up on the steps and I'm looking back and forth between him and his folks, the Dodger standing there grinning like a pumpkin with his jacket sleeve dangling empty because of his arm being tucked against him and Miss Liz-Beth and Chesterfield sporting looks on their faces like they ain't exactly sure what to think until finally Miss Liz-Beth explodes out the door and heads for Bopeep wagging her arms like she's trying to get rid of something that's wrapped around them.

"My baby!" she says. "Lord Jesus, it's my baby have returned!"

Bopeep laughs his great booming laugh, which sounds like pure music since I ain't heard it in so long.

"Like I said," he says. "Hey, Mama."

I watch her just about swallow him in a hug and then I turn back around toward Chesterfield, who extends to me a hand that's ever' bit the size of the ones on old Big-Big back in Dallas. I reach out and take it, best I can.

"Chesterfield Toups," he says. "Cantrell stepdaddy. He call me 'Pops' as I guess you heard. I take it y'all acquainted."

"Andrew Weems," I said.

He let go of my hand, finally. I wanted to rub it but didn't. Just put it in my pocket and tried to squeeze some life back into it.

"Yessir," I said. "We been on the road together for near about three years now."

Meanwhile, Miss Liz-Beth has let Bopeep go and is listening to him intently while he gives her a quick rundown about what happened to his arm. He pauses to do a handshake-hug with Chesterfield and then continues. Miss Liz-Beth's head is going slowly back and forth, and her eyes are glistening. Her hands are moving alternately from her mouth to somewhere on Bopeep—this time his chest, the next time his face, the time after that his shoulders.

"And Uncle Drew here took a pretty good pounding hisself," Bopeep said by way of finishing up that part of our tale.

It was then that I got introduced to Miss Liz-Beth, which Bopeep told me to call her because everybody else did, including most of the time him. I said I would and she hugged me near about as long as Chesterfield had shook my hand. Wrung me plumb out.

"I hate to think what you been through, child," she said.

"Oh, they's lots we done you wouldn't have to say that about," I said. "Being with Bo—I mean Cantrell—was worth every bit of it, too, the good and the bad."

"Well, let's go indoors and have something for y'all to eat," she said.

"How you traveling anyway?" Chesterfield said.

Bopeep pointed out the Hudson.

"Get out of here," Chesterfield said.

"Wait till you hear how we come to have it," Bopeep said.

"Ain't stole, I hope," Miss Liz-Beth said.

The Dodger and I exchanged a glance.

"Not technically," I said.

"But it is stole," he said. "After a fashion."

And so went the beginning of the end of me and Bopeep. We'd just about reached that point. I knew this as soon as Dolores come over bright and early the next morning. She was a goner for Bopeep, who was a goner for her. Two completely lost causes. It was like nobody else existed. You can just tell that about certain people. They're made for each other, you might say, and this pair had a bad case of the hooked-together hearts. First thing she wanted to do was take him over to Flint-Goodridge and have him looked over by somebody who knew what he was looking at. He of course acted like he hadn't had the idea cross his mind, much less been told repeatedly the night before by Miss Liz-Beth and Chesterfield that he needed to get over there.

The examination only verified what we already knew. They had all kind of terms for what it exactly was, but nothing said it quite as accurately as "a ruined arm." They did get him on some medicine to battle the internal infection he didn't know he had, that and some pain elixir. He said a day or two later that he'd got so used to hurting that it seemed like the way you was supposed to feel.

"A spoon of that syrup remind me it ain't so, Uncle Drew," he said. "Believe I prefer the relief."

"One extreme to the other," I said.

"That's right," he said.

"Just don't go getting to liking it too much," Dolores said.

We were sitting on the gallery having ice tea courtesy of Chesterfield's place of employment, Reily Foods. They mainly was in the coffee business over there, roasting and grinding, but they had got into tea not too long before and it had paid off. Fact, it would eventually pay off to the point where all these years later your mama served me a glass of it the other night. Luzianne. Look and see when you go to the house if there ain't a box of it in y'all's pantry.

And so we was having ourself a pitcher of Luzianne when Dolores asked me a question that kind of put the giddy-up into turning my thoughts toward the future. Simple question—and not a new one. Just a mite surprising to have it dropped in your lap by someone who maybe should've kept it to herself. But no. That's not fair to Dolores. She had every right to bring the subject up because she sensed that I was settling in a little too comfortably for my own good. Snapped me back to reality, you might say.

"What're you planning to do with yourself when you leave here, Uncle Drew?" she said.

They'd all taken to calling me Uncle Drew.

"What if maybe he ain't planning to leave here?" Bopeep said.

I felt a rush of blood in my face and thought about repeating what he'd said. But I knew I'd be wrong to. I knew she had a point. Much as I enjoyed my time in that fine house with those fine people, all of them, including the couple of dozen from the extended family and the neighborhood that regularly dropped by—much as I appreciated how far they went toward making me feel like one of the family—well, I wasn't. The Dodger and I might've considered ourself each other's brother, but with the very slight possibility that Miss Liz-Beth did, none of the rest saw it that way. And I ain't saying they should have. We wasn't brothers. We was close buddies who'd been through some extreme bonding-type situations together, but when it came right down to it we was from two different worlds and them two worlds wasn't quite ready to start looking for their similarities just yet. Not out in the open anyway.

"Don't know," I said. "Something. We'll see."

I took a last swallow of my tea and put the glass down

on the table. I guess they could tell I was irritated, which I was even though I already knew I shouldn't be and was trying not to let on. It was mostly at myself anyway, not at what Dolores had said.

"Y'all need to excuse me," I said.

"Aw, Uncle Drew," Bopeep said. "Come on now."

"I ain't gone yet," I said.

But I was as good as. I was getting ready to be. I went straight back to the sleeping porch where they'd let me settle and started gathering my things together.

"Were you mad?" Teddy asked.

"Irritated at myself primarily, like I said. Not mad. Change that *m* to a *s* and you'd have what I mostly was."

Teddy figured out the new word and nodded.

"I'm sad too, thinking about y'all splitting up," he said. "Seems like there ought to've been a way for y'all not to have to."

"Bopeep had Dolores," Uncle Drew said. "I didn't have nobody and wasn't inclined to look. Even if I had, what do you think the chances of me finding somebody willing, first, to put up with me and, second, to be friends with them—or, even less likely, a colored girl willing to step out with me? Not even slim is what. Not even slim. It was too complicated. We'd pretty much run our course."

There was a long pause. Teddy was thinking. He had something on his mind he needed to bring up, just to get a gauge on it. He didn't see any point in telling Uncle Drew about the letter. All he needed was an idea of how things would go once Mr. Kennedy answered it, which he would undoubtedly do by calling somebody on the telephone. Teddy hoped it would be him first, but it might be Uncle Drew. He'd covered that possibility in his letter, but he knew that grownups are not always reliable when it comes to doing what kids ask them to.

"Uncle Drew?"

"Yessir."

"When you said all this—all these stories you're telling me—that they're mine to do with as I please—is there any limitation on that, or do you mean it like they're literally mine to own and you won't mind what I do no matter what?"

"Quite a mouthful of a question there. Answer's yes and no. Yes, they're yours. No, I won't mind. Does that cover things sufficient enough for you?"

"It does."

"Good, because I'm hungry," Uncle Drew said. "You?"

"Sure am," Teddy said.

"Fine. I got something Miss Liz-Beth would make me and Bopeep and Chesterfield that I believe was my favorite meal in all of her vast repertoire."

That day they had breakfast—fried eggs, salty ham, biscuits, and fried green tomatoes. Dessert was an extra biscuit with fig preserves.

Chapter 24

If Teddy had made a list of how he wanted things to go, he would have had a hard time coming up with one as satisfying as what actually happened. First, Mr. Kennedy called him and not Uncle Drew. Second, Mr. Kennedy was *most* interested in the story of Bopeep Shines. Third, Mr. Kennedy assured Teddy that he knew a little something about how to get people who didn't want to talk to do it anyway.

"So," he said. "What do you think is our best course of action, young man?"

"I think you ought to just meet me here at my house about ten o'clock in the morning and we'll go over there together," Teddy said. "It'll be just like usual, except for you being with me."

"I'll see you then," Mr. Kennedy said. "Oh, and Teddy?"

"Yessir?"

"Thank you for thinking of me to do this with you."

"What do you mean?"

"I mean that you could have gotten in touch with the Shreveport paper or one of the TV stations over there. This is the kind of a story that—who knows? Somebody from ESPN might even be interested in it. It's an important story. So thank you. I promise to do it justice."

"You're welcome, Mr. Kennedy," Teddy said. "I wouldn't want anybody from somewhere else to know about it before somebody from here did, and I doubt Uncle Drew would either. We'll just have to see how he feels about the idea when we get over there."

Fourth, after Teddy told Uncle Drew when he answered the door that what he wanted to do with the story was pass it on to Mr. Kennedy for the newspaper, Uncle Drew did not balk.

"Your call," he said. "When's he coming?"

"He's already here," Teddy said.

He stepped back and motioned for Mr. Kennedy, who had suggested that it might be a good idea if he waited to see what Uncle Drew's reaction was going to be before coming over, lest the old man slam the door on them.

Fifth and finally, Uncle Drew and Mr. Kennedy hit it off immediately, Mr. Kennedy having spent some time on offshore drilling rigs himself by way of earning money for journalism school.

"Took a pay cut when you graduated I'd expect," Uncle Drew said.

"You got that right. Many's the time I've thought I couldn't have picked a worse profession, given the hours-worked, money-received ratio. But then the truck comes in with that week's edition and I couldn't be more content."

"Well, I know people appreciate your effort, whether they say so or not," Uncle Drew replied. "The record of a place has got to be kept."

They were sitting on the porch, Teddy in his lawn chair, Uncle Drew in his rocker, and Mr. Kennedy in a folding camp seat that Uncle Drew had brought out for him after the introductions. Each of them held a glass of Luzianne. Uncle Drew's was not doctored. Mr. Kennedy and Teddy took theirs with both lemon and sugar.

"I got one requirement for you, Mr. Kennedy," Uncle Drew said. "And that's that I am going to finish the story for Teddy here before we go back to the beginning. In other words, the first thing you're fixing to get is the ending."

"I'm perfectly fine with that, Mr. Weems," Mr. Kennedy said.

"Call me Uncle Drew, Mr. Kennedy."

"Please call me Rayford then, Mr. Weems," Mr. Kennedy said.

"So, Rayford, are you ready?"

"I certainly am, Uncle Drew," Mr. Kennedy said.

My original plan for a destination once I left New Orleans [Uncle Drew said] was naturally to head back on up here to Oil Camp. But a letter arrived in the mail the very afternoon Dolores asked the question that put me in motion, and this letter brought me temporarily to a dead stop. Now you will recall that every since Bopeep had gave me that $500 in Savannah I'd been regularly wiring sums home to my folks—thought I had, that is. In fact, though the money was safe and secure, they never got to see a penny of it. Didn't live to. The entire amount I'd sent was in the bank under my name because my folks and my sisters was gone, burnt to death the winter after I lit out with the Dodger in a fire caused by, apparently, a turned-over coal-oil lamp. That little house of ours went up in flames with no more resistance than a piece of parchment.

All this was in the letter, which was written by Mr. J. A. Adkins, president of the Planters Bank and Trust of Oil Camp. He had the address per my own last wire, in which I said I could be contacted in care of the Toups of such-and-such number on Dryades Street in New Orleans. Mr. Adkins said he regretted having to inform me of the misfortune that had befallen my parents and siblings but was pleased to let me know that he had taken it upon himself to place into an interest-earning account the money I had so generously been sending home without knowing what a cruel trick Fate had played—etcetera and so forth and so on. The upshot was that I had a good deal of money at my disposal. Every dime of what I'd sent, plus the interest it had accumulated.

Well, I didn't rightly know how to feel or what to do. I read the letter through a couple of times to make sure it said what it seemed to. I knew I should've been sad or angry or something. But I wasn't anything, just kind of empty. Lost. I'd been no more or less close to my mama and daddy than most youngsters. Couldn't say I knew my sisters all that well. They had their chores and me and my brothers had ours. We got along tolerable well. Course, my brothers was long since gone and I'd been away three years. Tell you the truth, when I left out of there I didn't feel any strong pull to go back, and I'd felt it less and less as time went on. I didn't particularly miss nobody or feel any but that one little tug of homesickness. I was too busy for it. Except for sending the money, my ties was fairly well severed. I hated it for the four of them naturally, but as far as any great overwhelming sense of grief or sadness, I can't say I experienced much, if any. Like I said, it was more like being lost than anything else. I was probably already feeling that way because of me and Bopeep fixing to say our farewells, so the news—old news in fact, which was strange to think about—the news just compounded the matter. I was in a fix because when you're lost you desire one of two things: to either find your way back to something familiar or to get found. In my case there wasn't nothing familiar available to find my way back to, Bopeep being ruined for baseball and all, and who in the world was going to find me?

Funny the decisions you make sometimes. I never told Bopeep or Miss Liz-Beth either one, neither them nor Chesterfield, what was in that letter. And they never asked. What I did was write back to Mr. Adkins and, in addition to thanking him for what he'd done and all, directed him to have my money wired to me at the Western Union in New Orleans. It come to a little bit over three thousand dollars, which was a good stake. Made me feel a little less lost, I guarantee you that. All that was left now was for me to bid my adieus and go see what I could find in the way of who Andrew Weems might be.

Miss Liz-Beth hugged me like she done the night I arrived. Had a tear in her eye too.

"If you ever, ever come back this way, I'll skin you alive you don't stop by for a visit and a plate," she said.

Chesterfield shook my hand and then surprised me by pulling me to himself and like to crush all the air out my lungs. He said it had been a pleasure and I said it surely had.

Dolores wasn't there when I left, which I wasn't too happy about because I'd been meaning to thank her for getting me up off my rusty-dusty and on my way. Bopeep said he'd try to talk me into staying a while longer if he thought it'd do any good. I said it wouldn't.

"Got to get, Bo," I said. "Got to go see what's next. Unlike you, I ain't sure what that is."

"Understand that, Uncle Drew," he said. "I ain't sure neither. Nobody is."

"Shoot," I said. "Y'all fixing to get married and start a family. You got you a nice job over at the coffee factory with Chesterfield. It's all cut out for you."

"Bothers me a little to think I be done rambling," he said.

"Don't let it," I said. "You rambled right to where you belong. I'm just sorry about your arm and baseball."

He cupped his hand on his shoulder and gave it a squeeze, moved it up and down a couple of times.

"Had us a time, didn't we, Uncle Drew," he said.

"Did," I said. "Reckon we'll ever see each other again?"

"Never know," he said. "Might do in the funny papers."

We were out on the sidewalk, the banquette as they call it in New Orleans. I was planning to get this over with, walk up to the streetcar stop, catch one, and start out to wherever it was I'd end up. We'd already had our final money conversation. I told him I had plenty—more than plenty—but he said that was old money already mine and that he wanted to give me what he owed me.

"Here we go again," I said. "You don't owe me a dime."

"Is we nigh on to blows over money after all this?" he said. "Ain't no sense in it, Uncle Drew."

"Ain't coming to blows over it, Bopeep," I said. "I just ain't taking no more from you. You the one earned it. But I'll tell you what. Don't think of it like I ain't took and you ain't give. Look at it like we both done them things and then I give it back to you as a early wedding present. That's the best I can do."

"I ain't like it," he said.

"You're welcome," I said.

He shook his head.

"You a fool," he said.

"We square?" I said

"I reckon," he said.

That was the night before. And now we was down to getting on our separate roads. Bopeep toed a rock with one shoe this way and moved it back that way with the other. I wondered if he resented what had happened to him as much as I did. If so, he'd never let on. But how could he not? He was bound to have some hatred built up in him, some fire. I decided I'd go ahead and ask him.

At first he didn't say anything. He just kept pushing that rock back and forth, looking down. Then he started nodding his head. He lifted his eyes.

"Do," he said. "Sure do."

I waited for more but that was it.

"Well, I guess we could stand here all day or not," I said.

"Got something I want you to have since you won't take your pay, Uncle Drew," he said. "It always been just as much yours as mine anyway. Even more if you think about it. Won't do me no good without you."

"What're you talking about?" I said.

He reached into his trousers pocket and withdrew the keys to the Hudson. I didn't even allow myself to get excited.

"I ain't taking the blankety-blank car, Bopeep," I said.

"Sure you is," he said.

He grabbed my hand, laid the keys on my palm, and closed my fingers over them for me. They were warm from his carrying them.

"Don't say nothing other'n 'thank you' or 'much obliged,'" he said. "Make you a pick. We ain't be arguing this."

I could see he was serious as a ant with a cake crumb. The car was mine.

"Thank you," I said. "Much obliged."

Bopeep laughed his great booming laugh and held out one of those bony hands of his. I took it. We stood there for some time holding that grip. I put my left hand on his shoulder. He couldn't return the gesture of course, his ruined arm being still tight against his side. Finally, he said something that I repeated and we let go of each other. I picked up my traps, put them in the back of the Hudson, and got behind the wheel. Pulling away I knew I was as all alone in the world as a feller can possibly be and I felt the weight of that fact all the way down into my bone marrow. I also felt like everything was going to be all right somehow. Far's I know it was.

"Did you ever see Bopeep again?" Teddy asked.

"Never did," Uncle Drew said. "Not too long after leaving him I found something in the back of the Hudson that I intended to return to him but wound up not ever taking the time to do it. One day follows the next, then it's another week gone, another month, another year. It goes by. I should've tried to keep in touch."

"What did he say that you repeated?" Mr. Kennedy asked.

"Said, 'Good luck.' We wished each other that."

"Not a bad thing to be your last words to somebody," Mr. Kennedy said.

"I reckon not."

Nobody said anything for a long time. Teddy wanted to ask the old man what it was he'd found but he decided not to. It was none of his business.

"Stay for a bite of dinner with us, Rayford?" Uncle Drew asked.

"Thank you, Uncle Drew," Mr. Kennedy said. "But I'd best be getting on back to the office. I'm going to go through my notes, look over those that Teddy sent me, and see what we have. What I'd like to do now is talk about a time we can get together to go through the front of your story. Sounds like it might take a day or two."

"Oh, come now, sir," Uncle Drew said. "It's dinnertime. You're bound to have a little bit of a growl going. I insist. As to our getting together, I'm here all morning every morning, up by five at the latest. Afternoons you might or might not catch me."

"Tomorrow morning too soon to get started?" Mr. Kennedy asked.

"Not a minute," Uncle Drew said.

"You'll wish you had stayed," Teddy told Mr. Kennedy.

"Will I?" he asked.

Teddy nodded.

"Well, I suppose whatever you have'll beat my peanut-butter crackers," Mr. Kennedy said.

That day they had chicken spaghetti, French bread with garlic butter, and green beans. Dessert was chocolate ice-cream pie.

Chapter 25

Uncle Drew and Mr. Kennedy spent the next few mornings sipping Luzianne and going through the story from the beginning. Teddy sat with them, listening to it all again. He was amazed by how close to verbatim the old man repeated the tale. There were minor differences, of course, but the episodes and the things people said were exactly the same. Mr. Kennedy captured it all on tape and promised that he'd make Teddy a copy. Uncle Drew finished by quoting what he and Bopeep had said to each other as they shook hands for the last time instead of just saying that Bopeep had said it and that he had repeated it.

"Finally he said, 'Good luck to you, my friend,' and I said, 'Good luck to you, my friend,' and we let go of each other. I picked up my traps. . . . "

When the story was over, Mr. Kennedy rifled through the notepad he'd occasionally been writing in, located an entry, and read to himself for a moment.

"The other day you said you found something in the back of the Hudson," he began. "You said you intended to return whatever it was but, let's see, 'wound up not ever taking the time to do it.' Then you said something about the passage of time."

He looked at Uncle Drew.

"What was it you found?" he asked. "I'm thinking it was some money Bopeep had put there for you just to get the last word in on that matter."

"He'd done that, I'd've sent it back as soon as I could

get to a place to do it," Uncle Drew said. "Wasn't money. Y'all sit a second—let me go fetch it. I got it out last night, thinking this might come up."

The old man rose from his rocker and entered the house. The screen slapped behind him. Teddy and Mr. Kennedy exchanged a look. Teddy shrugged. Mr. Kennedy raised his eyebrows. They sipped their tea, waiting.

"I'm fixing to get fat if he keeps feeding me every day," Mr. Kennedy said. "Good Lord, the man can cook."

"Beats my mama and my grandmama," Teddy said. "And that's saying something. He told me one time not to ever say that to them, but my mama knows. She's tasted what he does."

"Still good advice not to say anything."

They turned toward the door when they heard Uncle Drew approaching. He came out carrying an old suitcase. He held it out to Teddy, who stood up before taking it.

"This ain't . . . " he said.

"It is. I was surprised too. But that ain't all. Open him up."

Teddy set the case on the porch. It was a medium brown color with a darker brown handle and trim, including three decorative stripes. The latches had once been gilded but were now flaked and tarnished.

"Go ahead," Uncle Drew said.

Teddy put his thumbs on the latch triggers. Mr. Kennedy leaned in with his hands on his knees. Teddy popped the latches and lifted the top, half-expecting to discover packets of money. What he found instead caused him to bob his head and suck in a quick, involuntary breath. He noticed but was not put off by the strong smell of mothballs. It seemed fitting.

"Incredible," Mr. Kennedy said. "Unbelievable."

"It's all there," Uncle Drew said. "Both his Po' Boys uniforms, both his caps, his spikes, and his mitt."

The caps—one green with gold stripes and brim, the

other gold with green stripes and brim—lay atop two neatly folded jerseys, between which was a mitt so old and used that the leather had gone nearly black. The spikes were not visible.

"There was also this," Uncle Drew said.

He showed them a legal-size envelope that had once been white but had gone almost all the way to tan through the years. He removed the sheet of paper that was inside and handed it down to Teddy.

"It's wasn't really time passing that made me not return these things," Uncle Drew said. "It was this."

Teddy looked at the note, which was written in a small, uncertain hand:

To—my frin Uncal Drew Weems,
Dont rekon ill be needen any of this no more so here you
go do with them as you plese
From—your frin Cantrell Bopeep Shines

He passed the paper back to Uncle Drew, who gave it to Mr. Kennedy.

"One thing you can readily see there is that the Dodger wasn't going to win no spelling bees," the old man said. "Made me a little sad to get all his gear, because that meant the last littlest bit of a flicker of whatever tiny hope I might have fooled myself into maintaining was doused. But there it is, the baseball legacy of Bopeep Shines. Used to I'd wonder if he and Dolores ever had any kids and feel guilty if they did for them kids not having that suitcase."

"He might not have wanted them to," Mr. Kennedy said. "He might've decided to take the story to his grave with him."

"That's what kept me from trying to get in touch after while," Uncle Drew said. "Got to where if I heard somebody mention Bopeep Shines I wouldn't even bat an eye. 'Who?' I'd say. I already said goodbye to him once. Didn't want to have to again. Still don't. Till Teddy knocked that ball through my window I suppose I was willing to let the story die with me too. I guess that kind of woke me up to not allowing that."

"Well, I'm glad it did," Mr. Kennedy said. "And I hope you don't take this wrong, but I made a couple of calls to put out feelers in New Orleans to see if there's anybody left of the bunch you told me about, including perhaps Bopeep himself. You never know."

"Don't guess you do," Uncle Drew said.

"I'm not planning on doing any kind of an exhaustive investigation," Mr. Kennedy continued. "A couple of my old journalism buddies're down there. We'll see what they come up with. Probably nothing. Won't matter for our initial purposes anyway. You've given me enough information to fill more space than I've got. I may wind up putting out a tabloid. A special insert in the regular edition."

Teddy had ventured to pick up the mitt, which was comically small and stubby fingered. The pocket was as thin as a napkin. It didn't seem as if anyone could catch a ball in it. That it was for a lefthander compounded its oddness. He put it down and took up one of the caps. It was the green one with gold trim. On the crown were the interlocked letters N and O. The other cap, he noticed, had the letters P and B side by side.

"Why don't you put it on?" Uncle Drew suggested.

"No way," Teddy said.

"Go ahead. Ain't no cooties in there."

The cap didn't fit him perfectly, but it was only slightly too big. The brim was shorter than the ones he was used to. He took it between his fingers and adjusted the cap.

"Maybe that'll give you some good luck when y'all start playing," Uncle Drew said. "If that don't, the other'n might."

"We have our own caps," Teddy said. "Or we get them when we get put on teams."

"I don't think you understood what he means, Teddy," Mr. Kennedy said.

"What?"

Mr. Kennedy looked at Uncle Drew, who nodded.

"I believe he means the caps are yours, son," Mr. Kennedy said.

"But what about if y'all find Bopeep and he has kids?" Teddy asked.

Uncle Drew shook his head.

"Then they can negotiate with you," he said. "I'd give you the other things too, but they're no use except for a Halloween costume and too big for that right now anyway. They're just artifacts. Being an artifact myself I think I'll keep them a while longer, pass them on later. Imagine playing ball on a hot summer day in a wool outfit. Looks like they'd had heatstroke half the time."

"They were some kind of tough old boots, weren't they," Mr. Kennedy said.

"It's a fact," Uncle Drew agreed. "Had to be back then, don't matter what you done."

"Thanks don't seem like enough to say about these caps," Teddy declared.

"Well, I'll tell you what, Teddy," Uncle Drew replied. "That's something that ain't never changing as long as folks're civilized. Saying thanks and meaning it's always enough."

"Well, I mean it. Thanks."

"You're welcome," Uncle Drew said.

That day they had catfish po' boys, dressed.

"Very appropriate," Mr. Kennedy said.

"Thought y'all would appreciate the connection."

"Here's to the best of the Po' Boys," Teddy said.

He lifted his glass of tea. The men touched it with theirs.

"Hear, hear," Mr. Kennedy said.

Dessert was coconut pie.

Chapter 26

The *Oil Camp News* of the following Thursday contained an eight-page tabloid insert sponsored by local merchants in which Mr. Kennedy presented Uncle Drew's story of his travels with Bopeep Shines. The cover of the supplement was a collage of sepia-toned pictures of one ledger, the suitcase's contents, and the Hudson, under the headline:

UNCLE DREW
AND
THE BAT DODGER

There would have been a picture of Uncle Drew, but he deflected all of Mr. Kennedy's arguments in favor of it. Inside were no illustrations, only columns of words surrounded by the advertisements that paid for the supplement. There were six columns on each page, broken by a boxed quote from the story, which commenced after a brief introduction by Mr. Kennedy.

Editor's Note: Teddy Caldwell, nine, of Oil Camp, recently brought to our attention an extraordinary story that we are most pleased to present to our readers with this special insert. The speaker is Mr. Andrew Weems, 88, also of Oil Camp. While we have been forced by limitations of space to edit a good deal of Mr. Weems' tale, we feel confident that we have retained some sense of its scope. Extra copies of the tabloid are available for $2.50 at the News *office on Main Street.*

Teddy read the story in one sitting, hoping to discover that Mr. Kennedy and his reporter friends in New Orleans had come up with new information about Bopeep after he and Uncle Drew shook hands and parted ways that day. If so, there was no mention of it. Instead, the story started and stopped in the places Teddy already knew. Quite a bit was left out along the way, as the Editor's Note pointed out, but the main events were thoroughly covered. Mr. Kennedy had even kept in a good deal of Uncle Drew's comments regarding race, though he did not print the *n* word.

"We're so proud of you, Teddy," his mother said. "This is really a nice thing to have done."

"Well, all I did was break a window," he said.

His parents smiled, as he wanted them to.

"I'm just glad he let somebody record the story," his father said. "I was afraid he might not."

"So was I," Teddy agreed. "But he said all along it was mine to do with whatever I wanted to and this is what I decided I wanted to do. When Mr. Kennedy brought the first copy over for Uncle Drew to see he said it was on the Internet too. He also said he went in and updated that old entry that's been on there for so long about Bopeep's barnstorming being apocryphal and all."

"Good for him," his mother replied. "What did Uncle Drew think?"

"Oh, y'all know Uncle Drew," Teddy said. "First he told Mr. Kennedy he'd read the story later. 'In the paper,' he said, 'and not on the blasted Internet.' Then Mr. Kennedy said he sure was looking forward to getting his reaction. But after he left Uncle Drew told me he had no intention of reading the story anywhere at all, ever. I asked him why not and he said, 'I already know it fairly well, for one thing, and for another all I'd be doing is getting in a wad about things that after all that work Rayford done he wound up getting wrong anyway.'"

Teddy waited for them to quit laughing.

"Pretty good imitation there," his father said.

"Sounds just like him," his mother added. "At least from what I heard the other night. We need to do that again."

"Maybe he'll ask us over this time," his father said.

"I could take that as an insult, Mr. Caldwell."

"Don't, Mrs. Caldwell," his father said. "It ain't one. Take it as a compliment to Uncle Drew."

"Anyway," Teddy continued, "I told him it was all his words with just a few places where Mr. Kennedy filled in the gaps of what he was having to leave out, and he—Uncle Drew—said, 'Maybe so. But I hate to think they been run through the tape machine and a notebook and then typed and crammed into a space not near enough to fit them all.' After that he paused for a second, then he said, 'No, I'm sure old Rayford done a good job and didn't misrepresent us. I just don't want to see what he had to leave out because that'd of course become what I thought was absolutely the most important thing happened and I'd be down there asking him how a tin-eared illiterate ever got to be the editor of a newspaper, even just of one don't come out but once a week. Nosir, I'll leave it as it is and call it dandy.'"

Teddy himself was laughing now. His parents were rolling. Once he got his breath he continued.

"Y'all," he said. "Let me finish this. I asked him what he was fixing to do next time he ran into Mr. Kennedy and he said he'd tell him it was a good article. He said, 'Which of course I already knew since it's my story.' And I said, 'You won't be lying. He did do a good job.'"

"I should say so," his father remarked.

"It's all everybody's talking about down at Builders," his mother added.

"It's all everybody's talking about everywhere around here," his father said. "You ought to be proud of yourself too, Teddy."

"I kind of am," Teddy said.

The only problem wasn't exactly a problem, though it had caused Teddy and Uncle Drew to have to go to work in an unexpected way. The old man's mailbox was overflowing. The letters and cards began arriving the day after the tabloid appeared. By the third day, Mr. Bilberry was bringing Uncle Drew's mail in a special box.

"Ain't no way to answer it," he said. "I can't even read it all."

Teddy volunteered to help, thinking that doing so might solve an actual problem he had, which it did. Mrs. Delhomme listened to what he had to say and took only a moment to approve his substituting the mail he was going through with Uncle Drew for the book a week he had put down as his goal for the Summer Reading Program.

"Thanks, Mrs. Delhomme. I'm beginning to think I'm reading more words in the letters than I would in books."

"Well, the epistle has a grand tradition in literature," she said.

"Like in the Bible?" he asked.

"As in the Bible, yes," she said.

Each day Teddy and Uncle Drew would set a box of letters between them on the porch and work their way through it.

"Didn't know there could be this many people interested in a old man's story," Uncle Drew said.

"Me neither," Teddy replied. "But it ain't just that, is it? It's like they're wanting to tell you their own stories."

"History," Uncle Drew said. "Notice how most of them tell you how old they are and how high them numbers are. Bunch of old codgers like me that ain't got nothing to do but write a letter's what we mainly have here."

"I think it's great."

"I ain't saying it ain't," Uncle Drew replied. "Don't misunderstand that."

"And your story ain't no regular story," Teddy said. "It's like we saved Bopeep from being apocryphal."

"Except that about half of these letters are apocryphal," Uncle Drew said. "Me and Bopeep ain't never went to California, for instance. Here's a man saying he won two dollars off us in Fresno one afternoon, talking about how courteous I was giving it to him. Good Lord. Say, you decided whether you're going to get them to let you have a minute on the mound when y'all try out? That's coming up, as I recall."

Teddy looked up from the letter he was reading.

"I might," he said. "It's coming up all right. It's tomorrow."

"Do it," Uncle Drew said. "Won't hurt nothing."

"We'll see," Teddy said. "Know what I'd like to do for sure if you don't mind?"

"What's that?" Uncle Drew asked.

"I want to wear one of Bopeep's caps. You said it might bring me good luck and I think I'll be needing some, especially if I pitch. Mama put a safety pin in back of them and they fit just right."

Uncle Drew smiled with his eyes.

"You done decided, ain't you?" he asked.

Teddy nodded.

"Good for you," Uncle Drew said. "Wear you a cap."

"You sure?" Teddy asked.

"Why would I mind? You'll need a cap. Might be a little on the warm side, being wool and all, but it'll be plenty hot out there no matter what."

The idea of pitching for the coaches made Teddy's heart speed up.

"I wish my folks could be there," he said. "But maybe it's better they won't. I don't know. You really think I can do it, don't you, Uncle Drew?"

"Oh, for crying out loud," Uncle Drew said. "Here's another feller asking for my autograph. Sorry. What's that?"

Teddy smiled. He didn't really need to hear the answer.

"Nothing," he said.

As he had expected, Teddy was assigned to right field during Youth League tryouts the next afternoon. He took his place in line and gathered in all of the flies and stopped each of the grounders the coaches sent his way. His tosses to the cutoff man were strong and accurate. After they finished fielding, the players got six pitches to swing at. Teddy missed the first of his badly, foul-tipped the next two, then settled in and made solid contact with the final three. He was covered with sweat by the time the coaches called all the candidates in. He took his cap off and stuffed it in his back pocket. He'd worn the one with *N* and *O* interlocked on the crown. He was surprised that more of the others hadn't asked him about it, but he guessed they were concentrating on their performances and not on what somebody else was wearing.

"Good job, fellas," one of the coaches said. "We've been taking notes and are fixing to make our team selections this evening. Rosters'll be posted at the swimming pool by noon tomorrow so you'll have plenty of time to get your gear before the first games. We'll let you know when and where on that. Okay. All we need to do now is take a quick look at our pitchers so we can get y'all fairly placed. The rest of y'all are done. Thanks for coming."

Teddy raised his hand.

"What if we never pitched but want to try?" he asked.

The coach who had been talking, Mr. Durham, looked at his colleagues. All but one of them shrugged as if to say, "Why not?" The one who didn't seem to agree with them shook his head. His name was Mr. Williams. He was Lonnie's daddy.

"You're not telling us you think you can pitch, are you, Caldwell?" Mr. Williams asked.

"Yessir, I am," Teddy said.

Most of the players who weren't pitchers had started away, but when they heard this exchange they stopped. Several of them had looks of amazement on their faces.

"No need to laugh, y'all," Mr. Williams told them. "It takes a lot of guts for a guy who's a born right-fielder to say anything at all. Tell you what, Caldwell: let's us go ahead and see what you can do. You think you can pitch. Lonnie, get in there and show him what pitchers have to deal with."

Teddy knew exactly what Mr. Williams was doing. Lonnie had always been among the best batters in their group, and his father was giving him the chance to redeem himself for letting Teddy beat him in a one-lick fight. The two of them hadn't seen much of each other since that day. Teddy wondered if Lonnie would go back to his bullying ways if he got the upper hand in this duel. The two locked eyes. Teddy could read nothing in Lonnie's. He put his cap back on and adjusted it.

"Been meaning to ask you what's the deal with that hat," Mr. Williams said. "What's *N-O* stand for? No something— like maybe No Good?"

"Come on, O'Dell," Mr. Durham said. "Let's see what he's got. Can't hurt."

Teddy walked to the mound and waited for Lonnie to get situated. One of the other coaches set up as the catcher. His name was Mr. Blanchard. He had twin sons who played in the infield and always on the same team because they were so competitive that they fought when they were separated. Together they made any team better.

"Throw me a couple to get your arm loose, Teddy," Mr. Blanchard said.

Teddy's strategy was to show nothing in his warmup. He didn't even kick his leg. He just stepped forward and pushed the ball, barely getting it to the plate.

"You sure you want to do this?" Mr. Blanchard asked.

Teddy nodded.

"You got three pitches, son," Mr. Williams said. "No need to waste our time with any more than that. We done seen enough already, looks to me like. You other pitchers, go ahead and start loosening up."

Nobody moved. They were all waiting to see how far Lonnie would hit the lobs Teddy was sure to serve him. The other players were also watching intently, as were the coaches and the parents who had stayed for the tryouts. Both of Teddy's were at work. He hadn't minded that until now, when everybody was watching him. He suddenly found himself feeling small and nervous. If only his mother or his father—or better yet, both of them—could have made it over. He looked around and found no late surprises. He was on his own. He heard a voice or two encouraging him, but the majority of the noise was in favor of Lonnie.

"Hit one to the dump, Lonnie!" somebody yelled, referring to the rise in the outfield that separated the ballpark from the seventh fairway of the golf course.

"He may do it," Mr. Williams said. "Let's go, Caldwell. There's real pitchers waiting. Show us something."

The other voices crowded in on Teddy. They felt like blows.

"Smash one, Lonnie!"

"Kill it!"

"See if you can at least get one close enough for him to swing at, Teddy!"

"Three homeruns coming up!"

As he watched Lonnie step in and take his final practice cuts, Teddy became aware of the car that was moving slowly along the road between the baseball field and City Pool. At first he didn't fully register that there was anything unusual about it. Then he did. It was an old model of a make that few people knew had ever existed. The sight of it was like something from a dream. It was washed and polished and gleaming handsomely in the hot afternoon sun.

All of the nervousness drained from Teddy's body and

mind and was replaced by a calm certainty that filled him top to toe. Everybody who was watching expected a slaughter, but only one of them other than Teddy had the correct victim in mind. Lonnie touched the plate with his bat. Teddy touched the brim of his cap, acknowledging not his adversary but his friend, who had parked his car parallel to the third base line and was standing beside it. He lifted a thumb. He believed. Now Teddy was able to. He knew he was capable of the task at hand. He knew he was going to do well.

Before he went into his windup, he briefly considered saying something to Lonnie but decided against it. Instead he felt his face move into the slightest of smiles.

"Ready, sheeps?" he thought.

And then he showed everybody something.

Epilogue

Two items that only seemed to be unrelated appeared in the same edition of the *Oil Camp News* later that summer. The first was a letter to the editor.

Dear Sir,

A friend of mine directed me to your recent article concerning Cantrell Shines. I was amazed to learn that the stories Rev. Shines began telling during his final days were indeed all true. Although he rarely spoke of his baseball career, we were aware that he had played in the minor Negro Leagues, but we had no inkling of his depression-era travels. Although we listened to what he had to say, I must admit that we did so as we might have to a child recalling dreams. The stories seemed less the product of memory than the ramblings of a mind on the decline. Alas, it now seems as though we should have paid closer attention to those accounts than we did. Our hope is that from his vantage point in Heaven this dear man has forgiven us for doubting him. Thank you for setting the record straight.

Your readers may be interested in knowing that Rev. and Mrs. Shines were pillars of our community for many years, and by that I mean the entire community, not merely the black community, though it was of course there where their work started. If memory serves, the Shines were said to have come into their fortune as a result of the Reverend's shrewd investments. Little did we know how he obtained his original stake! As Mr. Weems mentions in the article, he (Rev. Shines) did indeed work for a time with his stepfather at Reily Foods. But, as he often told it from the pulpit, he had felt himself falling into the trap of being angry and bitter over the wrongs he saw in the world around him, wrongs that had been visited upon him and wrongs that had been visited upon his people. He did not like this about himself, but he felt the power of it taking him over. Still, he said, he felt that lashing out against the negative forces of the world would only lead to greater suffering and help no one. Further, he recognized that those forces are not biased; they visit themselves upon all races, all colors, all religions, all of mankind. Realizing this, accepting it, he made the decision to fight back peacefully, to help those in need regardless of who they were—in short, to minister. Our community is forever grateful.

Rev. and Mrs. Shines passed away within three days of each other in the autumn of 1989, Dolores preceding. Following her death the Reverend's decline was precipitous, and it was during those final days when, in something of a feverish state, he spoke almost exclusively of his travels with Uncle Drew Weems. The couple had been with us here at Heritage Trail for five years. They had no children of their own, but as you can imagine, their visitors of all ages were legion. Few were the evenings when we didn't have to shoo somebody away, as the "old folks" needed their rest. Attendance at both funerals was overflowing.

I apologize for going on so, but I wanted to provide your readers with this little update. I'll close by saying that I find Rev. Shines' old nickname most appropriate, for after a fashion he did indeed become a shepherd. I thank you once again for your article.

Sincerely,
Irma Jean Fontenot, Director
Heritage Trail Village
Luster, Louisiana

The second appeared in a box on page one:

YOUTH LEAGUE ALL-STARS NAMED

Teddy Caldwell of Oil Camp's nine-year-old Yankees team will take the mound as the starting pitcher for this year's Claiborne Parish Youth League All-Stars when the club travels on Saturday to Arcadia to face their Bienville Parish counterparts. The winner of the Claiborne-Bienville contest will take on the winner of the Webster-Bossier game in Minden, also slated for Saturday. The site of the winners' contest will be determined after Saturday's games.

The 18-man Claiborne Parish roster was chosen by a vote of area coaches. Caldwell, nine, of Gantt Street, was one of only three unanimous selections. Also thus honored were catcher Lonnie Williams of Oil Camp's Cardinals team and shortstop Bobby Ray Grimes, Jr., of the Pineview Giants.

"We're tickled with our group," said Claiborne Parish All-Star coach Jake Blanchard, whose Yankees took this year's round-robin team title. "The Caldwell kid is something else. He's got an unusual delivery, to say the least. It's like something out of an old newsreel. He gave folks a fit all year, and we expect him to do the same in these All-Star games."

Although no statistics are kept during Youth League play, Blanchard estimated that Caldwell struck out, on average, seven batters during the three innings he was allowed each outing.

Other Oil Camp players earning All-Star nods are the Blanchard twins, first baseman Nat and third baseman Pat, of the OC Dodgers.

Please see ALL-STARS, page 8, for a complete roster.